THE NEW KID

Temple Mathews

BENBELLA BOOKS, INC.
Dallas, TX

Copyright © 2009 by Temple Mathews
First BenBella Books Edition 2010

Big Gulp® and Slurpee® are registered trademarks of 7-Eleven.

BENBELLA

BenBella Books, Inc.
10300 N. Central Expy., Suite 400
Dallas, TX 75231
www.benbellabooks.com
Send feedback to feedback@benbellabooks.com

Printed in the United States of America
10 9 8 7 6 5 4 3 2

Library of Congress Cataloging-in-Publication Data is available for this title.
ISBN 978-1935618-27-0

Proofreading by Yara Abuata
Cover design by Laura Watkins
Cover illustration by Cliff Neilsen
Text design and composition by PerfecType, Nashville, TN
Printed by Bang Printing

Distributed by Perseus Distribution
perseusdistribution.com

To place orders through Perseus Distribution:
Tel: 800-343-4499
Fax: 800-351-5073
E-mail: orderentry@perseusbooks.com

Significant discounts for bulk sales are available. Please contact Glenn Yeffeth at glenn@benbellabooks.com or (214) 750-3628.

For William Thomas Mathews

TABLE OF CONTENTS

Chapter One: The New Kid

Will was on his back, falling through darkness, and the only thing he could think about was whether he had any reason whatsoever to go on living. He decided he did. There was someone he had to kill.

He was falling faster and faster, the updraft whipping at his clothes. He knew he'd have to get his body turned around to have any chance of surviving. He twisted his torso and wrenched himself sideways. The air was hot and getting hotter by the second. Soon it would be scalding. Dirt and debris shot up from below, pelting him in the face, as he plummeted through the dark tunnel, dropping fast as a sack of scrap iron. Tunnel entrances flashed by in a blur. He tried grabbing at the roots and outcroppings of rocks that zoomed by but he was going too fast. *This can't be it*, he thought, *this can't be the end, it just can't!* Sure, he'd made stupid mistakes; he'd miscalculated the power and cunning of his enemy. But there was still hope, wasn't there? He had to grab a root. It was either that or die for sure on impact. Impact on *what* he didn't know, but no way could it be anything but beyond horrible.

Will heard his father's voice echoing through the shaft.

"Let go, Will, you have to let go."

But Will couldn't, and his fingernails raked at the sides of the tunnel in desperation—and there, a root! For a moment he caught purchase, his hands grasping, palms burning, as the root slipped through his fingers until he wrist-wrapped it and was jolted to a halt, slamming against the side of the dank earth. He sucked wind and blinked away more swirling dirt. Maybe he was going to make it. Maybe he was going to live to see another day. But then he heard a hideous roar as something erupted from below. He was blasted with a wave of thick blistering air, engulfed in a torrent of fetid rain from below. He pulled on the root, his only chance at survival, and, feet scrabbling, tried to climb. Again he heard his father's voice.

"Let go, Will. You must let go."

But Will refused to let go and held on even tighter. And then the root snapped. Gravity yanked him backward and his head slammed into a rock. He was falling again and he saw the flames and molten lava below as he plummeted down and down. His ears nearly burst from the sound of an explosion and he felt the ground quaking, the earth splitting in two. The end was surely upon him. He thought he saw a face, the eyes swollen and pulsing with hatred, the mouth gaping open. Will screamed, his throat raw from the heat. This was it. In seconds he was going to die. The earth shook again, this time more violently.

"Wake up, Will. It's 7:09! Get your skinny butt out of that bed! You don't want to be late the first day at your new school, slacker!"

His heart still pounding from the nightmare, Will Hunter sat up, blinked twice, and the room came into focus. His nimrod stepfather Gerald was standing over him, one foot on the bed, shaking it with his foot. Hence the earthquake. His stepfather cracked one of his patented cannon farts, then did an about face and retreated into the hallway. Will looked around the room and saw the packing boxes that contained his life. Rising, he glanced out the window. The moving van that had disgorged all their stuff was gone. He looked down at the tracks the big Kenworth had left on the lawn when the movers backed it up to off-load his crates into the basement. He'd tipped the movers a couple of thousand each to ensure that they'd keep their mouths shut about the crates. To Will it was just part of doing business, because it was important that no one knew what his business was. If someone did find out it could prove fatal. The workmen's trucks were all gone, too, and Will was confident that they'd done as he'd ordered and the house's infrastructure had been modified to his exact specifications.

He looked around the neighborhood at the fall trees, the flowers in bloom. It was another town, another new school. Will was only sixteen but he'd already bounced around to so many schools he'd lost count. With a sigh he climbed into a pair of jeans, pulled a faded Caterpillar T-shirt over his head, then zipped into the bathroom to splash water on his face, run a comb through his hair, brush his teeth, and take a leak. Looking in the mirror he tried on a smile— best to at least try and appear friendly on your first day—but the smile looked phony so he settled on his usual stoic stare, grabbed his DC backpack, and bounded down the stairs two at a time.

In the kitchen he stopped when he saw his mother April at the stove. April—his favorite month. He saw her purse lying on the kitchen counter and quietly moved over and opened it. She only had five bucks in her wallet. Will took two crisp hundreds from his own wallet and slipped them into hers. He loved his mother more than anything on earth, and not a day went by when he didn't wonder what she'd done in a previous life to deserve winding up with a dorky loser like Gerald. The guy was a total jerk whose cheese had definitely slipped off his cracker. He could barely hold a job and his fashion choices would have been intolerable had they not provided Will with the occasional belly laugh. Gerald would wear green jeans with red socks and a blue T-shirt. Or a turd-brown old-man jumpsuit with screaming yellow socks and clogs. April made excuses, saying

Gerald was color blind, but Will was pretty certain the guy was just a garden variety idiot. After all, his biggest claim to fame was that he made his own beer. He was consistently flatulent and emitted massive blasts of gas that could knock out a junkyard dog. All in all, a great guy to have around.

Even though April worked full-time in market research she always took the time to make Will breakfast. This morning it was waffles with bacon and now he was careful to scuffle his feet so she wouldn't be startled. She spooked easily. To tell the truth, they all did.

"Morning, Mom."

She turned quickly, holding a plate, her eyes finding him with a quick smile that just about melted his heart.

"Will, I didn't even hear you come in. I made you—"

"A waffle bacon sandwich, I know, my fave. Thanks." He smiled back. "Gotta run."

Will grabbed the concoction, took a bite, and was halfway out the door when her voice stopped him.

"Good luck at school."

"Sure thing," he said.

Then she frowned and touched his arm. "Will, I'm so sorry we've had to move around so much. My job . . . sometimes you have to do what you have to do."

"It's okay, Mom, really. I totally understand. See you later."

Will gave his mom a quick peck and then exited. April had no idea that the real reason they moved around so much was because of Will, not her. He wished he could just talk to her. But then again he wished he could do a lot of things he knew were impossible. They'd been through one shitstorm after another and he wanted to keep things as stable as he could, for her sake and for the sake of the mission. Nothing was going to stop him.

The garage door opened and Gerald's Saab came lurching out in front of Will, almost running right over his Converses. Sometimes he wondered if Gerald did stuff like that just to annoy him, or if he was actually trying to kill him. Will quickly turned and hoofed it down the driveway toward the corner where some kids lingered, trying their best to look as cool as anybody can possibly look while waiting for a school bus. Will had a car of his own, a "rice rocket" Mitsubishi EVO. With its MIVEC turbo engine and six-speed, paddle-shifted dual clutch sequential transmission his baby generally blew just about everything in its path off the road. But on his first day in a new school Will always chose to ride the bus because he wanted to be as inconspicuous as possible. For any other kid this would have been easy. But Will was different and he always stood out like a sore thumb no matter how he looked or carried himself. He kept trying though. Mainly because he wanted so badly to fit in that his heart ached for it.

Gerald's Saab floated alongside Will as he walked down the sidewalk. A window powered down and Gerald's grating voice came clawing out.

"Will, I don't need to tell you how important it is for you to . . . toe the line this time."

If you don't need to tell me, then how about shutting your yap and putting the pedal to the metal, butt-wipe, thought Will.

"I get it, Gerald. I get it for sure."

"You know, when one door closes, another opens," Gerald added.

Will stared at the cracked sidewalk and clenched his jaw. He knew all about doors opening and closing. He'd had scores slammed in his face and he'd kicked down plenty more. He didn't like where most doors led because in his case, they almost always opened to someplace where a body could discover a whole new world of pain. He balled his fists and felt the red anger building up in him. But he breathed deeply and instead of exploding, conjured up a semi-cordial look and tossed it in Gerald's direction.

"Thanks, G. You rock. Got it, totally. Have a great day."

Gerald more or less scowled, looking like he'd swallowed a toad or something, or like he had yet another batch of dynamite gas building up. You could tell he was just itching to pull the Swedish tank car over, jump out, and knock Will around a little just to teach him some respect. But he knew he couldn't do that because no way would April ever stand for it. So he just sucked his saliva through his teeth, over and over—one of the many disgusting habits that drove Will nuts—until another gem of wisdom emerged.

"If you can't make it work this time, you only have yourself to blame."

Gerald apparently didn't need a response to this because he sped off, leaving Will to choke on Saab fumes. His stepdad was pretty much always like this, giving him grief for all the stuff that had happened to them as they'd moved from town to town to town. He knew Gerald despised him but what could either of them do? He was married to Will's mother so they had to keep the peace. But one of these days. . . .

Will walked down the street toward the corner, glancing around at the cozy pastel-colored houses, the white picket fences, the meticulously manicured lawns. It all looked so clean and neat and . . . welcoming. He gazed up at the local mountain, Mount St. Emory, a dormant volcano that stood guard majestically in the distance. It was pretty cool. Will decided he liked the look of Harrisburg and in the back of his mind, in a calm place, he wondered if the town was even infected. Of course he was reasonably certain it was—his calculations were seldom off—but he almost hoped that this time he was wrong, that this time he could spend a few months, or even just a few weeks, being a normal teenager, hanging out with the guys, skateboarding around, having fun just kicking back and watching something stupid on TV, wolfing down chips and bean dip and chugging Mountain Dew. A voice inside him said *not gonna happen, buddy boy, and you know it.*

Reaching the corner, Will quickly scanned the teenage faces. They were like a pack of wild animals taking stock of him, summing him up by appraising his worn Converse All Stars, his Gap jeans, his Caterpillar T-shirt, scratched Diesel watch, leather friendship bracelet, and faded DC backpack. They took great pains not to give him too much face time, averting their eyes to more important things like the weeds poking up through the concrete or the dried-out three-week-old squirrel flattened in the middle of the road.

High school rule number one: Whatever you do, don't let anyone think you might *like* them. The kids sizing up Will were wired, of course, pod punks numbing their ear drums listening to rich artists pretending to be pissed off at the Man. If they only knew who *The Man* really was, they'd tune in to something else, anything else, hell, church music or Wayne Newton, just to drown out their own screams. Will kept thinking to himself, they don't know me, they'll never know me, they have no idea what I'm capable of or what I've been through. Then he laid it on himself straight: They didn't know him because he wouldn't, he *couldn't*, let them, for their own good. It was nobody's fault. It was just sucky fate. He wished that this time he could let himself make a friend. Just one friend. But that wasn't too likely. Friends were for normal people, and the one thing that Will was definitely not was normal. One of the boys, an obese stoner with jowly cheeks, tore open a package of sour gummy worms and sucked them into his mouth with a slurping sound. As he chewed he glanced at Will like he was a bug on a windshield or something. Cute.

Then a pretty, self-assured-looking girl came running to the bus stop from the same direction Will had come. She looked strong and fast, and carried herself like she knew how to handle trouble should it ever come her way. She had clear blue eyes and dusty blonde hair with highlights, and wore navy blue cords and a long-sleeved Iron Maiden T. She gave Will a quick, neutral once over and quickly pretended he was pond scum or something equally appealing. And then their eyes met again as they both stole a second glance and their faces flushed with embarrassment.

Even though girls seemed drawn to him in a big way, Will was never all that smooth around them and, mercifully, the girl turned her back to him. But in a few moments he noticed she had angled her body and hung her head down so she could scope out Will through her bangs.

Will had been attracted to a few girls in the various towns he'd lived in but so far he'd been able to resist them. It wasn't like he was a big King Shit or something, but he had to blow them off because if his enemies ever found out he liked a girl she'd likely wind up in pieces. If she was lucky. So getting close enough to fall in love? Wasn't in the cards.

Trying to act cool and nonchalant, he took out his iPod and held it to his ear like he was making some important call on his cell phone. The only problem was he'd left his cell phone at home. He caught his mistake and jammed the iPod back in his pocket, then turned to see if she'd noticed his blunder. She had, and she half-smiled beneath her hair curtain. He wondered if she hoped she was the cause of his faux pas.

As the North Colone School District bus lumbered up the hill toward the corner, the kids bunched together in anticipation of boarding. But then a brand-new black on black Scion xB with smoked windows and cherry red spinners pulled up, pumping gangsta metal from Crimson at a gabillion decibels. Inside were two self-appointed alpha males, Duncan Walker and Todd Karson. Duncan was muscular and had short blond hair and green eyes and his skin was smooth and white. Todd was taller and darker in complexion but they both were unusually handsome, the kind of guys you'd see in a teen sports magazine ripping on a skateboard or dunking a basketball. They craned their thick necks out the car's windows in order to be better seen by the group and smiled. Their teeth were perfect. But they had no manners, a fact that Duncan demonstrated as he hocked a green projectile onto the sidewalk and sneered at the bus riders.

"Check it out, pussies, the Dunc's got his license to thrill. Guess where I got this puppy! I WON it on KXMC radio! That's right. I was the last one still awake at the mall, my tongue jammed up this baby's tailpipe! Some of us are winners, and the losers get to ride the short bus!"

Todd and Duncan barked out staccato laughs, and then Duncan leered at the girl Will was still pretending not to watch.

"Hey Natalie, you wanna ride? The backseat's full, but you can sit on my lap. You better hurry, though, 'cause it's filling up fast!"

Duncan pumped his lap up and down, an act which he apparently found greatly amusing as he cranked up the volume on his stupid donkey laugh. Natalie rolled her eyes as if she couldn't believe how idiotic this guy was. Will just stared at Duncan calmly, studying him as though he were some sort of lab rat. Duncan stopped laughing and pointed at Will.

"What are you looking at, ass face?" he growled.

I'm looking at an idiot, thought Will. But he said nothing and with Herculean effort just stared dumbly at the ground.

"That's right, a-hole! Keep your ugly mouth shut!" Confident he was victorious in this minor skirmish Duncan then stomped on the gas, the xB spitting forward into traffic looking like some freakish troll delivery truck. Shaking his head, Will quietly boarded the school bus, moved all the way to the back, and plopped down, putting his iPod earbuds in. He stole another glance at the girl, Natalie, and for a moment he thought he'd seen her before somewhere. But he couldn't think of where or when so he pushed the notion out of his mind. She was just some girl. Period.

A large crow sat on a telephone line on Route 16. Common wisdom has it that crows are incapable of having human thoughts like hatred. But this crow felt power surging within him, and his pea-sized brain was on fire. This bird was pure malevolence, a mean-assed sucker, a killer ready to spring into action. His black eyes flared slightly red and he swooped down off the line and glided down the road.

In the bus Will peered out the window, watching the town of Harrisburg go by. It was a normal-enough looking town, no better or worse than the others he'd lived in. Just like all those other towns, it had a polished surface that made it feel safe and welcoming. And, just like all those other towns, underneath was another story. Always another story, and usually not one with a happy ending. The hairs on the back of Will's neck prickled and he immediately went on alert. His seventh sense told him that the wind of the Dark One was blow-ing. He glanced at the faces on the bus. Normal kids. Just normal teenage kids. But that could change any second.

BAM!

Something hit the top of the bus. Then something else hit. And something else. It sounded like gravel but it wasn't. It was hail. Kids gawked out the window.

"Cool!"

"Holy crap, look at it come down!"

Flying right through the hail the crow located its target and tucked its wings in to gather speed. From its point of view the world was shades of brown, a sepia view of suburbia. As the bus roared along Will sensed the crow coming and looked out the window. The crow was flying erratically by the bus. For a split second Will dis-missed it as just an ordinary crow but as it swooped right down at his window as though taunting him he concluded differently. Espe-cially when he saw its eyes.

A few seats away Natalie leaned up and opened her window, reaching an arm out to feel the hail. Will sprang forward and dashed down the aisle, bumping whoever got in his way.

"Sorry, excuse me!"

"Hey, watch it!"

"What's he doing?"

He reached Natalie's seat and there was no time to do anything else but bull his way right over her to get to the window. The crow was rocketing right at the opening, emitting a horrifyingly un-bird-like cry, a guttural braying sound more likely to have come from a dying farm animal.

"Hey, do you mind?!" yelled Natalie as Will not only stepped on her foot, but brushed his face against her forehead and inadvertently elbowed her boob. She might have done more—like protested with a kick to his privates—but she must have finally seen the crow jamming right at the open window. She screamed. Hearing the scream, the bus driver glanced in his side mirror just in time to see it. BAM! Will slammed the window shut and the crow crashed into the safety glass, breaking its neck, splintering its beak, and cracking the window before bouncing backward onto the pavement. The bus driver yanked the wheel and the front tire smacked into the curb, sending kids flying from their seats. On the pavement, the crow's eyes fluttered and its claws grasped for life, but life was saying adios, amigo. Blood spilled from the crow's eyes and then it died.

Inside the bus, everyone had moved to Natalie's side to see the action, gawking out the windows and marveling at the bird bleeding on the sidewalk.

"Cool! Did you see that?"

"Man, this is just like that old guy's movie, Hitchlock!"

"It's Hitchcock, dipweed."

"Whatever."

"Crows live longer than any other bird."

"Not this one."

Will was gazing at the cracked window and the pattern of blood that the crow had left there. It looked like someone had hastily painted a sloppy little symbol. In the shape of a pentagram.

Natalie was staring at Will, her eyes narrowing.

"How did you know that crazy bird was gonna—"

BAM! Another crow slammed into a window three rows back. And then another, and another. The bus was being swarmed by a murder of crows and they were out of their minds, diving and slamming into windows like kamikazes trying to sink a destroyer. The bus erupted with shouts and screams. The hail came down harder. A couple of freshman girls started to cry and the bus driver sat there in dumb shock until Will shouted up to him:

"DRIVE!"

The driver stomped on the gas and the bus lurched forward. A few more crows dive-bombed the bus, cracking the back window, and then the attack was over. The hail stopped abruptly. The bus was stone silent the rest of the way to school. As it pulled into the unloading area the shock began to wear off and was replaced by excited talk. Just about everyone on the bus shot at least one suspicious glance at Will. They all wondered the same thing: How the heck did he know that the first crow was going to attack? Will kept his head down and pretended to groove to music on his iPod, taking care not to return their gazes. Best to appear nonchalant. No big deal.

He tried to tell himself that the crows were acting crazy on their own accord, that it was just some freaky nature thing and had nothing to do with him. And he'd probably just imagined the bloody symbol. But deep down he knew better. He always did. It was the same story wherever he went. Things looked good and pure and wholesome on the surface, but underneath the whole place was evil and sucked beyond words. *They* already knew he was here in Harrisburg. *They* were here, too, and he would have to battle them. *Demons.* The crows had been a nice little twisted welcoming committee. Back on the pavement, the dead crow lay still for a moment longer, then rose on crushed legs, flew up into the sky, and banked toward Mount St. Emory.

Will looked out the bus window at Harrisburg High—HOME OF THE MUSTANGS!—as kids poured out of the bus and chatted excitedly, spreading the story of the hail and the whacked bird attack to all their friends. Will was the last one to exit the big yellow bus and Natalie was waiting for him, her eyes full of questions.

"Hi, I'm Natalie."

"Um, I'm Will."

"Nice to meet you, Will."

He smiled thinly and started to walk away but she blocked his path, looking at him with her searching eyes.

"Can I ask you something? How the heck did you know about that crow?"

"I just . . . had a feeling."

"Some feeling. Thanks. If you hadn't slammed that window shut that freaky bird might have pecked my eyes out."

"It's no big deal."

"Well, my eyes are a big deal to me."

"I didn't mean. . . ." Will was flushing now, flummoxed and inept. He could usually avoid chicks without too much trouble. But *this* girl—he was thrown off balance by her. Not only was she totally hot—in a natural way, an unconventional way—she also seemed mature for her age. She held a kind of sadness in her eyes and she looked haunted, like she'd lost something, or someone, important. Maybe Will was imagining it or projecting his own feelings on to her, but he couldn't help feeling connected with her because of it. Then it hit him again, this feeling that he'd *seen* her before.

She looked so appealing, just standing there, defiant, ready for him to make the next move. Will told himself he had to stay aloof. Better for everyone that way. But hell! Given half a chance, he might really dig this Natalie. She was so pretty that his brain went numb. He stood there and the only thing he could think of was to ask her how long she'd had her shoes. Moron! Numbskull! He kept his mouth shut and stared at her kneecaps. Exasperated, she shook her head.

"Whatever," she said as she left.

He watched her walk away and was inexorably drawn to her. He liked the way she got right in his face, liked the sparkle in her eyes, liked the way she wore her cords. He'd never had a girlfriend; just the thought of such a thing seemed way too perilous. But that didn't mean he couldn't dream. He was a guy, after all. Again he shoved Natalie out of his mind. It was time to take care of business, time to start in at yet another school.

A couple of white panel trucks were parked next to the school. Some painters had the shrubbery covered with drop cloths and were rolling out a coating of primer onto the masonry walls of the school. No doubt they'd come up with some innocuous institutional color for the place. Schools always did that. He guessed this one would be some shade of boring beige. On another wall, the main wall of the front of the school, the painters had already laid down a coat of primer and someone, probably members of the art class, had sketched a huge rough outline of a galloping mustang. Whoopee.

Then Will looked over at the parking lot where some cheerleaders were pinning paper roses to a homecoming float anchored by an ancient Ford flatbed truck. The dominant girl, who clearly knew she was the most beautiful, seemed to be asserting herself over the others and as she gestured for them to do this and that her eyes wandered over and found Will. She froze for a moment then, as if she was catching herself, blushed then tossed her hair like a filly and went back to bossing the other cheerleaders around. Will studied her, noticing how her skin shone in the sunlight, how her hair spilled onto her shoulders like she was in some TV commercial for shampoo.

Will pulled his eyes away from the cheerleader—*don't go there, you know you can't go there, you gotta stop acknowledging girls*—and further inspected the school. The old part, the anchor to the new additions, had to be the oldest structure in Harrisburg. A three-story ashlar edifice, it looked like the stones had been cut from some quarry in Europe where the sun never shone. The place had a look of finality about it, as though the Four Horsemen of the Apocalypse would be right at home here. *How fitting*, Will thought to himself as he looked at the surrounding grounds. On one side of the school stood an imposing old-growth forest choked with towering pines. On the other side the ocean crashed against a rocky bluff. Perfect. Just perfect. Will's nemesis always did have a flair for the dramatic. He glanced again in the direction of the cheerleader who along with her cheer squad had paused in her efforts on the float and was checking him out. As soon as they saw him look their way they turned up their noses to make sure he knew they wanted nothing to do with him, that he was beneath him.

Refocusing himself, Will eyed the school entrance and headed for it. He'd done this walk more times than he wanted to remember but never quite got used to it. He thought to himself, *When you're the New Kid, it's like you've got a big neon sign flashing on your forehead blinking, "Check me out! I'm THE NEW KID!"* At least that's what it felt like. And sure enough, as the sea of kids parted and Will waded through, they whispered and pointed and scoped him out. Fresh meat. Most of the girls looked like they either wanted to run away or lay a big wet kiss on him. Half the boys acted like they wanted to beat the crap out of him and the other half wondered if he was going to beat the crap out of them. High school, you had to love it. Or maybe not. Duncan was hanging with some of his buddies by a bench and he glared at Will as he walked by. He used his fingers to make the "I'm watching you" sign. *No*, thought Will, *I'm watching you. All of you.*

Will checked in with the principal, a large oafish man with adult acne, small eyes, and a neck that was thicker than his head so his whole body sort of came to a point.

"Welcome to Harrisburg High, I'm Principal Steadman," said the pointy head as it looked down at a folder. "Do you like to be called Willie, Bill, or William?"

"It's Will."

"Good for you." Pointy-head—Steadman—smiled, revealing overlapping front teeth. Will mustered a smile in return and studied the man. He could be safe or he could be one of them. It was hard to tell, especially with adults. It usually took a while to smoke them out. Will's enemies were nothing if not clever.

Steadman's administrative smile evaporated as he opened a file, read a little, then tapped it as though he was a hot shot TV cop or something. Guys like Steadman made Will want to puke, but he thought it best to abstain for the time being. Steadman tapped the folder again.

"You know what this is?"

Will kept mum, figuring Steadman would get around to answering his own question sooner or later. They always did.

"It's your *permanent record*, your transcripts from the schools you've attended. You've been around, haven't you, William?"

"We've moved a lot, yeah," said Will.

"And you've had some rough patches, haven't you? It says here you blew up the boiler room in the basement of Wellington High School in San Diego?"

"Accidents happen," replied Will, though he knew good and well his blowing up the boiler was a totally necessary act of self-defense and not any kind of accident.

"Yes, they do," said Steadman, "and apparently they happen to you with frightening regularity. The bus crash on the Porter Bridge overpass in Corpus Christi, Texas. The gas main explosion at Jordan Manning in Greenhaven, North Carolina." Steadman flicked the folder with his middle finger. He looked frustrated, like he knew he had to hand down some stupid edict but didn't particularly feel like it. He was clearly conflicted. Either that or he really had to go to the bathroom. Finally, he sighed.

"I want you to know that I'm a fair man, and that as far as I'm concerned you have a clean slate to start with here at Harrisburg High School. Here's your class schedule and your instruction packet. *You're* responsible for reading it and following the rules. Here's your locker number and the combination. It's *your* responsibility to keep your locker clean and free from drugs, contraband, and alcohol. I run a tight ship but a fair ship, William."

The name's "Will," thought Will, but he didn't bother correcting Steadman. He just wanted this over. Everywhere you went there were rules, but they were trivial compared to the rules of *his* world, and those rules Will lived to break in the worst possible way.

Principal Steadman pinhead stood up, indicating the brief meeting had come to an end. He reached over and grabbed a couple of forearm crutches and then came around the front of the desk to shake hands. Will felt ashamed that he'd held even an ounce of malice for Steadman. The poor guy had multiple sclerosis. Then he remembered the time an enemy had come at him disguised as a blind drooling quadriplegic and decided he'd better stay on the alert even though Steadman seemed like a basically nice guy to whom life had dealt a crummy hand. Steadman shook Will's hand and Will squeezed tightly, trying to feel for moisture in the center of the palm. They sometimes had mouths or eyes there. But Steadman's hand was as rough and dry as a chunk of tree bark. Will left the office.

He passed dozens of kids as he made his way down the hall to his locker. They all stared at him and did their usual whispering and pointing thing again. He stood out like an orange on an apple tree. *Does everybody know everybody else in this school?* wondered Will. *Of course they do. It's your typical small-town, inbred, socially incestuous scene.*

He found his locker and as he did he saw a crowd of boys gathering down the hallway, fidgeting with anticipation. *Oh God*, thought

Will, *not another lame locker prank. What's it going to be this time?* At Wellington High School in San Diego they'd filled his locker with pizza dough. At Kennedy in Corpus Christi they'd used rats from the biology class and Will remembered how angry he was, not because he was embarrassed but because they'd injured one of the rats and he'd had to take it to the vet. In Greenhaven, North Carolina, at Jordan Manning High they'd used an "anatomically correct" inflatable doll (always a favorite) and at Steele High in Brunswick, Vermont, they'd used horse manure. So of course nothing would surprise him. Knowing this sort of thing was inevitable and not wanting to disappoint the doofuses down the hallway he slowly dialed the combination and opened his locker. Out tumbled two dozen water-filled condoms. *How original.* The goons down the hall fell all over themselves laughing and high-fiving each other. Will sighed, trying once again not to let this kind of crap get to him. But it always did, deep down. He knew kids did stupid stuff like this to make them feel better about themselves; he understood the psychology, but it didn't soften the blows.

"You'll have to clean that up, William," said Principal Steadman as he crutch-walked up to Will. "Don't take it too personally. This happens with every new kid. Just buck up." Steadman patted him on the arm and crabbed his way down toward the faculty lounge.

Will disposed of the condoms in a nearby trash can and then headed for class as the first period bell rang. He followed the school map Steadman had given him and walked with his head down and took a left at the second hallway past the trophy case. He noticed a commotion in his peripheral vision and told himself to just keep on walking. But he knew there was trouble in the air and he was drawn to trouble like a shark to blood. There was a banging noise coming from the boys' restroom and two chiseled thugs stood guard by the door like gargoyles, muscular arms folded. As he walked by Will heard muffled voices and the straining high notes of someone who was not at all happy. Will stopped. He knew at this point he should just ignore whatever juvenile games were being played. Something told him this *wasn't* a game, but he decided to ignore his instincts and walked on past the boys' room. Let whoever was in trouble go ahead and suffer. It wasn't worth revealing himself for.

He was almost to his chemistry class when he heard the scream.

Chapter Two:
Rescuing Rudy

Will stopped, turned around, and walked back to the boys' room where he eyeballed the thick-necked gargoyles.

"The restroom's closed," said Thug One.

"Yeah, it's out of order, so take a hike," added Thug Two. Will stared at them.

"Hey, are you deaf?"

Will stood his ground and stared at them.

"We said there's *nothing* in here, just keep your butt moving!"

"If you know what's good for you!"

Will almost always knew what was good for him, but he rarely followed that path, the one of least resistance. Ever since he could remember he'd more or less been forced to follow the path of *most* resistance. He pushed right past Thug One and Two and though they were much taller and outweighed him by a combined forty pounds, something about this New Kid told them they'd better *back off* or suffer.

Entering the restroom Will shook his head. Why *does this always happen?* he asked himself. What was it about adolescent males that compelled them to distribute cruelty like it was candy on Halloween? The nasty alphas from the bus stop, Duncan Walker and

Todd Karson, had a short skinny kid by the legs and were head-dipping him in one of the toilets. Will's voice was calm but firm.

"Put him down."

Duncan's head turned slowly as he kept up the torture. He eyed Will, and then barked at the two muscular gargoyle guards who had followed Will in.

"What the hell did I tell you? Man, you two are so stupid!"

"He just sort of got by us," said Thug One. Thug Two studied a knuckle and kept his mouth shut. Duncan turned his attention back to Will as he kept dunking the hapless skinny kid's head in the porcelain pond.

"Listen up, hero, I'm gonna let your intrusion slide because you're the New Kid and you're too dumb to know any better, but I'm sure as hell not gonna put 'Roto Rudy' down. So just turn around and march your butt outta here, pussy face."

Will clenched his fists and breathed deeply. He knew he had to keep his anger in check. He didn't want to hurt anyone. Check that. He wanted to hurt them, just not put them in intensive care. He breathed deeply again.

"Put him down. It's over," said Will evenly. Duncan's grip tightened on little Rudy's ankles.

"Well I can't do that, partner. You see, my name's 'Duncan,' and I'm compelled to do just that. See, I'm dunkin' Roto Rudy!"

Duncan spat out an ugly laugh, then hissed at the thugs.

"Will you puleeeeze kick his ass now?"

The thugs looked at each other and measured which was worse, not following Duncan's command or messing with the stranger. They chose wrong, and stepped toward Will and threw punches. Moving lightning fast, faster than any kid they'd ever seen, Will ducked the first punch and Thug One's fist smacked into the tile wall with a sickening crunch. *He's not going to be taking notes in class anytime soon,* thought Will. Thug Two swung hard and his punch glanced off Will's shoulder. Will dropped and spun and neck-whipped the guy, then kicked his ankles out from under him. Two down, two up. He looked over at Duncan and Todd.

"You see where I'm going with this?"

"Holy crap!" said Todd, amazed at Will's unreal display of speed and strength. He was like some super zombie mutant warrior you'd see on a video game, not a high school kid. Duncan was apparently not as impressed because he intensified his torment of poor Rudy, who by now looked like a cat who'd just crawled out of a rain barrel. He was quite a sight. His sleeves were too long and his pants were too short. Nothing about him seemed to fit. His hair looked like a soggy bird's nest.

"Nobody listens," said Will. He heard the sound of a jet taking off in his head and saw the red curtain drawing closed across his mind's eye. He fought to remain calm. *Can't let anger rule my being!* He closed his eyes tightly and a lone tear from his exertion escaped and slid down his cheek. Duncan's face lit up with glee.

"Oh look, the New Kid's crying. Oh, boo hoo—"

When Will opened his eyes again they harbored such fury that Duncan paused, releasing Rudy, who squirmed sideways as he hit the floor. In a flash Will was across the room. His blinding speed took the bullies totally by surprise. He buckled Todd's knee with a thrust kick and then kidney-punched Duncan. Then as they swung at him he used their own momentum to duck and twist and bang their heads together. Then he stuffed their heads in the toilet one at a time then shook them like wet rats, and shoved them on their butts. Totally stunned, Rudy found himself liberated, and skittered sideways like a crab until he reached the door.

"Hey, what the hell?!" Duncan yelled as he felt the lump already swelling on the back of his head where he'd slammed against the wall. The toilet had jammed and was gushing disgusting skanky water and the floor of the boys' room was now flooded. Rudy stood on shaky legs and stared at the New Kid. Will turned on his heels and exited, Thugs One and Two, who were still nursing their injuries, giving him a wide berth.

Out in the hallway Will walked back toward the chemistry classroom. Maybe with a little luck he'd actually make it to his first class. After an altercation such as the one he'd just experienced he always felt an odd mixture of shame and exhilaration. What kind of a person was he that he could so easily see the red and unleash his violent side? He was afraid of it and didn't like letting it out. Okay, that was a lie he was telling himself, he loved letting it out. It just felt wrong.

Rudy caught up to Will and skipped alongside him. The little guy was totally in awe of the New Kid. With a sideways glance Will got a good look at Rudy, who had the usual teen pimples and hair so ragged it looked like he was wearing a mop. Right away he could tell that Rudy was amongst the walking virgins, dorky guys who'd never have a chance in hell of scoring with a girl. But right now Rudy wasn't thinking about girls, he was still pumped up over being rescued and he bobbed up and down as he walked like he heard some silent funk.

"Hey, you're the New Kid, right?"

"You're pretty quick," said Will as he kept on walking.

"Very funny, New Kid. You got a name?

"Will."

"I'm Rudy."

"I heard."

"Anyway, hey, thanks. I mean, in the long run it's probably not gonna do much good—I'm like perpetual cannon fodder for those jerks—but thanks anyway. I do think you're going to regret throwing yourself under the bus for me, though."

Will stopped and looked at him. "And why is that?"

"Well, Duncan's the über-alpha male in this school and he's got like his own skanky army of commando drones who do whatever he says."

"So?"

"So, my guess is that he's going to spread the word to have your head on a stake before lunch," said Rudy.

"I can take care of myself."

"Yeah, I scoped that out, but you don't know what you're dealing with."

"Neither does he," said Will.

Rudy smiled broadly, totally impressed. "Man, you got some big brass ones, for sure!"

"You ought to go change into some dry clothes."

Rudy shook his head and danced around the hallway like he was the happiest kid on earth, not someone who'd just had his face toilet-trained.

"Naw, I like being wet, it reminds me of running through the sprinklers in summer."

Will gave Rudy a sideways glance. "Rudy, you're whack, you know that?"

Rudy smiled. "Hey, thanks, man!"

The boys' room door slammed open and Duncan and his bullies blasted angrily out into the hallway. Duncan raised his fist and yelled at Will.

"Hey, New Kid! So you got in a lucky sucker punch. This ain't over!"

"I never said it was," said Will calmly.

Then he opened the door to his class and entered as Rudy watched in awe, a humongous smile spreading across his face.

"Cool. . . ." Rudy was beyond impressed. This was huge, this called for rejoicing! Someone finally had the cojones to stand up to the great Duncan Walker! He heard footsteps—which he knew had to be Duncan and his butt-faced cronies—and sprinted away from them down the hall.

Will breezed through his chemistry class, taking a pop quiz and purposefully missing a few of the rudimentary questions to make it look good. Inside he was laughing; he could teach this class himself. He skated through his trigonometry and government classes as well; all the information was stuff he'd learned years ago so the biggest challenge was to appear interested and not tip the teachers off that he knew more than they did.

Will saw Natalie again in his English class, where his ears perked up as he heard the teacher, Mrs. Nevins, a thin woman awash in freckles and good cheer, call Natalie "Miss Holand." The face, and now the name—it was all too familiar. As the smiling teacher passed out copies of *Romeo and Juliet*, Will slouched in his chair and prayed not to be called on. He didn't want to interact with Natalie like this. It worked. Mrs. Nevins assigned some other kid the role of Romeo and Juliet to Natalie. Will watched as Natalie and the kid performed a scene "with feeling" in front of the class. Natalie went first. As the color rose steadily in her cheeks, kids snickered.

"Wilt thou be gone? it is not yet near day. It was the nightingale, and not the lark That pierced the fearful hollow of thine ear; Nightly she sings on yon pomegranate-tree: Believe me, love, it was the nightingale!"

Will knew the play fairly well. He wasn't a big fan or anything but since he could speed read with about ninety-five percent comprehension he'd devoured every book he could get his hands on. He watched and listened, just like he always did; always on the sidelines, never in the social game in school. The kid mumbled his way through the passage, embarrassed.

"Um . . . It was the lark, the herald of the morn, no nightingale: look, love, what envious streaks . . . uh . . . the severing clouds in yonder east: Night's candles are burnt out, and jocund day stands tiptoe on the misty mountain tops. I must be gone and live, or stay and die."

A few chuckles rippled through the room. Will just stared at the floor. Finally, he couldn't help himself and looked at Natalie. She was still blushing.

When lunch time rolled around Will found himself in line at the cafeteria and immediately felt queasy. It was amazing how, at nearly every school, the lunch ladies were so freakish and hideous-looking that they were almost as scary as demons. Not a single one had turned out to be a demon yet, but he still watched carefully as they slopped the gut-busting institutional food onto those big, ugly green plastic trays. You never knew when patterns would suddenly change and if he wasn't careful he might just get poisoned. He chose today's special, the "rockin' pizza combo," then sauntered into the lunch-room and found the most appropriate table for a New Kid, the one populated by the school's loser/misfit club, including Roto Rudy, who scooted uncomfortably close to Will and gawked up at him like he was some kind of Greek god or something.

"Where you from?" asked Rudy.

"San Diego, Corpus Christi . . . a few other places."

"Yeah, you have that look about you."

"What kind of look would that be?" asked Will.

"Like someone who's been around and seen some things."

Rudy had no idea. Will had been around all right and seen things; the kinds of things that nightmares are made of. Will took a bite of his pizza and glanced out at the parking lot. The cheerleaders from that morning, including the one who'd caught his eye (her name was Sharon Mitchell, he had learned in chemistry class), were out working on the float again.

Rudy tapped his fingers on the table top. He wanted to know more about his new hero. "You must be some kind of army brat or something, right?"

"Something like that," said Will.

He was growing increasingly nervous because of the scene unfolding in the parking lot, where one of the super-cool unbelievably-beautiful totally-wonderful-in-every-way cheerleaders was using an ancient ball peen hammer to pound away at something on the old Ford that held the float. Will had a bad feeling, and when he had bad feelings, most often Hell came calling. He shifted uncomfortably in his seat. A group of black-clad punks who thought they were wicked were walking across the parking lot toward a gray van tricked out with skulls and crossbones on the side. He sensed that these two disparate groups would collide; he could feel it in his gut. He just didn't know how, or whether it would be his problem when it did. Rudy tapped Will's arm to get his attention.

"Hey, are you a gamer? Because if you are, maybe we could hit up. I'm on level 3 of *Demon Hunter*. I've got over a hundred kills." Rudy beamed as if he'd won the state wrestling title or something. "In the Village of Madness I never saw the Rat Man Demon coming, I kept looking at the sewer grates and he like comes swooping down off the roof."

His attention still drawn outside, Will spoke matter-of-factly.

"He hated the sewer, wouldn't go anywhere near it. He hid in the rafters, mostly. That's where I nailed his ass. Caught him totally by surprise."

Rudy gave Will a questioning look. Will cleared his throat.

"At least that's what I figured. Who knows? It's just a game."

Rudy nodded. "Hey, again, thanks for saving my butt earlier. That was really cool of you. And nobody's hardly ever cool to me. I don't have a lot of friends in this school. Or any other school for that matter." Rudy snort-laughed and then hiccuped until milk shot out his nose. "Sorry, I guess I took too many dork pills this morning," he said, blushing.

Will dropped his pizza and stood up abruptly, extricating himself from the lunch table. Whatever was going down outside was going to happen soon. Then he saw it. The old float truck's gas tank was leaking, thanks to the ditzy cheerleader's ball peen hammer blows.

"I talk too much, I know. I'm sorry, I'll shut up if you want," said Rudy.

But Will was already out the door.

. . .

In the parking lot he moved as fast as he could without running; he didn't want to tip the freaks off. They were handsome but at the same time scummy-looking leather Goths, punks who were smoking behind their skull van. One of them was attempting to light a cigarette with a plastic lighter. The scene went slow-motion in Will's mind as he saw the rivulet of gasoline from the old truck's tank snaking down toward the Goth puffers. Sharon Mitchell and her cheerleader friends were still going on about decorating the float and yammering about who they thought was cute and how they were going to have their hair styled for the fall dance. They were clueless.

The Goth alpha prick now sensed Will and as he opened his mouth in a lecherous smile Will saw the beast had, in place of teeth, rusty screws. Fury rose in Will like a storm and he felt his muscles tense and his jaw tighten as the violence struggled to be released. Will's only chance to save the girl and her friends was to get the lighter from the monster and he took two powerful steps and went airborne, slamming into the Goth smoker punk . . . who barely yielded. *This sucker's strong!* thought Will. The punk's jaws were snapping, preventing Will from getting a good grip on him as he scrabbled with the lighter, creating sparks. Then came a flame and as he bit into Will's arm with his rusty screw teeth he dropped to the ground and held the flame to the rivulet of gasoline. Will managed finally to snatch the lighter away but it was too late—the gas was aflame and snaking its way toward the truck. With time-bending speed Will threw himself forward, catching up to the streaking fire, overtaking it, and knocking into Sharon Mitchell, their bodies colliding full on. Will's powerful anger immediately evaporated. He was totally relieved to feel it depart. After all, he *was* lying on top of the head cheerleader.

"What are you doing?" shouted Sharon, "Get off of me!"

Will shoved himself off and then rolled toward the flame river, snuffing it out just a couple of feet from the float. His jacket was soaked in gas and burst into flames and as the girls screamed he shrugged it off his body and stomped it out. Sharon and the other cheerleaders stood gaping at the crazy New Kid standing in front of them with his shirt half ripped off, chest heaving. He looked like some sort of character from a comic book. But was he good or evil? They were still too shocked to notice the Goth punks laughing as they drove off, their van backfiring. Will, though, had no time to appreciate their stares as he shoved Sharon and her pack of cheerleaders away from the old truck. Another tendril of gas was aflame and shooting toward its target.

"Go! MOVE! NOW!"

They shrieked indignantly but did as he commanded.

"GET DOWN!"

They hit the dirt and then the old truck and the float erupted in a fireball. The girls were terrified. The smoke billowed. Will turned and faced Sharon, still holding the lighter in his clenched hand.

"They were. . . ."

Will gestured to where the Goth punks had been, but his voice trailed off—of course the creeps were long gone. He wondered if the girls had even seen them in the first place. Will knew he looked like some insane petty arsonist. He wanted to explain that the scummy Goths were infected souls, servants, but he knew the girls would never believe him. No one ever did. All Sharon and the other cheerleaders saw was some lunatic kid. *Great*, thought Will, *I've met two cute girls today and managed to alienate them both.* It wouldn't be the first time he'd saved the butts of kids who'd ostracized him. And it most likely wouldn't be the last.

What Will didn't know was that secretly Sharon had been totally electrified by her brief physical contact with him. She thought his hair was the bomb, his eyes were rock and roll, and as he walked away from the scene, she checked out his butt and gave him a 10 on her cheek scale. But of course she couldn't let on that she felt that way. No, she had to make sure the New Kid thought she held him in callous disregard. So those were the signals she sent out.

An hour later, after the Harrisburg fire department had completely doused the flaming float, Will sat across from Principal Steadman, who tapped a pencil tip on one of his crooked teeth and stared at Will with irritation.

"We're not getting off to a very good start, are we, William?"

It was of course a rhetorical question but Will nonetheless gave his stock answer, the same answer he'd given over and over whenever he'd found himself in similar situations.

"I made a mistake. I'll try and do better."

"A MISTAKE? You call burning down a homecoming float a *mistake*?" The veins in Steadman's forehead looked like they were about to pop. He took several deep calming breaths, closing his eyes and touching his fingertips to do some Yoga thing, acting like Will wasn't even in the room. Will wished he wasn't. Steadman opened his eyes and forced a smile onto his lips.

"Forgive my outburst. I'm working on that. It's good, William. What you said was good. All is good. Admitting our mistakes, our . . . weaknesses, admitting who we really are is the first step to improving our lives." Principal Steadman smiled. "I'm going to have to assume this was, as you say, an accident. I promised you a clean slate and that's just what you're going to get. So even though you have a history of this sort of thing, I'm going to let this slide and let you off with a warning this time. But please remember, if you cross the line again, the consequences could be . . . severe."

Will nodded, his nostrils flaring, not out of anger but because he smelled something coming off of Principal Steadman. Slowly Will lifted his head and met Steadman's eyes. For a split second Steadman's eyes darkened. Then he smiled and shook Will's hand.

"William, I'm a good judge of people. And I happen to think that even though you have a pretty damn dodgy past, I believe in my heart that deep down you're a good boy. I hope you don't prove me wrong."

As Will left the office and made his way toward the bus loading area, kids stared at him and whispered to each other and pointed. There he goes, Torch Boy the fire freak. The New Kid. Will boarded the bus. His first day at his new school was finally over. But his adventure in Harrisburg was just beginning. The hail and the crows might have been a coincidence but the Goth punks were real. As Will rode the bus home he could think of only one thing: *He's here.*

Chapter Three:
Will's Sanctum

Will got off the bus with Natalie and a few of the other kids but didn't look back at her as he walked toward home. He knew that just being in her orbit was a bad idea; he was pulled toward her like the planets to the sun. He wasn't sure exactly how he was going to handle the feelings he was beginning to have for this stranger but he knew he would have to keep his distance. Even if she did have a smile that cut right through him.

His house was two stories and constructed of brick with ivy crawling up the front and had a large porch jutting out like a big strong jaw. It had green shutters and a gray slate roof and an attached two-car garage. Will anticipated his mother's singsong voice asking him how his first day of school had been. *Well, gosh, Mom, let's see, the bus was attacked by demonic crows, I made the toilet in the boys' room flood while saving some skinny kid I don't even know, I inadvertently blew up the homecoming float, forever alienating myself from the head cheerleader and her gang of pretty faces, and now the whole school thinks I'm some kind of whacked out arsonist. How was your day?* Of course Will would say none of that, he would smile and nod or grunt some monosyllable answers like all teenagers. Sometimes being sixteen came in handy—you could gloss over tons of bizarre behavior and have it all chalked up to being a teen and going through "those awkward years."

He called out as he entered the house, "I'm home."

No answer. Good. Will slouched off his backpack, made a quick raid of the refrigerator and scarfed down a couple of brownies with a cold glass of milk, and then, after locking the front door, went down into the basement. Flicking the lights on he saw that all his crates had arrived intact. The basement itself was huge and as such suited Will's purposes perfectly. He pretended to be an old-school photographer, shooting on film in addition to digital, so he could construct a "darkroom" and thereby restrict entry and keep his real work away from prying eyes. He would get around to building the false wall later. For now all he really needed to do was unroll some thick black plastic and staple it to the overhead floor joists to seal off the first phase of his workspace construction from his mom and Gerald. The basement was always Will's domain. His mom backed him up unequivocally on this and Gerald, though he grumbled, went along with the edict. Will was sure it was because as long as Will wasn't anywhere to be seen or heard, Gerald was happy. Out of sight, out of mind. That's the way it worked. *If only it worked that way with everything*, thought Will.

Two hours later Will heard his mom and then Gerald come home and, rather than risk an awkward intrusion, went upstairs and shared perfunctory greetings with them. While Gerald opened one of his homemade beers and extolled its taste, Will nodded like he gave a crap, had a quick bite of chicken and biscuits, mumbled something about homework, and then went back down into the basement. Two hours after that he had the darkroom set up in the first chamber. Anyone trying to enter had to do so by means of a "light lock," which meant completing an S turn and then moving through a flap door so that by the time you were in the amber-lit room you were completely turned around, a fact that worked entirely to Will's advantage. Any parental unit snooping around would surely miss the fact that Will had put up a false back wall, creating a secret chamber that only he knew about.

Now that his secret chamber was in place, at least with temporary walls, Will went about setting up his futon and unpacking his crates of equipment. He had geological sensor probes and infrared motion detectors and spelunking supplies. He had a well-stocked chemical lab setup and another for weapons design. He had a crate that held his cache of weapons, which he unpacked and inspected. The pulse generator pistol had shifted in transit, but he examined it and it looked fine. And of course he had his computers. Lots and lots of computers; enough computing power, in fact, to service a small university. He was wired in and dialed in to the max. He had to be. His survival was at stake.

He set up his largest monitor, connected to his most powerful XTC 9000 computer, and fired up his *Demon Hunter* game. He fed in some data and the hero on the screen came to life, charged down a hallway, and using a microartillery bracelet, unleashed a barrage of firepower that blasted a horrifying winged demon. He glanced at his kill count. 642. Will smiled. The microartillery bracelet kicked ass, but was nothing compared to his power rod.

Turning his attention away from the game program, Will opened several more crates and set up his chemical analysis and modification lab. Once it was operative he concocted a cleansing healing potion. Rolling up his shirt sleeve, he applied it to his forearm where the Goth punk had sunken in his rusty screw teeth. The salve stung at first but as it began to simultaneously disinfect and heal, the pain lessened. Will watched as his skin repaired itself, the wounds pussing, then scabbing, then smoothing over in a matter of seconds instead of the usual days. It said a lot about how much he had to use it that he'd recalled his precise formula off the top of his head without having to consult the data on his mainframe.

He was rolling his shirt sleeve back down when he heard a noise. His head jerked up to the right and he saw the barest flash of an image. Eyes, a pair of eyes. Silently cursing himself for leaving a small corner of one of the basement window wells exposed, he grabbed a boltdriver and sprinted out of his secret warren. He took the stairs three at a time and burst up into the kitchen and out the door.

Outside he ducked into a crouch and quickly scanned the yard for movement. There! A figure was darting through the shadows. Fortunately the guy didn't look too big or strong so Will pocketed the boltdriver and took off running across the dark yard, his feet slipping on the wet grass. The interloper was fast and evasive but Will had experience, *lots* of experience, not to mention time-bending speed, so when the guy zigged Will zagged and leapt into him, knocking him sideways and taking him down with a flying tackle. The guy was slender and strong and had arms taut with muscle, but Will swiftly overpowered him and flipped him over. Then his jaw dropped. It wasn't a guy, it was a girl. It was *her*. Natalie.

"Back off, you freak!" she shouted.

"Whoa! Um, it's Natalie, right?" he stammered.

"Yeah, that's right, it's Natalie. I don't think we really met properly before."

Will was stunned and didn't see the punch coming. But he sure felt it. Not only was Natalie strong, she had one heck of an uppercut. Will blinked up at the stars, and now she was looking down at him. She looked pissed. "Do you always go around tackling people?"

Will got up rubbing his jaw. He couldn't help but notice again how she seemed even prettier when she was mad as a hornet.

"Why are you in my yard?" he asked.

"I was out walking, and I was . . . curious. This is my neighborhood, too, you know." Natalie's eyes sparkled with life and Will was again flummoxed, this time by his attraction to her.

"What were you doing spying on me?"

"The question is, what were *you* doing in your basement that you didn't want anybody to see? And what is that thing?" She pointed to the boltdriver, which had fallen out of Will's pocket.

"It looks like some kind of taser or something. Are you a hood?"

"It's just a . . . prop. Sometimes I make videos." Will hastily shoved the boltdriver back into his pocket.

"Uh-huh." Her tone said she didn't buy it. "And that goopy stuff you were putting on your arm?"

Will couldn't answer immediately; he had to think about this. He decided that sometimes the best defense was a good offense.

"I should turn you in for being a peeping Tom," he said. He started walking back toward his house but stopped at her next words.

"Fine, do that. And I'll tell everyone I know about your secret little mad scientist laboratory in your basement."

A voice suddenly blurted from the hedge, "What secret mad scientist laboratory?"

Both Will and Natalie jumped at the sound but relaxed as Rudy emerged from the shadows, crawling out of the hedge, brushing debris off himself.

"What are *you* doing here?" demanded Will. This was not good. Things were quickly getting out of control.

"What's it look like? I'm snooping, eavesdropping, detecting."

"Well, you can cease and desist now, and depart," said Will.

"No way, José!" said Rudy. "I have as much right to know what's going on here as she does."

Will looked to Natalie for help.

"He's not mine," she said, then added, "So what's it gonna be, you show-and-tell, or we tell and then you show?"

He would have to make some kind of concession or he'd never get rid of them. He thought quickly. "What do you want?"

"Well, for starters, you could slop some of that magic goop on this," she said, holding up her elbow. Her long-sleeved T had torn and her elbow was bleeding.

"Magic goop? Cool! Oh, she's bleeding, I think I'm gonna faint."

"Please do," said Will. "That would definitely be your best move."

"Nobody's fainting and nobody's leaving, not until you share, cowboy," said Natalie.

Will looked around at the trees, which were gently swaying in the night wind. The area looked secure, at least for now. And he couldn't risk Natalie following through on her threat. These two seemed relatively harmless and he didn't have to really show them much, just enough to get them off his back. Part of him wanted to show them, wanted to let them in on his secrets. He couldn't, of course, but surely them seeing a few things wouldn't hurt. He'd take them down and put on a little dog-and-pony show and be done with it. Shaking his head, he motioned for Natalie and Rudy to follow.

"All right, come with me."

Entering Will's house they ran smack into April, whose face lit up with delight. Rudy's jaw dropped. This woman was so retro, she looked like June Cleaver from that old black-and-white show *Leave It to Beaver*. She wasn't wearing pearls or anything, but she did have on a cotton dress and the way she smiled made him think of old-fashioned moms, not modern ones like his own mom, who wore workout clothes most of the time. Rudy smiled right back at Will's mom as she spoke.

"I see you've already made friends. How wonderful. I'm April, Will's mother, and that's Gerald."

Gerald was in the adjacent room, wearing the world's ugliest mismatched terry cloth shorts and shirt outfit, complete with ketchup stains. He was glued to the TV, watching the golf channel and chugging his homemade beer, and didn't even bother grunting in their direction. He did, however, treat them to one of his fire-cracker farts, which delighted Rudy to no end.

"I'm Natalie," said Natalie, hiding her wound and extending her other hand, which April took. She was about to go on when Rudy butted in.

"I'm Rudy, and your son, Will, I mean, he really stepped up to the plate and saved my butt today, let me tell you!"

"Oh, he helped you with your schoolwork?" asked April.

"No, I was practically in the jaws of death when he—"

Will saw Gerald's head bob up like he couldn't wait to hear what a screw-up Will had been on his first day as the New Kid. Will cut Rudy off.

"Yeah, Mom, schoolwork, something like that. Listen, I'm gonna show them my darkroom real quick and then they're gonna leave."

"I can bring you some—"

"We don't need any milk and cookies," said Will.

Rudy frowned.

"We don't?"

They clomped down the basement stairs and then Will led them through his maze of black plastic and into his secret chamber where they were visibly impressed. Rudy let out a low whistle.

"Something tells me this isn't just some science project. Whoa, your computers, your database, it's all so . . . massive!" Rudy marveled at the bank of flat panel LCD displays and the whirring servers and modems twinkling with dozens of lights. "Hey, that's *Demon Hunter*! But what version is it? I haven't seen this one yet!" Rudy was just about jumping out of his skin with excitement as he stared at a game loop going on one of Will's monitors.

"It's an old version," he said.

"No way, I have them all and I haven't seen that one." Then Rudy's eyes went way wide with shock. "Six hundred and forty-two kills? Are you KIDDING me?"

"It's just a glitch in the program."

"I WANT that glitch, dude! How'd you do it? Come on, tell me!"

Sometimes not saying anything at all was the best way to deal with inquiring minds and Will just simply dumped the subject, ignoring Rudy and turning his attention to Natalie.

"Let's have a look at that arm." He touched Natalie's hand gently, without thinking, and they both blushed. He ignored that and focused on her injury. Her wound was minor, just a scrape, and he knew he would have to do a little sleight of hand here so she wouldn't freak out watching the rapid healing process. He applied some of the ointment and then looked into her eyes and asked her to do the same.

"Who do you think you are, Count Dracula? Why should I look in your eyes?"

"Because I want to check your pupils, this is very important."

"You can be one very intense guy, you know that?" she said.

"I get that a lot. The eyes? Look into my eyes?"

Natalie obeyed him and they locked eyes. It was instinct for any animal, including the human animal, to want to examine its wounds; and Will just had to keep her distracted long enough to put a bandage over the already healing scrape. Once he'd succeeded, it finally occurred to him the position he'd put himself in. He was standing right in front of Natalie, their faces close together, as he held lightly onto her arm. His face burned again. They quickly looked away from each other.

"Keep it totally covered and don't take the bandage off for at least three days."

Will was so distracted he didn't even notice Rudy picking up the boltdriver that he had set down on the workbench earlier. KABLAM! The shot rang out like a thunderbolt, which of course it was, albeit a mini one. All three of them stared at the smoking hole in the wall.

"Give me that!" Will snatched the boltdriver out of Rudy's shaking hands.

"Whoa! That is soooo cool! Fire that sucker again!"

"I'm not going to fire anything! And please don't ever touch anything in here again."

"What IS that thing?" demanded Rudy.

"It's just a little electro-magnetic voltage stimulator, a stun gun I made some minor modifications on."

"Minor modifications?" asked Natalie, waving away the smoke from the smoldering hole in the wall. She stared hard at Will. "Hunter, isn't it? Will Hunter?"

"Congratulations, you got my name right."

"Well, Mister Will Hunter, who exactly are you and what are you doing in Harrisburg?"

"What do you mean? My mom got a new job, so we moved here. I'm just a guy, a junior in high school, the New Kid. That's about it."

Will caught an image on one of his huge plasma screens behind Natalie and Rudy, an unmarked grid of Harrisburg. A yellow glow emanated from one of the sectors. Will cleared his throat and purposefully knocked over a canister.

"Whoops!" He bent down to pick it up and secretly hit a switch for his equipment. Everything went dim and on standby. Will smiled a friendly guy smile, his best "Hey, I'm just a normal kid like you" smile, and began to herd the two snoops out of his domain. "If you don't mind, I'm like totally slammed with homework and could use some me time."

He escorted them out and stood watching them walk down the street, Natalie shooting wary looks back over her shoulder at him and Rudy weaving down the sidewalk, engaged in some game of chase happening entirely in his own mind. Will couldn't help but smile. He liked the kid. Even though Rudy was roughly the same age as he was, Will couldn't help thinking of him as a kid. He himself had been made older by experiences, few of them the kind a sixteen-year-old kid should have. He wished he'd had a different life, a life in which he could fall for a girl like Natalie and be friends with goofy

Rudy. But that just wasn't possible. Not with the quest that awaited him each and every day of his life.

Natalie turned and looked at him one last time before turning the corner, and he remembered. He *had* seen that face before. Only the name attached to it wasn't Natalie.

Chapter Four:
The Vanishing

Natalie entered her house and went up into her room. Even though the rest of the house was pretty much style-deprived, she'd done a sweet number on her own digs. The walls were dusty rose and she'd sponged her ceiling to look like clouds. A prodigious reader, she had scads of books and had them lined up in alphabetical order on a couple of wooden bookshelves she'd rescued from the alley, sanded down, and painted teal blue. She worked at her desk doing homework for twenty minutes but her brain was elsewhere. She got up and stretched, then fell onto her bed and thought of Will.

When she'd seen him at the bus stop that morning, she couldn't believe how hot he was. She'd spent most of the wait for the bus stealing glances at him, noticing how trim and muscular he was, how well his jeans fit, how his blue eyes caught the light. She hadn't been sure then if she'd seen right or had hallucinated but it seemed as though one of Will's eyes was lighter, almost crystal blue, while the other was a deep, piercing sapphire. But she'd confirmed it in his basement, staring right into them as he fixed up her arm.

She looked at the bandage on her arm and even though Will had instructed her to keep it on for—what did he say, three days?—she was curious because she felt no more pain and peeled the bandage back. She felt like a caterpillar crawled up her spine when she saw that where the wound had been, her skin was smooth as silk. Not a trace of the injury remained. She shuddered and whatever yearning she felt for Will increased exponentially.

She didn't like being so attracted to some new neighbor whom she hardly knew; it made her feel weak and vulnerable and the last thing she needed now was to feel more out of control than she already did. She tried not to think of him but she couldn't because the thought of him was like something clinging to her skin. She decided to take a shower. One of the old movies her grandmother used to love to watch had a scene where some women sang, "I'm gonna wash that man right out of my hair," and Natalie thought it was worth a try. She stayed in the shower a long time, washing and rinsing her long hair, and then turned off the water and toweled off. She got out and put on her pajama bottoms and a camisole and again fell onto her bed.

She closed her eyes and felt the stinging of tears, tears that came upon her suddenly. Why was this happening? She went to her night stand and picked up a picture of what looked like her with shorter hair. But it wasn't her; it was her twin sister Emily. Same nose, same chin, same cheeks, same blonde hair only shorter, same sparkling eyes. Natalie held the framed photograph up to a mirror and positioned it next to her face. *So alike they could hardly tell us apart*, she thought. *But we were different enough, and we knew it*. Natalie watched as another tear emerged from her eye, not her tear but her sister's; no one but a twin could ever understand. *Why are you crying?* she asked the photograph. *What have they done to you? Where have they taken you? Please tell me, Em, please?*

Natalie shut her eyes again, opening all her intuition, all her channels, making herself ready for a sign, a message, any kind of communication from Emily. She received them frequently. But there was nothing tonight. By her bedside sat a scrapbook. If she'd opened it like she had a thousand times before she would have seen the newspaper clippings about how Emily drowned while swimming in Green River, how even though her body had never been found, the police concluded that there was no foul play. Because of the drugs. Emily wasn't a heavy user, she only experimented. She was just a chipper. Natalie had warned her dozens of times that nothing good could come from using drugs, but Emily always laughed in that little bird-like way of hers and blew her twin sister off. Natalie knew now, too late, that she should have been more proactive, she should have demanded Em stop using, even turning her in if she had to.

She remembered the night it happened like it was five minutes ago. They went on a double date with Jim Sparrow and Hal Stellini in Jim's dad's Range Rover. The guys and Em fired up joints and passed them around but Natalie refrained. She never saw the point of becoming impaired. She enjoyed her life *au naturale*, organic, without the use of chemical additives or *addictives* for that matter. She was already flying high. The music was fantastic, the warm night air like a blanket around them.

They drove with the windows down and then pulled in and parked by Old Mill Restaurant next to the river. The moon bathed the riverbank in a silver band of silk and they cranked up the stereo and danced. Natalie felt free as a nightbird. She loved watching her sister, who always danced like there was no tomorrow. Emily danced so hard and so fast that she was soon soaked in sweat and she kissed Jim and he whispered something into her ear. Shrieking, Emily ran into a thicket of trees, peeling off her clothes, and Jim followed. Natalie was blushing and feeling awkward because she knew Hal would be entreating her to do the same and there was just no way that was going to happen, even though Hal was cute and played guitar like Ben Harper. They just danced, and when the music slowed, they slowed down with it. Hal tried to kiss her but she didn't feel that way about him. She felt bad because he was such a nice guy and she hated to hurt people's feelings. So she let him kiss her on the cheek and he seemed for the moment satisfied.

When the sudden cloud cover blacked out the opal moon they hardly noticed. When the rain began to fall it was so warm that they laughed but when the trees shook and the river began to rise, Natalie became worried. She heard her sister shriek and her heart started hammering in her chest.

"Emily? Em?"

She ran into the thicket where Emily had disappeared. In her peripheral vision she saw the earth moving. Not the whole landscape, just patches of the damp, leaf-strewn earth—shapes, ugly, awful shapes that rose up too swift for the eye to see and then disappeared down again. Then in the distance through foliage she saw sets of eyes in the river, each with one green glowing eye and one yellow. The eyes blinked as the creatures in the river moved rapidly about, then disappeared. Natalie thought that surely she was hallucinating. Maybe she'd inhaled some of the weed and it was laced with something. Whatever it was, her head was spinning, and she heard things, too. Low, guttural sounds, the kinds of sounds animals make. She ran toward the river.

"EMILY?"

Natalie burst out of the thicket, onto the riverbank, and found Jim lying on his side moaning, his scalp bleeding.

"What happened?"

Jim just moaned again and felt his head.

"Where's Emily? Jim, where's my sister?" she demanded.

"Hey, take it easy on him, can't you see he's been hurt?"

Hal had arrived and was holding Natalie back as he leaned down to examine Jim, handing him his clothes, which Jim began to slowly pull back on.

"Jim, did you slip and fall?"

"No, they . . . hit me."

"WHO hit you?" Natalie screamed.

"I . . . I don't know . . . I didn't really see them."

Natalie's eyes frantically scanned the riverbank, both sides, and the river itself. Her nostrils stung with an astringent smell, a strong chemical odor. It was so potent for a moment it burned her eyes. Then she saw the mismatched eyes in the river again; sets of eyes: yellow and green, those horrible, horrible eyes! She took one look at Emily's clothes strewn on the rocks and then splashed into the river, screaming her sister's name, her throat going hot and raw with the pain of dreadful possibility. What if, what if. . . . Her mind racing, heart banging in her chest, her eyes bled tears as she called for Emily again and again, then turned on Jim like a feral creature and bore into him with accusing eyes.

"Where is she, Jim? Where did she go?"

"She . . . she was right here, and then it got dark, and. . . ."

"What, Jim, WHAT?"

"And then I don't remember." Jim held his head and Natalie hated him in that moment for being so pathetic, so clueless. He should have protected her sister, not just let her *disappear*. Tearing her eyes from the river, Natalie looked back at the dark woods and ran upriver.

"Emily!"

She raced through thick brush and stinging nettles and blackberry bushes with stalks thick as her wrist. Thorns tore at her skin, and still she ran, crying out, her feet slipping in her wet shoes. But there was no sign, no sound, of Emily. Natalie staggered back down to the riverbank where the boys were huddled.

Hal tried to reassure her, "Don't worry Natalie, she's probably just downriver, they'll find her. They will," but voices whispered to her in the night wind, tiny evil voices like bones being crushed. *No, they won't.* Natalie shook her head and the voices became the sound of the river. Had they spoken, or was it just in her head? The pain she felt was like a thick narcotic, slowing time as it coursed through her veins, her brain now sluggish, energy spent. Natalie looked up at the moon, the smiling face now a nasty grimace.

"Don't leave me, Emily, don't you dare leave me!" And then Natalie cut loose with a scream that rose from a place she didn't even know existed, a scream that lifted birds from their nests and drove rodents farther underground—the howl of a twin torn asunder. And just as suddenly as the sky had darkened the clouds above parted and the river seemed to calm down. For a split second Natalie thought she saw eyes, yellow and green eyes, again in the river, near the bottom. Fury cleared the sluggishness from her body and she ran and dove in.

"Jesus, what are you doing?" yelled Hal. He hesitated, and then dove in after her. They were both underwater, their thrashing kicking up silt that swirled up from the river bottom and turned the water a murky green. Hal's hands found Natalie's wrists and, gasping, he pulled her from the river and onto the bank.

It was a night that Natalie prayed to forget and yet her heart would never allow it. It was the night when it seemed as if the river itself had risen up and claimed her soul mate, her sister, her other half. Without Emily, Natalie felt utterly incomplete.

In her bedroom Natalie put the picture of her twin sister back on top of her nightstand. The night of terror and loss was the past. The only thing that mattered now was getting her back. Everyone thought Natalie was crazy, thought she was just another wounded twin who lost her sibling and would be forever haunted, a loony who held out hope when there was none. But Natalie knew different; she knew her twin sister was alive.

On the streets of Harrisburg a chilly wind buffeted Will as he rode his turbo scooter, carrying the megaspatial awl in a small telescope case that stuck out of his backpack. He had a rule about weapons, which was never design anything that couldn't be jammed into a backpack. This device, though technically not a weapon, was capable of exuding great force, so he had to be covert. Like all his weapons and gear it was of his own design and manufacture and

Will knew he had to be careful hauling it around. The boys at the Pentagon would love to get their hands on any one of Will's inventions, including this one.

Any curious onlooker would no doubt conclude that Will was riding his scooter up to high ground, up to the local lover's lane, Netter's Ridge—some called it Makeout Heaven—to set up his telescope and gaze at the constellations. What a good boy, studying the stars for his science class. In fact Will loved to stargaze, but he had no time for that tonight, not after seeing the blip on his geothermal radar screen.

When he reached an intersection, instead of heading up the hill he turned and took a long street that sloped down to the lowest part of town, the city blocks that held the Harrisburg Cemetery. As cemeteries go it wasn't bad, no better or worse than others he'd spent far too much time in. This one had a rustic split-rail fence surrounding the perimeter, as though the land held sheep or cattle instead of decaying corpses. Using his infrareds Will scanned the grounds. No creatures larger than a small rabbit were in attendance, so he unpacked the megaspatial awl, loaded it with blast cartridges, and then powered four sensor spikes into the ground in a quadrant enclosing the cemetery. Then he zoomed down another street and every few hundred yards or so blasted another spike into the ground. It took him more than three hours but he eventually had Harrisburg plugged in, letting him monitor demonic movement as far as the city limits. When he was done he was thirsty enough for a Big Gulp and swung by a 7-Eleven.

Inside the small convenience store he pumped himself a root beer Slurpee, paid for it, and took it outside where he found a low wall to sit on, enjoy his drink, and feel the cool night breeze against his skin. Sometimes it felt so good to be alive that he ached. On occasion he would allow himself to enjoy these simple moments, quaint pleasures of a normal life, but invariably his thoughts would bring him back to reality. He wasn't normal and he never would be.

He looked up at the sky and closed his eyes. *I miss you, Dad*, he said in his inner voice. And he thought he heard his father say, *I miss you, too, son.*

Will was sitting in the shadows so he was pretty much obscured when the beat-to-crap '91 Taurus pulled in, blaring "Sista Killer" from six speakers and two huge subwoofers in the trunk. A couple of gansta wannabees chugged down the last of some cheap tequila then pulled ski masks over their heads. *Crap*, thought Will, *I'm so not in the mood for this. Can't a guy take a break, enjoy his freakin' Slurpee, and commune with the cosmos without the long slimy arm of crime reaching out to him?* He guessed not. He watched the punks carefully, studying their eyes. They were bloodshot, pupils dilated from drugs, but not liquid black. Maybe these two were just a couple of drunk, doped-up losers. They sure looked that way on the surface. When he saw the 9mm come out and the clerk so scared he was going to wet his pants, Will sighed and knew what he had to do.

As the robbery was going down Will felt his anger bubbling up but he kept cool and calmly walked over and knelt down behind the swinging front door. He loaded up the megaspatial awl with a spike and blast cartridge and waited and watched the scene unfolding using a parabolic mirror. If the guy with the gun had put his finger on the trigger Will would have had to go on inside. But the money was being handed over without a fight so he aimed the megaspatial awl at the Taurus. *Bye-bye.* He fired a spike into the gas tank and KABLAM! The Taurus went up in a ball of flames, all four doors blown cleanly off their moorings. The punks turned and mouthed the obligatory F-words and then charged out the front door. That's when Will stood up and clocked them both at once with dual upper-cuts that rattled their pea brains and dropped them in the doorway like two sacks of yesterday's rotten apples. He felt a thrill course through his body, a feeling so seductive and pleasurable that it scared him. He shook his head, ashamed, willing the feeling to go away. *It shouldn't feel this good to hurt people*, he thought.

Will picked up the gym bag they'd used to grab the loot and returned the cash to the open-mouthed clerk, who was still in shock but not so numb he couldn't mutter a croaking, "Thank you." And then, as Will started to cruise away into the night on his turbo scooter, the clerk came out from behind the counter, dialing the cops, and called after Will. "Hey, who ARE you anyway?"

Will just muttered to himself, "The New Kid."

Fifteen minutes later Will was back in his basement refuge, powering up all his monitors. He studied the one linked to the geothermal sensors and the spectral scalar and vector magnetometers he'd just planted. The magnetometers had the capability to measure the component of the magnetic field in a particular direction, which meant that in combination with his ground-penetrating radar he could detect movement underground.

The cemetery looked dormant, no corpses rising, no catacombs active. The rest of the town was quiet, too. He moved to his main computer and hit some keys that began the recording process, then pushed his chair back and rubbed his eyes. Even Will Hunter needed sleep, and right now he needed it badly. He dimmed the lights, exited his lair, and climbed upstairs. Moments after he did, the monitor showed movement, a tiny red light flickering in one of the sectors. And then the light grew brighter. And began moving.

Upstairs, Gerald was multitasking, brushing his teeth and scratching his ass. He grunted as Will passed by him, then blurted out something nearly unintelligible. Will ignored him.

"May, I'm dalking do doo!"

Yeah, you're talking doo-doo alright, thought Will. He sometimes wondered if Gerald wasn't a human but a monster of some sort, but knew that was just his bitterness talking. The guy wasn't anything so spectacular as a monster; he was just another middle-aged washout, and Will was duty-bound to make nice for his mother's sake. So he smiled his good teenage boy smile.

"What's up, Gerald?"

"How'd it go at school today? You didn't cause any trouble, did you?"

"No more than usual."

"That's not funny. Be straight with me."

Gerald grabbed Will by the arm, and Will stiffened. The red curtain formed in his brain and could have closed easily, in which case Gerald would have sustained grave bodily injury. Will was shaking, his anger coming to life swiftly and powerfully. But he knew better. He was tempted to give Gerald a good panda kick that would send him through the wall and probably crack his skull. Instead he thought of how much he loved his mother, remembered the smile on her face when he'd surprised her with daffodils on her birthday, and the scarlet curtain faded away. Will forced himself to stay in this quiet place while he relaxed his muscles and actually managed to produce another saccharin smile for Gerald.

"It was just another day, Gerald. I hope you enjoy your delicious cleansing beer while you watch Leno tonight. Goodnight."

Gerald let go and muttered something foolish and vaguely threatening while Will quietly retreated to his room and collapsed onto his bed. Another violent storm averted. Will remembered how his father told him to choose his battles and make them few. Gerald wasn't worth a battle.

There was but one vehicle parked on Netter's Ridge, Duncan's black-on-black Scion xB, and it vibrated with the sound of heavy metal death rappers enticing someone, anyone, to do something that they would perhaps enjoy now but no doubt regret later, doing twenty to life. Sitting next to Duncan was Mookie Heller, the handsome but thick-necked Thug One whom Duncan had earlier charged with guarding the boys' room door. Their heads bobbing to the music, Duncan and Mookie smoked from a small metal pipe and sucked down rocket blasters, a combination of vodka and a popular purple energy drink, Zing. While he bobbed his head, Mookie flipped through one of the many tattoo artist magazines he had on his lap. The Mook was a tattoo freak, no doubt about it.

"I was hangin' out at the Puke Parlor, watchin' Black Dog lay down some ink. He let me practice with one of the needle guns. It was sooo cool!" boasted Mookie. But Duncan just fixed him with a hard cold stare.

"The hell you thinkin' about that shit for when you can't even do one simple thing I ask?" To punctuate his words Duncan smacked Mookie on the back of his head.

"Sorry I messed up today, Dunc, it won't happen again."

Duncan didn't acknowledge Mookie's answer, just kept bobbing his head to the music and clenched his jaws, bringing up thick veins on his temples. It wasn't the music that Duncan was responding to; it was a voice that only he heard. It was a voice that told him what he must do. The voice was fathomless and raspy and gave Duncan the chills.

"Someone has come. I will need your help now more than ever."

"Whatever, sure . . . you know I'm there, man," stammered Duncan. Mookie looked over.

"You talking to me?"

"Shut up, Mook!" shouted Duncan. And then the voice spoke again, crawling into Duncan's head through his ears like a snake.

"It's time to prove your loyalty," said the voice.

Duncan could hardly believe it. What more did he have to do? When the voice told him to single out a kid for a beating, Duncan listened and did as he was told. Yesterday the voice told him his mother was a whore and the paint salesman she was currently dating deserved to die. Duncan couldn't agree more. But the voice hadn't told him to kill anyone. Yet. Last week when the voice requested that he steal drugs from a local dealer, Duncan had no problem setting up the phony buy, meeting the skinny hippy freak in an alley, and then using a pipe to beat him bloody and steal his

$500-an-ounce skunk. What could the voice be wanting him to do now, tonight?

"Higher, fly higher, Duncan," said the voice.

And so Duncan smoked more, and drank more, smoked and drank until he could see the music rushing out of the speakers in neon hues, until his head floated up and parked itself above his body and watched while he patted Mookie on the shoulder and said, "Let's go for a walk."

They got out of the xB and Duncan led Mookie to Lover's Leap, past the "Danger" and "Caution: Steep Cliff" signs to the craggy bluff from which you could see the whole of Harrisburg stretching out like a vast black carpet speckled with twinkling lights.

"You know what I look like when someone doesn't do what I ask?"

"Of course I do, Dunc, you look bad, that's why I said I was sorry. You know I'm loyal to you, hell, I'd jump in front of a train for you."

"Really?" asked Duncan, his bloodshot eyes struggling to find Mookie's shape, let alone any expression of truth or dishonesty on his face.

"Yeah, man. We shouldn't even be having this discussion. We're tight, we're solid," said Mookie.

"Okay, then show me. Put one foot out there, over the edge."

"Aw, man, Dunc, don't make me do this."

"You said you'd jump in front of a train. This should be nothing."

Mookie's balance was already severely impaired by the booze and drugs but two thoughts took hold in his soggy brain. One: He *was* loyal, dammit. And two: This would be over soon, he could do it. He lifted a leg up and reached it out over the ledge while he balanced on the other. He felt good, he had an incredible buzz on, Duncan was right, this was nothing. Mookie was so high he felt like he could fly. He was invincible. He turned and smiled at Duncan.

"There. See? You trust me now, Duncan? Huh?"

"Yeah," said Duncan.

And then he pushed him. As Mookie screamed and fell, Duncan closed his eyes and felt a sudden gust of wind, warm as hot breath. His nostrils stung as he smelled the familiar acrid smell that assaulted him whenever he had these kinds of hallucinations. Because that's what they were, weren't they? They had to be. This whole thing couldn't be real. It just couldn't be. But it was. Duncan was infected, rotten to the core—a servant, a soldier, a slave.

Mookie didn't die, but he broke both his legs and suffered compression ruptures in two disks in his lower back, an injury that confined him to a wheelchair for an indefinite period of time. Instead of funneling his anger, bitterness, and hatred toward Duncan, Mookie turned it all back on himself, channeling it inward. It was his fault, the voice told him, and the only path toward redemption was through servitude. He must serve *him*. And Mookie made up his mind that he would. He would shave the hair from his body. He'd always been into tattooing and now he threw himself into the art with a vengeance. His numb legs weren't useless, they were a canvas and he would spend his days alone in his basement as the Michelangelo of tattoo artists, emblazoning himself with the perfect pagan symbols to prove his worthiness. He would be a soldier in the New Army, the Army of Rage, loyal only to the Dark One.

Chapter Five:
The Challenge

Just as she had last year as a sophomore, Sharon Mitchell led the cheers at the lunchtime pep rally to help drum up support for this year's gridiron campaign. The Harrisburg Mustangs had been perennial conference doormats but all that had changed last year. They started out 0-3 but had a miraculous turnaround, finishing 9-3 and tying for the conference title. This year they were 7-0 and were steamrolling opponents in a punishing fashion. Will sat in the bleachers not far from Natalie. Rudy was right by his side.

"She's looking at you, man," said Rudy, elbowing Will and indicating Sharon.

"She's looking at everybody," said Will.

"Hey, get a clue, she's definitely checking you out. Gawd, I can't believe how lucky you are! You know what I'd give to have her look at me just one lousy time?"

"You're telling me you've been going to school with her for years and she's never ever looked at you?"

"No, she did look once," said Rudy.

"Well, there you go."

"I don't think it counts. She only looked at me because I was throwing up on one of her friends."

"Thanks for sharing," said Will.

"Man, she is just nailing you with her eyes, dude!" quipped Rudy.

Sharon Mitchell *was* staring at Will as she did her routine. She had stunningly beautiful eyes but Will didn't need the distraction. Instead of staring back at Sharon, Will scanned the entire gym. All the kids looked healthy and vibrant, the gym brimming with excitement and color. The hardwood floors gleamed and the glass backboards shined. Everything was squeaky clean. It was like an advertisement for chewing gum or some soda drink; this was the ideal, this was Americana at its best. How could there be anything evil in the midst of these wholesome young teens? In situations like this sometimes Will had to pinch himself to break the spell. He knew that even when things looked wonderful and pristine on the surface, underneath there would be pain and suffering, young minds full of malice. As he scanned the gym he was looking for *them* but he saw only regular normal teenagers and a smattering of adults. The creatures he sought knew full well how to hide in plain sight, though, and strike when you least expected it. He had a feeling there was at least one of *them* in the gym. But who was it? He kept looking at the eyes, always the eyes.

"Stand up, it's time to shout, come on fans, yell it out! Say it proud, Go Mustangs, Go Mustangs, Go Mustangs!"

Sharon and her cohorts were in fine form, working the crowd up, getting everyone into the spirit, though truth be told, most of the boys in the stands were not thinking about the upcoming football season but praying for some miracle wardrobe malfunction. Natalie's eyes ping-ponged back and forth between Sharon and Will, noticing how Sharon was openly locked in on Will as she bounced and shook her green and gold pom-poms in a syncopated rhythm. Then Sharon leapt forward and as she shook her hips she did a solo yell.

"Salt makes you thirsty, pepper makes you sneeze, but when it comes to football we make you buckle at the knees! Go Mustangs!"

She high-kicked her way closer to Will and then tossed off her pom-poms, backed up, and with a running start executed a magnificent handspring front flip, landing breathless and flushed right in front of Will. The spectacular gymnastics move brought the most ardent fans in the "Pony Power section" to their feet, screeching. But Duncan wasn't cheering. His eyes were dark and he stared at Will and Sharon as though they were terrorists. If looks could kill.

Moments later in the hallway Will walked along with Rudy.

"I hear Coach Kellog's looking for a new running back. What about you? Can you run?" asked Rudy as he joked around and handed off an apple into Will's stomach like a football. Will just kept walking.

"Well then, maybe you can throw. Hit me, I'm going long!"

Will smiled and waited a few beats, took a bite of the apple, then tossed it down the hall.

Rudy made a juggling, overly dramatic catch. "He scores!"

"Trust me, the jerk's *not* going to score."

Will heard the familiar voice and turned around to see Duncan right in his face. His breath smelled acrid and his eyes were bloodshot.

"Keep your creepy eyes off my girlfriend," he snarled.

Will didn't want to deal with this right now, but he was also sick of guys like Duncan. Every school had way too many of them and they needed to be put in their place. He knew he should keep his mouth shut but somehow he just couldn't. He figured Duncan couldn't be one of *them* because that would just be too easy. Still, He often went for the cruelest alpha males, luring them with power and glory, so anything was possible.

Will baited Duncan even before he knew he was doing it. "Your girlfriend was in the gym? Gee, somebody must have left the barn door open."

Rudy howled like that was the funniest thing said in the history of mankind and even Duncan's acolytes couldn't help but burp out some muffled chuckles.

"I'm *talking* about Sharon Mitchell, the head cheerleader. The most beautiful and bootylicious girl in the whole school, dipwad. I saw you gawking at her. Knock it off, she's mine."

"Funny, I didn't see your name tag on her," said Will.

Duncan's fuse had been lit a long time ago—probably at birth, thought Will—and this set him off. He grabbed Will by the collar and slammed him into a locker, hard. Will closed his eyes and breathed, thinking of the surface of a pond, the skin of the water so calm it was like glass. The trick worked and he remained relaxed and unfazed. Duncan's nostrils flared like a stallion and he yelled in Will's face.

"She's wearing my pin! We're going steady!"

"Not anymore."

Sharon's voice rang out soft and sweet. Rudy thought it sounded like liquid candy and he let out a low whistle as Sharon removed Duncan's two-year football pin and handed it to him. Farther down the hallway Natalie was watching Sharon put on her little show for Will's benefit. Natalie told herself she didn't care and stalked off, but only got ten feet before turning back around and taking it all in. The truth was she did care, and she watched in horror as Sharon continued with the public dump.

"Sorry to do this now, Dunky, in front of all these people. Wait a minute, no, I'm not, because this definitely makes it officially official."

Smiling politely and then tossing a come-on look at Will, Sharon walked off with the other cheerleaders laughing and trailing behind her, leaving Duncan floundering in a pool of humiliation. If he was angry before, he was seriously, dementedly, borderline-brain-exploding furious now and he sucker-punched Will, who was momentarily dazed, stunned just enough so that when Todd and another of Duncan's muscular bootlickers shoulder-jammed him against the lockers it took him at least two seconds to react with a couple moves of his own, spinning and kicking. The melee was on and Rudy jumped up and down.

"Kick their butts, Will!"

Will had had it with these punks and was just about to go into time-bending mode when a stentorian voice rang through the hallway: "That's enough!"

It was Coach Kellog, a towering bulky man who you could tell was once in fantastic shape but had hoovered way too many Whoppers since and had gone mostly to flab, straining his Sansabelt slacks. Still, on the football field and in the hallways he was the law, and the skirmish subsided as swiftly as it had begun.

"So, you like to hit, huh?" he asked Will.

"Not especially. But if somebody hits me, I hit back."

Will noticed the coach wore a Patek Philippe Calatrava watch that ran around twenty grand. He made it a point to be able to spot expensive jewelry because sometimes it tipped him off. Demons were often too proud and too stupid to hide the fact that they were suckers for expensive jewelry. But then, so were a lot of so-called normal people.

Coach Kellog's eyes narrowed. He grabbed Will's arm by the bicep and was pleasantly surprised at how strong the kid was.

"Nice attitude. Let's see you bring it to the field after school. You got a problem with that, Duncan?"

The coach turned to Duncan and his boys. Duncan hung his head.

"No, Coach," he said, and then stomped off.

"Well then, it's all settled, we'll see you after school, New Kid."

Will watched Coach Kellog cut a swath as he swaggered down the hallway.

Rudy sidled up next to Will and grinned. "Looks like somebody's trying out for the team after all."

Then he went into his goofy primate dance and in a singsong voice talked about the one girl in school that he'd thought about every single day ever since third grade.

"Sharon Mitchell. Oh, man, I can't stand it! *Sharon Mitchell!*"

The rest of the school day passed without incident and as he trudged toward the football field after the final bell rang Will wished he'd never antagonized Duncan. He should have just backed down and hidden behind a cloak of bogus cowardice, something he'd done many times before in order to get the job done. But not this time, this time he'd put himself out there in the thick of it and he wondered if he'd made a mistake. But then he answered his own question. Of course he was doing the right thing. Just how *bad* were these bad boys? He had to find out. It wasn't the first time finding out the truth would mean enduring some pain.

Rudy, who was making it a habit of being ubiquitous, appeared beside Will crunching a bag of chips. "'Sup?"

"Not much. I'm just going out to get my head pounded by a bunch of pubescent gorillas."

"You don't know how lucky you are, having a chance to make the team."

"It's not that big a deal," said Will.

Rudy shook his head back and forth in disagreement. "Spoken like someone who's never had a problem being on a team, or being popular, or being a chick magnet. Me, I'm the opposite. I've never been on a team in my life. I'm an only kid, I don't even have brothers or sisters."

"I'm an only child, too," said Will.

That made Rudy feel a little better, but he still ached over the fact that no matter how hard he tried, he just never quite felt like he *belonged* anywhere.

They reached the field and Will watched as Duncan and the other football players jogged onto the new turf and began stretching.

Will returned his attention to Rudy. He wasn't sure exactly why, but he wanted little Rudy to be happy.

"Every school I've been to has tons of clubs you can join if you want to. How about the chess club or something?"

"You figure just because I look like a pencil-necked geek I'm a brainiac nerd, right? Well, I suck at chess. I'm also no good in science, I hate math, and I'm totally hopeless at every sport known to man, even darts."

"You must be good at something," said Will.

"Well, I'm pretty darned good at making Sharon Mitchell look like she wants to toss her cookies every time she lays eyes on me." Rudy sighed. "The stone cold truth is I'm pretty much terrible at everything except eating, sleeping, and wishing I was someone else."

"That's a sucky way to think."

"How would you think if you'd never been any good at anything? I tried Cub Scouts but I couldn't even earn the penmanship badge. Believe me, I've thought about this a lot and I finally came to a conclusion."

Will glanced out at the field and saw Coach Kellog motioning for him to join them. "I gotta go. What's your conclusion?" he asked Rudy.

"That I'm a one-hundred-percent certified, official-with-a-capital 'L' Loser!"

Will couldn't help but offer Rudy a smile and a pat on the shoulder. "You're not a loser, you're my friend. And you'll find your place. Everyone does sooner or later."

Rudy stood in shock. He couldn't remember the last time anyone had referred to him as a "friend," and now he was friends with the coolest guy in school! He danced around in a circle and watched as Will jogged over to Coach Kellog, who pointed to the locker room.

A few minutes later Will was suited up in pads and cleats and on the field thinking, *Okay, guys, go ahead and lay down the gauntlet.* The other players all looked at him and their eyes said they wanted to punish him, make him pay for thinking he could just walk onto their turf and take over. They did wind sprints and Will not only kept up with the group but pulled ahead, just a little, stopping himself before the extent of his abilities became obvious. Then came the jumping jacks, the squats, the pushups, all in the hot sun, all with full pads on, under the watchful eyes of Coach Kellog, who paced back and forth flipping a football and had his gaze locked in on Will as though he was expecting something. Will wasn't even particularly winded or anything but he had to play the part and he pretended to struggle. He knew he could wax these suckers anytime he wanted but that would be stupid. He wouldn't find out anything that way. He had to bide his time.

"Okay gimme two more sets of twenties!" yelled Kellog as the players groaned and did more wind sprints to the twenty-yard line and back. Coach cocked his arm and tried to blindside Will with the football but Will instinctively spun quick as a cat and caught it.

"Nice catch," said Kellog. "Now let's see if you can run. Listen up! We're doing end-around 88 double B!" Two squads formed quickly, and the ball was snapped and handed off to Will. He didn't know the exact play but he knew what an end-around was. He also knew he had to hold back and was tackled for a loss, hard. There were a couple of late hits, too, but Will jumped up afterward like a good sport and patted his adversaries on the helmets.

"Nice hit. Good footwork," he said.

"Come on, Hunter, don't sandbag! I've seen your wheels, now give me some heat!" growled Kellog. "Slant left!"

They lined up for another play and this time when Will got the ball he feinted inside like he was going to slant but shifted his footing and sprinted outside the tackle, and when the tight end laid down a decent block he was around the corner. Nobody was going to lay a hand on him now. He cruised into the end zone and did it all without time-bending.

"That's more like it!" shouted Kellog, and then he spit and yelled at the defense. "You girls want another shot at boy wonder or shall we call it a day?"

Duncan was sucking wind and he snorted and pounded his chest. "Run pretty boy again, Coach, we'll stop him."

"Green T5! Green T5!"

The quarterback told Will that Green T5 was a halfback option. Will nodded and when the QB flipped him the ball he looked down-field but the receiver was purposefully dragging his heels and was totally covered. Will had only one option and that was to run. He did, but Todd Karson laid down an illegal trip and caught Will's toe, slowing him down just enough for Duncan to hit him full on and hold him up while three more defensive players plowed into him, helmets first. Then Jocko Morgan, the biggest kid on the field, flew into Will low and hard, trying to take out his knees. Morgan was big but dumb and telegraphed the move, so Will was able to twist just enough to save his kneecaps from being shattered as he was knocked to the ground face-down. Will was lying there wondering if they were going to simply surround him and kick him to death when he heard Coach Kellog's shrill whistle pierce the air.

"Alright, gimme a lap and then hit the showers!" he yelled.

As Will got up and walked gingerly toward the showers the coach stepped in front of him. "I looked at your transcripts. All that talent and you never went out for the team?" Coach Kellog stared hard at Will.

"I guess I'm just not much of a team player," said Will.

"Things change."

"Yeah, sometimes they do."

Coach Kellog nodded slowly. "I like you. Now take another lap and then get your butt outta here."

Minutes later in the locker room Will showered alone. When the steam cleared he found himself suddenly surrounded by a half-dozen players led as usual by Duncan. They were in their street clothes, holding towels. Will wrapped a towel around his waist as they formed a circle around him.

"You shout for help and we're only gonna make it worse," said Duncan.

"Do you hear me shouting for anyone?" said Will. "If you girls have something in mind, get on with it. You're boring me."

Will knew what was coming. He stood and took it, his teeth clenched tightly as they snapped at him with the towels, the stinging tips bringing up welts on his chest and back. He felt tears welling in his eyes, felt the fury swelling up within him but managed to keep it corralled. For now.

Duncan and the others kept at it until Duncan raised a hand. Some of the guys looked at each other, wondering what the heck this New Kid was made of that he didn't even let out a peep when any one of them would have dropped to the floor and whimpered like a baby after such a beating. He just kept staring at them with cold steel eyes and it freaked them out so much they backed off a step.

"Are you done?" asked Will calmly.

"Not even close. Midnight. No pads. Fifty-yard line. Be there."

They left and Will closed his eyes, trying to find a serene place to park his roiling anger while he composed himself. He'd learned a long time ago that controlling his mind was the key to directing his own life. Feelings started with thoughts and if you thought of things that made you happy, or strong, that's the way you felt. It was a Zen kind of thing and he'd mastered it years ago. When he opened his eyes his anger was gone and he was ready to face the next challenge.

When he got home he entered through the side door, slipped past his mom, and went right to his basement chamber where he applied his healing balm to the myriad of welts that crisscrossed his back and chest. Minutes later he was completely healed. But midnight was coming and would be upon him before he knew it. He checked his computer monitors and noted that the readouts on the cemetery showed recent activity. It didn't surprise him to see that *He* had been recruiting the dead again. It was nothing new.

Will went to the far corner of his chamber, moved a large trunk aside, and lifted a floor panel to reveal a safe, which he opened with his thumbprint. He pulled out an object about the size of a track relay baton. It was a smooth shard of crystal, with a metal handle in the middle and intricate carvings on its surface, and had the heft of a short length of metal pipe. The power rod was the most valuable thing he had in his possession and he hadn't used it in weeks so he knew he needed to test it. Attaching a tiny flesh-colored patch to the back of his neck, he slipped the power rod into the back of his jeans and exited the basement.

A half mile from his house Will found a wooded thicket in a deep gully with good surrounding cover. It was unlikely he would be seen by anyone. His only audience would be a smattering of birds, some croaking frogs, and the chirping crickets. He took out the power rod and thumbed a symbol. The weapon whirred to life.

He thumbed another symbol and long laser-like spikes shot out from either end. They were like stationary molten lightning, so powerful was their burn, and formed a double lightning saber, a kind of deadly javelin with burning hot blades on either end. Holding the weapon in the middle he twirled it and smiled at the thrumming sound it made as the lightning blades knifed through the air. Leaping sideways he calmly touched the shimmering blade into a thick maple, instantly burning it. He knew he could cut through it if he applied enough pressure but this was just a test. Function one, double-tipped lightning saber: check. Will quickly deactivated the saber function and then squeezed another symbol. The power rod vibrated as it built up a blast charge. Will whirled and pressed a spot and the power rod fired a golf ball-sized fireball that slammed into a rock, which exploded on impact. Will quickly ducked down and turned the power rod off. He looked and listened. Silence. The frogs and crickets were suddenly mute. Function two, fireball blaster:

check. Finally Will touched yet another spot on the rod and aimed it at a leaf dangling from a maple about twenty feet away. In two seconds the leaf froze solid and dropped from the branch. Function three, freeze beam: check.

Now it was time to test the retrieval patch. He pressed the patch, which was perfectly disguised as part of his skin, the exact color of his flesh. Upon the touch of his index finger the patch glowed briefly before becoming invisible again. He then threw the power rod into the sky like a boomerang. It arced high up into the clouds where it hovered, pulsing and finding an invisible shelf where it remained until Will activated the retrieval patch, at which point the power rod swooped back down right into his waiting hand. Good. The power rod was up to speed and ready to rock and roll with the best of them. He returned to his house, chowed down on a couple peanut butter and jelly sandwiches and a tall glass of milk, then breezed through his English homework, an essay on Lord of the Flies. It was familiar territory: the two sides of human nature, civilization versus savagery, good versus evil.

He set his watch alarm and slept for forty minutes, then awakened at 11:45. He shoved a couple of pillows under his blankets to form a teen-sized lump in his bed. It was a lame ruse but it was better than nothing. Then he snagged his backpack, slipped out his window, and made his way through the shadows toward the high school.

Chapter Six:
The Hazing

Will knew he had to go to the midnight tryout, not to save face but to check the players out. They thought they were going to put him to the test but they were wrong; *he* was the one testing them, using himself as bait to see if he could draw them out. Because if any one of them was infected he would spot it and then maybe they would lead him to the place he knew he had to go.

The sky was overcast, making the night seem thicker, darker, more foreboding. A block before the stadium Will saw the lights blazing. He removed the power rod from his pocket and sent it into the sky where it would wait in the clouds until called. Then he walked toward the stadium.

If he'd been as careful as he should have been he'd have noticed that during his walk to the high school someone was following him, watching his every move. But he was too busy thinking about what was ahead to pay much attention to what was behind him. He paused to stash his backpack in some bushes, then walked into the stadium and as soon as he hit the track the lights suddenly went off. When his eyes adjusted only a sliver of moon gilded the gridiron, making it seem like a scene from a dream, or a nightmare. He walked out to the fifty-yard line and stood waiting. A football sailed out of the darkness and he caught it. Then he saw them, emerging from the darkness like a band of Mongol warriors. They were wearing pads, but not the usual kind; these were painted hot red and fretted with bands of metal. Getting hit with them would be like being hammered with giant brass knuckles. *Cute*, thought Will, *I'm so glad they told me no pads.* They wore face paint and sported heathen deity tattoos drawn in henna on their bulbous biceps.

Will knew what was expected. They were there to punish him, pure and simple. It was a blood gauntlet and he knew he'd be hit ten times harder than he had been on the practice field today. He tried to read their eyes from a distance but they wore eye black and he couldn't see much of anything.

"Are you ready, New Kid?" growled Duncan, who had shaved his head for the occasion and topped off his dome with a pagan symbol for death.

"I thought you'd never ask," said Will, doing his best to control the dread that was creeping through his veins. *Never let them smell your fear*, he told himself. *They're pack animals and the weaker you appear the more bravado they muster.*

"Then bring it, dipwad!" shouted Duncan.

They spread out and crouched down and Will slipped in the mouth guard he'd brought along and began to run. He was either going to have to spill blood or have his blood spilled, probably both. He ran straight at Duncan and lowered his shoulder and at the last second he planted his left foot and danced right so the blow from Duncan's heavy pads only glanced off his shoulder. The next two hits he took he wasn't so lucky. Todd Karson slammed into him and Jackie Boy Weaver, another drone warrior thug, threw a vicious forearm uppercut that knocked out Will's mouth guard and made his gums bleed. But Will kept on running, feinting and slipping off tackles and stiff-arming his way down the field to the forty, the thirty, the twenty. By then they were routinely smashing into him two at a time, then three at a time. But he was built like a Mack truck and had probably endured more punishment in his travels than all these steroid freaks put together. He knew all about pain; pain was his constant companion.

"Give it up, stupid, lay it down!" shouted Duncan as he jammed a shoulder into Will's face for the umpteenth time. But Will wouldn't quit and kept pumping his legs like a plow horse. The hits kept coming. Will felt his ribs crack and cartilage in his knees give out.

By the time he staggered to the ten-yard line he'd been hit in the ears and nose and had rivulets of blood running out of both. Still his legs churned, his heart raced, his head throbbed. And he kept on going until there were simply too many of them, mobbing him now in a scrum.

"Hold the son of a bitch up!" yelled Duncan, and Jackie Boy and Todd pushed defensively into Will, propping him up like a target. Then Duncan got a good running start, went airborne, and speared Will's chin with his bald head. Will's head snapped up, whiplashing like a crash test dummy in a head-on. The skin on Will's chin split, as did the skin on Duncan's noggin. Both of them staggered from the blow. Will's strength gave out and he collapsed onto the turf just across the goal line. He rasped: "Touchdown. Looks like I scored after all."

He briefly passed out then regained consciousness and rolled onto his back. He gazed up at the pack of brutes surrounding him, staring down at him. He wasn't sure, because his bell had been rung but good, but he thought he saw the irises of their eyes go that sickening liquid black. *Son of a bitch*, he thought to himself, *they might all be infected, every last one of them. They might be the real deal. Demonteens.* But he shook his head and the image went back to normal, or as normal as it could considering his blurred vision.

As his world went black again Will heard a rumbling, coarse, animal-like voice that rose the small hairs on the back of his neck.

"Bring him on down."

• • •

"Down" meant a little-used corner of the locker room where they laid Will on a trainer's table. He was only half-conscious but his brain was clearing quickly and he heard voices.

"How'd you like that, pretty boy?" asked Duncan.

And then another voice, a voice that was animal-like, growled: *"Where is it?"*

Will's skin crawled. He turned his head in the direction of the voice but only saw a dark corner. Was there a shape there? He was so dizzy from the head shots that he couldn't tell for sure.

"Wake up, fart brain!" said one of the football players as he slapped Will's face. Then Will heard the creature growling again. He was confused. Who was speaking here? The players? Or someone, some*thing*, much more sinister?

Duncan circled around and clapped his hands on the sides of Will's head, making his ears ring. The players were laughing now, their voices bouncing around the room, all distorted. Will's hearing was suddenly out of whack but he could have sworn he heard a guttural roar erupt from the dark corner followed by a hissing sound like air escaping some hideous orifice like a blowhole. The room suddenly stank, awash with acidic microparticles, an excretion of pure malevolence.

Again the question came at him: *"Where is it?"*

But all the players' lips were moving and they jabbered and poked at him and sneered as they began performing a "fart down," blasting Will with as much flatulence as they could muster. Maybe that's where the smell was coming from. They were so tightly cloaked around him now that seeing into the corner was nearly impossible but—there! Was it *the Dark Lord*? Did he just see a pair of eyes peering out from the black corner? Creature eyes? Yellow eyes?

Will's vision was blocked again but he thought he might have seen a figure in the corner nod its head, and Duncan and the other punks loaded sweat socks with baseballs and began pummeling

Will's body. His body's natural reaction was to toughen up and it did, his muscles contracting, his skin thickening. The rage began to build inside him and he knew he wouldn't be able to hold it in for long. The beating lasted only thirty seconds but felt like thirty lifetimes. Will was hit more than a hundred times but he just took it, absorbing the pain. He wouldn't make his move until the precise moment. The power rod was waiting, but he wasn't going to blow it by going off half-cocked. Still, his ribs were on fire and these creeps deserved a thorough thrashing.

He heard the raspy beast voice give an order: *"Search him!"*

Again Will was so woozy from the beating he couldn't be one hundred percent certain that the command hadn't come from one of the bad boys. The voice he heard in his battered head was one he'd heard many times before. And no matter how many times he heard it, it still felt like a lance piercing his very soul. Duncan and the others did as they were ordered and searched Will roughly. They came up empty-handed. Will was dizzy. Maybe they'd done more damage than he'd thought.

"Nothing. He's not carrying."

"His skin. Check his skin."

Duncan and the others continued to search Will but were unable to locate the cleverly concealed retrieval patch. They were fumbling fools.

"Cut him open if you have to!" said the beast.

"Gladly," said Duncan as he produced a deadly looking hunting knife. The blade looked sharp enough to cut through bone like butter and it glinted in the light as Duncan lowered it slowly toward Will's face.

Duncan touched the knife to Will's chin, ready to being flaying him. "I'm going enjoy this. Let's see how Sharon likes your face now. . . ."

Will reached behind his neck, placing a finger on the retrieval patch, and was just about to call his power rod down to try and pull his ass out of the fire and hopefully save his life when the overhead fluorescents in the locker room banged on and the scene was flooded with a harsh white light. Principal Steadman stood in the doorway, leaning on his forearm crutches. Next to him were Rudy and Natalie.

Natalie's heart felt like it was going to break; she ached to the bone seeing Will lying there, his body red with welts and bruises, his face grimacing in pain.

"Will!" she shouted and ran to him. She touched his forehead gently.

"Don't worry," said Will.

Principal Steadman puffed up with anger and indignation. "Will someone please explain to me what's going on here?"

Duncan and the punks stood mute. Natalie helped Will sit up and he glanced into the corner. The creature was gone. Will had to wonder if he was ever there in the first place. There was the sound of a toilet flushing, water running, and then Coach Kellog emerged from the adjacent room, drying his hands on a paper towel.

"Coach, you know the school's policy about hazing!" said Steadman.

"You bet I do, and the whole crazy rite of passage makes me sick, but what are you gonna do? Boys will be boys. It's a stupid tradition. I was up in my office working on the playbook when I heard a commotion. I came on down and told them to knock it off straight away."

Duncan and the others just stared stupidly at the concrete floor, saying nothing. In their war paint and festooned football pads they looked more foolish than dangerous in the light, more like bad boys than demonteens. Coach Kellog approached Will and used a damp towel to clean him up.

"Trust me, it's not as bad as it looks," he said to Steadman.

No, thought Will, *it's a hell of a lot worse*. His mind was starting to clear and as it did he knew it had just been wishful thinking before that he'd been imagining the voice and the players' eyes.

"I'm fine," said Will, and climbed gingerly off the table and then joined Natalie and Rudy.

Natalie's eyes were full of fire. "Are you all insane? Look at him!"

"I said I'm fine, and I'm fine," repeated Will, and he squeezed Natalie's arm as he said it, a signal for her to play along. "They just wanted me to feel like I was part of the team. The thing is, though, like I told Coach Kellog, I'm not really a team player. If you don't mind, Principal Steadman, I'd like to get out of here." Then Will turned to Duncan and the others. "I'll catch you later," he said, even giving Duncan an affectionate pat on the shoulder as he passed by him, leading Rudy and Natalie up and out.

As they exited they heard Principal Steadman delivering another edict about the dangers of hazing. At least Will knew now that Steadman was one of the good guys and wasn't infected.

Will had made it about halfway across the football field when Natalie stepped in front of him. He tried to walk around her but she blocked his path again.

"No, no way, José! We saved your butt, you're not just gonna walk away. Look at you! You're a mess!"

"She's right, New Kid," added Rudy.

"Come on, Will, let me help you. We've got to get you home and get some of that magic goop on you."

"No need to go to my place," said Will.

He went over to where he'd stashed his backpack and took out a small tube. Then he sat down on a bench and pulled up his shirt to rub the healing balm liberally all over his chest, arms, neck, and face. But his back was still in pain and he couldn't reach all the bruises. He held out the tube to Natalie.

"Would you mind putting some on my back?"

Pulse racing, Natalie accepted the tube, squeezed out some of the gel, and carefully rubbed it over Will's bruises. Then she stared disbelieving at Will's skin. She knew the balm worked fast because of her arm but it had been mere seconds and his back was already looking better.

Will was amazed at how tender Natalie's touch was—especially when he turned around to find her standing with her hands on her hips, demanding, defiant, and beautiful. She almost glared at him. Even little Rudy looked all puffed up with bravado.

Natalie spoke first. "We saw that freak show in there and we are soooo calling you out! You are going to give us the *whole* story this time, tell us who you are and why you're here."

"Whole what story?" said Will.

"Don't even go there," said Natalie. "We know something big is going down and you're going to tell us!"

Will measured them again, the pretty, pushy tomboy and the skinny, pimply-faced ninety-pound weakling. Natalie was muscular and quick on her feet, but overall they weren't exactly the dynamic duo. He'd have preferred more formidable confidants, but these were who had arrived like the cavalry. Maybe he would have gotten the power rod in hand and kicked ass and maybe he wouldn't have. Maybe Duncan and his cronies would have skinned him like a deer and left him to die. It was a close call—way *too* close. So he made up his mind to do something he'd never done before: share his life with someone.

It would feel good to let it out. He hadn't had real friends before, ones he could truly confide in. Maybe this would be a good thing. He'd never let himself get attached to a girl before, either, but maybe it was time to change all that.

"We're waiting," said Natalie.

Will took a deep breath, then let it out slowly. "Before I say anything I'm going to warn you."

"Warn away," said Natalie, her arms crossed.

"Okay, then listen and listen good. What I'm about to tell you will make you change the way you look at things."

"What kind of things?" asked Rudy.

"Everything."

A silence followed as Will watched their faces. Natalie still looked determined but Rudy seemed nervous and a part of him clearly didn't want to go down this particular road. Will wasn't going to drag anybody into this who didn't want to be involved, so he said, "Why don't you take off, Rudy. Go rock on some game or something."

"No," said Rudy, now crossing his arms, too. "I'm staying."

"The truth of the matter is," said Will, "that the less you know about me the safer you will be. If I let you into my confidence it could be dangerous, for both of you."

"Um, the thing is, Sir Lancelot, what you don't know is that it's already dangerous," said Natalie. "So enough with the dire warnings and talk already!"

Will shot a look over at the field house. "Let's get out of here. I'll talk, but not here." He began walking and they caught up and walked beside him. As they left the school grounds and moved through the small town Will pondered what he was about to do. Things were heating up and something bad was going to go down. There could only be one outcome. What he was about to tell these two would either save them, or kill them.

Chapter Seven: Origin

The night sky had cleared and the stars winked down as Will led his new friends to the verdant park in the center of town. Under a canopy of massive oak trees Natalie and Rudy sat on a bench while Will paced back and forth. As he spoke they barely moved. They might have been statues if it weren't for their breathing, so rapt was their attention. He told them about a fateful night that had changed the course of his life forever, a night that had bound him to his eternal duty.

He was just eight years old and coming home from fishing up at Fallen Leaf Lake with his father, Edward. They'd been to a baseball game that same weekend and had gone out for ice cream, too. Edward had been so loving and attentive to Will that he'd even let him hold his prized railroad watch. It was an Elgin pocket watch, the watch Edward had inherited from his own grandfather. As young Will held the watch to his ear and listened to the ticking, Edward smiled and hugged him and told him someday the watch would be his.

It was as if Edward had known what was coming and was trying to cram in as much face time with his son as he could before . . . it happened. As they arrived home to their modest three-bedroom Craftsman in Palo Alto they were greeted with a freak storm that whipped up punishing hot winds, winds hotter than any Santa Anas. And even though the winds were hot the sky was ragged with angry clouds. Will's mother had gone to visit her sister during the "boys' weekend" so the house was dark. As the winds grew to gale force Will's father did his best to secure the house but it groaned under the sheer force of the assault, shingles ripped asunder, debris raking against the windows.

Normally a calm, grounded, steady-handed man, Edward was suddenly nervous and twitchy and Will saw fear in his father's eyes for the first time as Edward gazed at the roiling sky.

"Come down in the basement with me, Will, I have something to show you. Hurry!"

Down they went. The basement was Edward's domain and Will had not been allowed this kind of access until now. Sure, he'd snuck a peek or two and wondered what the big deal was about a workbench and a bunch of tools and junk in the basement. Why had he been refused entry? His father had told him it wasn't a safe place for a boy to play and Will's mother had backed him up. But tonight all bets were off; tonight was a rite of passage.

Edward moved quickly past his workbench and flipped a switch and a fluorescent bulb flickered on in the far corner of the basement. Will craned his neck to look past his father as Edward unlocked and opened a thick old oak door and saw a secret room full of different kinds of futuristic-looking tools and weapons—weapons!—the likes of which Will could never have conjured up even in his wildest imagination. His father picked one of the weapons up. It looked like a shotgun from the future and Will was filled with excitement despite the ominous howl of the storm outside.

Kneeling down inside the secret room, Edward dialed a combination on a floor safe and removed a crystal key. He then brought the key out of the room and locked the oak door behind him. He rolled the clothes dryer aside, revealing another, smaller door to a hidden compartment. Using the crystal key he unlocked the compartment and pulled out an ancient box adorned with intricate engravings. He used the same crystal key to open the box, and from the box he lifted out a book. Or rather half a book.

Closing the secret compartment, Edward brought the book out and set it down on his workbench. Will's eyes were filled with wonder as his father opened the thick, age-old volume. The pages were made of what he later learned was cabretta leather and the front cover was made of marble and embedded with emeralds. The back cover and an indeterminate number of pages were missing.

"Inside this book," said Will's father, "are things you will need to know if you are to survive."

Will wished that his father had not used the word "if" and his young heart thudded in his chest as he awaited further instructions. Gazing down he saw that the pages were covered with ancient symbols. Though Will had learned to read at a very young age and read at a tenth grade level already, he had no clue what any of these symbols were. How could a book he couldn't even read ever help him? His father had anticipated Will's confusion and immediately addressed it.

"You will have to learn to decipher the code. Don't be concerned with this now, Will, you're not to open this book until one minute past midnight on your thirteenth birthday, do you understand?"

Will nodded, even though he had dozens of questions swirling around in his head. But there would be no time for questions. Will shivered, for the room had gone suddenly cold. There was a crack of thunder and it sounded as though the heavens had split open. Will thought the sky must surely be falling! The basement windows blasted open and the door to the upstairs flew off its hinges. The basement filled with swirling snakes of smoke as the whole house shook on its foundation. Edward hefted the book and, placing it into Will's hands, shoved him under the workbench.

"Take care of your mother, Will! Do you understand?"

"Yes, Dad, but—"

"Stay silent! And close your eyes! Do NOT watch this!"

Will tried to do as he was told, grasping the book and ducking under the workbench as the room continued to fill with smoke and debris. There was a horrifying clicking, screeching, clattering sound. A swarm of cicadas appeared. And what Will saw next caused his young mind to twist inward and fold up upon itself. He was so terrified he could only watch with one eye barely open. Still, through his eye slit he witnessed the unthinkable. The cicadas melded together and out of their mass formed a humanoid creature! It had a spiny coat, a massive head topped with goat-like horns, and eyes of putrid saffron. The creature opened its mouth and out came a blast of wilting hot air, thick with malice and hatred, air that stank of acrid chemicals, the rotting of all things good. The creature was surely speaking, but the tone and pitch were so unearthly that young Will could not make out words. He only knew that the monster was demanding something of his father and his father was refusing to cooperate.

The noise was deafening and Will held the book between his knees and covered his ears. But he could not for the life of him close his eyes. So he kept one eye open and because of the roaring in his ears what he witnessed was a pantomime. His father drew the futuristic weapon and fired—but the creature moved swiftly out of the way of the blast and was on the other side of the basement in a manner that no human being could ever accomplish! Though he fought valiantly, Will's father appeared to be no match for this inhumanly fast creature, who quickly overpowered him, pressed his slimy forehead to Edward's own, and spoke again in its frightening tongue, demanding answers that did not come.

In a rage the monster ripped off the big old oak door to the secret room and with its clawed hands tossed the contents, all the while roaring. Will thought he saw the monster breathe fire. As seconds passed like lifetimes the creature's fury reached an apex, apparently not finding what it was looking for. It grabbed Edward and lifted him, and shook him as a lion would shake its prey to break its neck. As his father's body went slack Will couldn't control himself. He began to emerge from his hidey hole, his mouth opening into a scream.

But the scream never came because as the creature fled with Will's father slumped over its shoulder the basement was suddenly engulfed in flames. Will was certain he was trapped and doomed to burn to death. Then he saw it. The crystal key. His father had dropped it on the floor. On purpose? That didn't matter now as Will's trembling fingers groped for the key. He was so nervous he kept dropping it and could barely slip it into the lock on the front of the secret compartment. Fire licked at his heels as he turned the key. Then the door opened! He collapsed inside, pulled the book in after him, and closed the door, taking refuge in the tiny cabinet while the fire raged. His ears were ringing and his throat was sore and his head throbbed.

Safe for the moment, he started to cry thinking of what had just happened to his father, the person he loved more than anything else on earth, and prayed that this wasn't real, that it was all just a bad dream, a horrific nightmare from which he'd soon awaken. But he knew it was real. And that realization crept through him like a virus. His stomach churned and he sweat buckets. Finally, he fell into unconsciousness. An indeterminate amount of time later Will opened his eyes. The ringing in his ears had stopped and he heard the blessed sound of near-silence. He peeked at the crack under the secret cabinet door, no longer a slit of burning orange, now just dark.

Will opened the door gingerly and as he crawled out he saw that the basement had flooded, the overhead sprinklers his father had installed still showering the entire area with water. He called out, his voice weak with his utter lack of hope.

"Dad? Daddy?"

He was met with stone cold silence; the house was empty. Will sat for the next twenty-four hours, until his mother returned, rocking and holding the book and praying for a miracle. A simple miracle, really: *Just bring my father back to me*, prayed Will. But even though he was only eight years old he knew this one incontrovertible fact: If he was ever to see his father again he would have to bring him back himself. Hell had come to get Will's father, and Will might very well have to go to Hell to get him back.

When his mother returned and the dust from the incident settled, it was decided by those parties concerned—Will's mother, the child psychologists, the minister, teachers, and other relatives—that Will's version of what had transpired the night of the storm and subsequent fire was not, in fact, an accurate account of a young boy's father being abducted by a demon, but rather an emotional defense mechanism, a tall tale conjured up by a boy in terrible pain. They all believed that Will had made the story up to deal with the supposed "fact" that his father had left him and his mother, most likely to run off with a woman. They also believed that it was Will, and not some rampaging demon, who had set the house on fire, a young boy abandoned by his father acting out his pain. After a while Will stopped trying to convince them that he was telling the truth and retreated. He went about his business like any other kid, going to school and doing his homework, watching TV and hanging out with his friends. But he did all these things in order to appear normal, in order to bide the time necessary. Inside he was waiting—for one minute past midnight on his thirteenth birthday.

Will knew he was different; the demon had left a mark on him in more ways than one. There was a hole in his heart where his father had once been, but there was also the matter of his eyes, which were now two different colors. While one of his eyes was the same normal blue it had always been, the other one, the one he'd witnessed the abduction with, had faded into a lighter crystal blue with gold specks. He wondered if he looked like a freak or some kind of pubescent god-like warrior. He chose the latter.

Halloween, long Will's favorite holiday, was a day of the year he now shunned. He had once loved to make himself appear ghoulish, to wear colored contact lenses and scar tattoos and bite down on fake blood capsules to scare his mom and dad silly. But no more. Now that he knew there were actual ghouls and demons roaming the earth he'd lost his taste for pretending.

Mostly, Will kept his eyes and his ears open. He watched over his mother, like his father had asked, as she endured the loss of her husband. It was not a pretty sight. Before, April had been gregarious and loved to paint and play the piano and sing. After, April changed dramatically. She suffered from depression and was often times wan and withdrawn. She still painted occasionally, but her paintings, which had been bright and cheery renditions of colorful birds in flight, now featured barren landscapes and, while beautifully crafted, were infused with grief. Time passed. And Will grew. He was determined to save them: his father *and* his mother.

For the next seven years young Will worked hard at his studies, learning absolutely everything there was to know about demons, spirits, goblins, ogres, warlocks, and other creatures of the dark side. He was drawn to the subject matter like no other kid before him; he was obsessed. It was his life. He knew what he'd seen was real, even if most of the descriptions and depictions of demons throughout human history were wildly inconsistent and frequently absurd.

As he grew mentally he also grew physically and by the time he was ten years old he knew beyond a shadow of a doubt that he was physically gifted; he was a boy like no other, a specimen so superior to his peers that he dared not partake in athletic competitions lest he bring the world's curiosity down upon him. He didn't dare allow himself to be found out, instead lying in wait, getting stronger and faster each day, developing reflexes more akin to feral creatures than young boys. He was proud of his new body, proud

that he could jump higher and run faster than any of his class-
mates—so fast sometimes he scared himself. It was as if he could
bend time itself, slowing it down as he ran past it. He was so strong
and so fast he knew he could kick the crap out of guys twice his
age. He longed to show off, to tell a friend his secret. But that was a
luxury he could ill afford. Though at times he gained strength from
his solitude, in his heart he was lonely. In his mind he would howl
at the moon, calling out to his father. *I will find you. If it takes the
rest of my life, I will find you.*

He trained himself, running and lifting weights. With each
stride, each breath, each strain of a muscle, he thought of his father,
thought of how much he loved him, how much he missed him, how
much he wanted him back. And he *would* get him back. That much
he knew for sure. He hated the creature that had kidnapped his
father with every fiber of his being and he dreamt of a hundred ways
to slaughter him.

As he trained and did pushups and worked on his upper body
strength he knew he was gifted for a reason. The heavens had
endowed him with these abilities for a reason, and that reason was to
be ready when it came time to rescue his father. He studied karate
and Tae Kwon Do and Kung Fu and taught himself every offensive
and defensive technique in the disciplines, always in private, away
from prying adult eyes.

Only one time did he slip up and allow others to see his powers,
when he was eleven years old. It was a foggy night and he'd been in
a funk because his mother had started dating this creepy new guy
she'd met on the Internet. So he was carrying some anger to begin
with. He felt like he might explode if he didn't get out and do something, and lately he had been feeling compelled to test himself anyway. So he ventured down to the rough part of the city, past the
mattress factory and junkyards, past the boarded-up old slaughter
house. He explored the rows of seedy bars and kept on walking until
he found himself surrounded by a trio of vagrants who had nothing

but malice on their minds as they corralled him, greedily eyeing the expensive watch and jewelry he'd purposefully worn and the digital camera he'd brought along. He was bait and he knew it, and his heart raced in his chest as he flexed his muscles.

When the three of them made their move young Will sprang into action. Though it seemed to him the world was suddenly in slow motion, his transformation was actually quite rapid. He felt as though his skin grew tougher, like he had some kind of hide instead of the regular human epidermis. His vision became astonishingly clear, as though he was seeing everything in HD while the real world was in analog. And he was fast. His speed was just out of this world and he felt hot, like his blood was suddenly boiling, coursing through his pumped-up veins.

Using a series of powerful kicks and chops Will laid the three grown men out flat in a matter of seconds. Afterward, as the heat in his body faded, he was terrified that he'd killed them and quickly felt for pulses on all three. They were alive but when they regained consciousness they'd remember this night for the rest of their lives. Maybe they'd even stop drinking, convinced they'd hallucinated the little kid who'd transformed into a whirling dervish before their very eyes and kicked their asses from sin to Sunday. Will left them the watch, camera, and jewelry, went home, and locked himself in his room.

He cried for two solid hours, wondering how he could possibly have enjoyed inflicting pain on another human being. He tried to deny the pleasure he felt while hurting the men, telling himself that they probably were due such a beating, that they'd most likely done horrible things to people anyway and were owed. But he felt shame. He was terrified of how exhilarated he felt while in the heat of battle and he feared the red curtain that fell over his mind when he was in the fighting mode. When he stopped crying he vowed never again to test his newfound strength and hand to hand combat skills on hapless human beings, only on creatures that deserved it. And he knew that waiting for him somewhere was a creature that deserved it very much.

The day before Will's thirteenth birthday was a normal day like any other, at least as normal a day for a young man like him could be. Although nervous in anticipation of the events he suspected would unfold early that next morning, he played it cool, only venturing down to the basement five or six times to stare at the small cabinet door he would open at precisely one minute after midnight. He played a couple games of Scrabble with his mother, letting her win as always. Then she quaintly tucked him in at 10:30 and told him how proud she was that he'd grown so strong and smart and how much she loved him. She'd repeated these words so many times over the years that he knew they came from deep within her heart.

He also knew that she missed his father like a caged bird misses the sky. She'd waited three years after Edward "disappeared" before finally being talked into filing for divorce by her sister. Six months after that she'd met Gerald on TrueLove.com and he'd courted her vigorously, treating her as though she were an angel, the perfect woman, the only woman for him. He'd said all the right things and at times Will even believed he might permanently lift his mother out of her depression. But after their marriage Gerald revealed his true self, a simple-minded angry man, a drinker who wanted things his way and thought Will was a nuisance. Gerald had miraculously managed to mask his flatulence during the courtship but once he had the cheap ring on April's finger he relaxed and walked around like he had grenades going off in his Jockeys. He was a fool and he smelled bad and Will could not help but dislike him.

At ten minutes to midnight Will stood holding the crystal key and staring at the door to the secret cabinet. At five minutes to midnight he paced nervously back and forth, snapping his fingers, cracking his knuckles, building up courage. At one minute to midnight Will's hands began shaking. He counted off the sixty seconds.

At exactly midnight he heard his father's grandfather clock upstairs chime a dozen times. He counted another sixty seconds, slid the crystal key into the lock, and then opened the small door.

Will used the key to open the box and there it was. The book. He lifted it out and was surprised how light it felt to him. *Of course*, he thought. *I'm bigger and stronger than I was back then, I'm almost a man. I am ready for the book.*

He laid it on the workbench, opened the cover, and stared at the first page. He felt a sudden wind and turned in fear, expecting the worst: that the beast had come back to claim the book! But it was only a draft from upstairs. Will calmed himself and began to study the volume. He'd brought his digital camera and laptop computer down to the basement and methodically photographed the pages and then ran program after program utilizing pattern recognition software designed by the world's top archeologists. Four hours later he was no closer to understanding the strange language than when he'd first started. But no way would he even think of giving up.

He was on spring break from school so his mother and Gerald allowed him to spend his time alone in the basement with what Gerald referred to as his "geek toys." Will began designing his own pattern recognition software that learned as it ran until finally some semblance of a language emerged. It dawned on Will that the reason the book was in code was so that no one who was less than exceptionally intellectually gifted could ever have a hope of under-standing it. It took seventy-two hours but by the end of the week he finally had the entire ancient manuscript translated and as the amazing sense of accomplishment washed over him he proceeded to read.

He read it cover to cover, skipping school for seven days, using his computer voice-enhancer to place calls to the school nurse from his "mother" informing her that he had chickenpox. The contents of the ancient book not only amazed him but led him onto a path he knew he must follow. It forged his destiny.

He learned that his father, Edward Hunter, like *his* father and grandfather before him, was an "everto venator"—a demon hunter. The book contained all their combined wisdom, knowledge, and skills in the art of tracking down and doing battle with demons, and identified the various permutations of the beasts as well as identifying the main demon, the ruler, as the *Lord of Darkness*. He had many monikers, including Devil, Satan, Beelzebub, and Lucifer. In more recent times he'd been referred to as Darkmaster, Bonecracker, and the Dark or Black Spirit. But the truth was, he had no name, because how could you give a name to pure evil?

Throughout history Will's ancestors had done battle with this terrifying creature but had never defeated him, a task that was now apparently left to Will. Will was tempted to run and ask his mother a zillion questions. But as he read further he learned that the matriarchs were never informed of the exact nature of the family business. It was determined that the less they knew the safer they would remain. So Will's mother April knew little or nothing of Edward's demon hunting and Will, too, concluded she was better off if he kept it that way. Will ached to tell her his discovery. If she only knew the truth about Edward's disappearance she might leave Gerald; her entire life might change. But for her own good she had to remain uninformed.

Will vowed then and there that he would find the Lord of Darkness and destroy him, right *after* he liberated his father. Then he could tell his mother everything, the whole truth. He prayed that he was not too late and held onto hope, figuring that if the demon had wished to kill his father he would have done so right on the spot. But he didn't; instead he knocked him stupid and kidnapped him, took him hostage. But for what purpose? Will didn't know but he swore he would find out.

In addition to explaining and detailing a plethora of skills needed to become a master demon hunter, the ancient book also indicated the existence of something called a power rod and gave a cryptic set of instructions revealing its location. Will decided his first step would be to follow the directions and recover the power rod immediately. He made a couple peanut butter and jelly sandwiches, packed them up, and took a bus from Palo Alto down to Carmel. From the funky old bus station he hiked to the San Carlos Borromeo de Carmelo Mission, a restored California mission first built in 1771.

The mission was a magnificent old pale orange stucco structure and as soon as he stepped onto the grounds Will felt safe and protected. His heels echoed on the tiles as he entered the cathedral and while part of him felt secure and warm and welcomed, another part began to feel terribly uncomfortable, like an unwanted guest in a stranger's house. Eager to locate the power rod he shook off the feelings and focused, again studying the map he'd copied from the ancient manuscript.

He soon found the herb garden and the graveyard containing the remains of the priests who'd given their lives in service of the mission. Marking off thirteen steps due north he located a sheet of flagstone and lifted it. Digging into the moist dirt he unearthed an old oilcloth and, unwrapping it, saw that it held the soiled but intact power rod. Wiping away some of the dirt and grime he noticed that the center of the rod—just as the book had said—glowed bright blue. It was a crystal of power and Will couldn't help but smile because if this thing he held in his hand was anything at all like what he'd read about he'd just found the single most amazing weapon any kid had ever owned. He felt like a king.

His body tingling with excitement he slipped the power rod under his jacket and walked away from the old mission. For a moment he thought he heard angry whispering but when he turned he realized it was just the wind brushing the needles in the pine trees. No one, or rather no *thing*, was after him. Yet.

As he boarded the bus back to Palo Alto and watched the world going by in a blur; all his thoughts were on the power rod under his jacket. When a rough and tumble-looking older boy jostled him with his backpack and glowered at him threateningly Will kept his cool and just smiled at the jerk.

"Hey, dipwad, who did your makeup?" sneered the tough guy.

Who taught you your manners? thought Will, but kept his words to himself. When the bully kicked Will's seat he thought of taking the rod out and activating it. If the ancient book was correct then the rod would enable him to slice the cretin in half. Anger surged within him and he saw the red curtain begin to draw over his mind's stage. So he prudently got up and walked to the back of the bus. He sat down and stared out the window as the tough kid chuckled victoriously. If he only knew.

"That's it, chickenshit, you better move it."

Will dialed the creep out. *Save your anger, there will be bigger battles to fight. Much bigger battles.*

The rest of the trip passed without incident and Will took the power rod home. As soon as the sun contracted into the dying light he climbed out his window, walked to the woods, and tested it, cutting through tree branches and shooting fireballs into the river where they hissed out harmlessly.

His power rod was a weapon like no other, but it wasn't the only weapon of its kind; there were two more identical to it. And the book prophesized that when the three rods were joined together they would form a triangle, a Triad of energy with such awesome power that whoever possessed it would surely be able to subjugate mankind and rule with impunity. It also prophesized gravely that if the three power rods were ever joined together, the being that held it would gain the ability to use a mysterious key—a key that would unlock a portal and unleash incalculable terrors upon the earth.

However you sliced it, Will knew that it would be disastrous if the Darkmaster got his hands on Will's power rod, so he designed and built the retrieval sleeve and patch, allowing the rod to normally remain hidden but be handy whenever he needed it. The crystal inside it possessed infinite power, which enabled the rod to soar and hover, cloaked safely in the clouds. In the years that followed Will learned to use the power rod judiciously and it served him well in his battles against the minions of the Lord of Darkness as Will tracked him across the land wherever he took refuge—usually in and around high schools, where he recruited impressionable teenagers, infecting them with his vile thoughts and turning them into wicked souls, the way he was in Harrisburg.

Chapter Eight:
All In

Natalie and Rudy had barely moved as the tale unfolded. Now they blinked and breathed the night air in deeply. Quite simply, Will had blown their minds.

"I've been tracking him . . . them . . . since I was fourteen, going from school to school. You see, he can only infect you in your sixteenth year. If he gets to you, you're one of them. If he doesn't, if you make it to seventeen without being infected, then at least he can never take you over wholly."

"I'm sixteen," said Natalie.

"So am I," added Rudy.

Will nodded, and added, "But even if you're seventeen or older, that doesn't mean he can't affect you, or use your body as a host. He does that all the time, uses adult bodies as temporary hosts."

"How can you tell who's infected and who's not?" asked Rudy.

"It's difficult. If you see someone who's gone through a rapid physical change, or is suddenly getting straight As or something or looks a little too . . . perfect, chances are he's hooked them not only by invading their thoughts and tormenting them but by rewarding them with all kinds of crap. Also, lots of people look like demons—

you know, bikers, Goth freaks, punks, just about anyone who thinks it's cool to wear freaky jewelry and tattoos and piercings like badges. But just because they want to look like a pirate or counter-culture commando or fly their freak flag or whatever doesn't mean they're demonic. The Black Prince's recruits can look perfectly normal, even angelic, you just never know. He has many converts and they are totally, utterly vigilant and do his bidding without question. And actually, I can never be one hundred percent certain what evil is his doing and what's just . . . human nature. So I poke around and try to follow him. Sometimes I catch a whiff of him, sometimes I just encounter his soldiers."

Natalie looked at Will with sympathy.

"So you're always the New Kid in school?"

"That's right."

"You never get to really settle down and make friends?"

"Not really, but it's cool."

Will looked away, pretending to study the night sky so Natalie wouldn't see the moisture in his eyes.

"I'm sorry, Will, that must be really hard."

She touched his hand and though he tried to remain stoic he felt his muscles slacken slightly, felt his hand going warm, the blood rushing to the place she was touching him. His face flushed and he withdrew his hand.

"Like I said, it's no big. And besides, I'm used to it," he said.

"You said *infected* . . . how does he do it? How does somebody get 'infected' anyway?" asked Rudy.

Will's eyes narrowed.

"You sure you want to hear this?"

Both Natalie and Rudy nodded enthusiastically. There was nothing like a good scary story to pique one's interest. The fact that this wasn't a story but was real didn't seem to bother them.

"I caught a demonteen one time and he told me all about it. Just before I wasted him. You've heard of tinnitus?" asked Will.

"That's like ringing in your ears, right?" said Natalie.

"Exactly. Most of the time it's a ringing, but sometimes it sounds like a buzzing or a crackling or a hissing. It's the sound your brain makes when it's trying to rewire itself."

"Oh man!" said Rudy, clutching his ears, "That's happened to me like a billion times in my life!"

"It doesn't mean anything, it's just how it starts. It's like he's calling you on the phone or something," said Will. "When the ringing stops you hear him say your name, three times. Then he tells you to embrace the dark side. It can be just a thought or it can be something you do, something you know is wrong. And if you think it, or do it, you feel this incredible rush of energy surging through your body. He tells you to open yourself to him, to make a mark. It can be as small as a prick on your finger or a little cut, just as long as you raise at least one drop of blood. Once your blood is exposed to air then that's it, game over, you're infected."

Rudy and Natalie were silent, allowing the full impact of Will's narrative to sink in. A cool breeze swept through the park and Natalie felt her skin prickle with goose bumps.

"I've always known there was something going on here in Harrisburg," said Natalie. "I knew it even before they took my sister."

"Your sister Emily?" asked Will. When Natalie looked surprised and then suspicious, he said, "I read about her in the paper before I moved. As soon as I saw you I thought I knew you but I didn't work out why right away. I saw her picture and then I saw you and. . . ." He stopped and cleared his throat. "Emily's disappearance was part of why I thought he might be here."

"The cops and the paper and everything said she drowned, but they never found her body," added Rudy.

"That's right," said Natalie. "And I just know she didn't drown. She was on the freakin' swim team, no *way* that river took her. It was him. Or them, or whatever you call them. That night. . . ." Her voice trailed off as though she was too scared to even utter what happened out loud.

Will stepped closer to her and put a hand on her shoulder.

"How did it happen, Natalie?" he asked. "You can tell me. You know I won't think you're crazy."

"I heard things. Voices. And the air. . . ." Again her voice trailed off into the dark night.

"Was there a smell?"

"Yes! How'd you know?"

"I know a lot of things. Did you see anything?"

"No. Yes. I mean, I'm not sure. I thought I maybe saw something, some . . . eyes. Underwater."

"Oh God!" said Rudy. "This is so creeping me out!"

"Good," said Will. "The more creeped out the better off you are. You'll be safer if you stay alert."

"Will, you have to help me," said Natalie.

"Help you what?"

"Find Emily."

Will frowned.

"Natalie, we don't really know for sure what happened to your sister."

"They took her and I know it!" said Natalie.

"The question is, *how* do you know it?"

"It's just . . . a feeling I have. Don't you trust your feelings?"

"I always trust my feelings," said Will.

"Well then, there you go. This time you can trust mine." She turned to Rudy and touched him on his shoulder. "We both know there's been something weird, something that really sucks, going on in this town for a long time, right, Rudy?"

"Yeah, you pretty much nailed it."

"Now that we know why you're here, we can help you," she said to Will. "And we're going to."

"We are?" asked Rudy. Then he added, "I'm kidding. At least I think I am."

"Look, you guys," said Will, "I came to Harrisburg because I did research and found out the crime rate here spiked a few months ago, especially crime involving minors. That's usually a sign that he or his servants are doing their dirty work. And I read about the kids who disappeared. About . . . Emily."

He looked at Natalie.

"Of course Emily is important, but I have to look at the bigger picture. I have to do my thing and poke around and see if I can draw them out into the open. If I can do that, then maybe I can get some face time with an Underlord."

"What's that?" asked Rudy.

"You know, like a captain or something, a middle manager, someone who reports to the big boss."

"Right, I know all about that," said Rudy proudly. "I did a paper on the Mafia. So the Devil is like the *capo di tutti capi*, the boss of all bosses, and the Underlord would be like the *sotto capo*, the second in command. And then you got your *soldatos*, or soldiers."

"I guess it's something like that," said Will. "Listen, I hardly know you guys, but from what I know of you, I like you. I don't want to see you get hurt. You deserved to know what you saved me from back there, but I need to do this alone."

"No more warnings, Will. I'm going to find Emily. And we're going to help you whether you like it or not," said Natalie defiantly.

Will knew he should tell her no but he couldn't figure out how. She'd suffered a loss not unlike his. They both knew what it felt like having a loved one disappear. They both knew that the worst part was *not knowing* what happened to them or if they were still alive. Will thought he understood his attraction to her now. It wasn't just superficial, they were bonded by their shared pain, their determination to get their loved one back. They were *connected*. How could he deny her when she only wanted the same thing he did?

A fine mist had settled over the night and everything felt damp. Will looked at Natalie and Rudy and pondered what it meant that he'd finally shared his life with someone. He knew that no matter how much he wanted to he couldn't take back the information he'd entrusted to them. It was obvious that they were going to keep sticking their noses in his business, the family business. But it was too late now, the die had been cast. Will just hoped that their determination to be involved wouldn't end up costing them their lives.

Chapter Nine:
The Invitation

Will dreamt he was in a meadow. A soft wind caressed the long wild grasses and blew dandelion seedlings around like tiny angels. He was lying in the grass next to a girl. Her features were vague, ever shifting; sometimes she would appear to be Natalie and a moment later she'd morph into Sharon Mitchell. In either incarnation he and the girl were moving closer together, laughing, holding hands, the blanket around them rotating slowly, and Will found himself only inches away from kissing either Natalie or Sharon. As their lips touched the image of the girl clarified: it was Natalie, and she tasted of strawberries. Happiness surged through Will. His whole body was warm from the sunlight, warm from the kiss, warm from happiness. And then the blanket began to wrap around Natalie's legs and transformed into thousands of red demon ants, now biting her, now pulling her down as the earth yawned open and claws reached up. Natalie was screaming as she was pulled down and though Will tried to help he was paralyzed, his arms frozen at his side. The sun dropped closer to the earth and became so hot it began to burn Will's flesh.

He woke up. The morning sun was streaming through his curtains and he sat up and wiped the perspiration from his face. His first instinct was to call Natalie and see if she was okay. But he knew that she was perfectly fine—after all, it had only been a dream.

He showered and shampooed his hair, checked himself out in the mirror, and decided he needed a haircut, or a least a trim. But who had time for that when the weight of the world was bearing down on your shoulders? He still wasn't certain if Harrisburg was the right place, or if he'd made an error in calculating this small burg as a likely place for the Lord of Darkness to spawn a nest of depravity and destruction. Sure, he'd encountered demonteens, but the country was crawling with them. Had he really seen and heard the Lord of Darkness? His gut told him he was on the right track. But he still wondered. Rudy had said that Harrisburg used to be a really nice place to live, but that lately things had gone south. The streets didn't feel safe anymore at night. Graffiti had made a sudden inexplicable appearance. Kids seemed to be wearing more leather and getting more body parts pierced. Natalie had agreed, but said all that stuff could be explained by TV and the fact that Harrisburg's population had surged in the last five years with the construction of a computer chip facility in nearby Waterville. What gave Natalie the creeps wasn't the way kids dressed or the increase in vandalism or the violent misogynistic music that filled the air. It was something else, something she called an epidemic of anger. It was as if the town had been infected with some disease that caused its citizens to lash out at each other. Will knew exactly what could cause that. *Him*. His poison was potent, his ambitions limitless. And it was up to Will to seek him out and destroy him and his kind.

At school Will was finally beginning to blend in a little; at least he wasn't pointed at and whispered about everywhere he went. Some kids had actually started smiling at him (mostly girls) and nodding at him (mostly boys). He ate lunch now at a table with Natalie, Rudy, and a few of Natalie's friends, but whenever the conversation strayed too close to who Will was, where he came from, or how he became so buff, he would clam up and ask questions about boring teachers that would lead to someone else bringing up something more titillating and Will would be off the hook. Each time he did this Natalie would smile knowingly at him and one time even reached under the table and pinched his leg.

After school the next week, the three of them went to Stoner's Park but it was empty except for some skateboarders so they opted for a trip to Highland Mall instead. It was just like every other mall in every other town in the country, full of chain merchants, stores like the Gap, Old Navy, Banana Republic, Lucky, Guess, Hollister, and A & F. Will wondered how many of the shoppers knew that all these retailers, the purveyors of the "cool" brands that made consumers feel like individuals, were in fact owned by just a half-dozen huge parent conglomerates. It was like a big spider web that trapped shoppers and sucked the money out of their wallets. Ninety percent of the clothing was made in sweatshops in poor countries halfway around the world. *But hey, who cares*, thought Will. *Certainly not the kids bleeding their parents' Visa cards dry.*

As they walked through the mall Natalie paused outside a store called Bebe that Will wasn't familiar with, seeing a top that made her eyes sparkle. And then Will saw a hint of sadness in her eyes and he concluded that this shop was stupidly expensive and that the top Natalie was yearning for was out of her price range.

"Hey, do you think we could go in here?" he asked innocently.

"Um, sure," said Natalie.

"Are you kidding me? You're kidding me, right?" said Rudy.

But Will and Natalie were already heading inside. Will went right to the rack where Natalie's holy grail top was hanging and pulled out a small.

"Try this on."

"Why?"

"I noticed it in the window and I need to get something for my aunt. I'd like to see what it looks like on. But if it gets you all cranky. . . ."

"No, no, I don't mind," said Natalie.

Rudy was so bored he was thinking about what it would be like to kiss a mannequin. Will waited patiently and when Natalie came out of the dressing room wearing the top she was so flushed with excitement that it made Will's heart thump. He knew he was sliding further and further down a slippery slope but he didn't care. It felt good, making Natalie happy, and he told himself that after all the years of deprivation he deserved a little pleasure.

"Um, do you like it? I mean, for your aunt?" asked Natalie, turning around as she modeled it.

"It's perfect." Will signaled for a sales clerk, a college girl who came right over and immediately felt herself drawn to Will even though he was at least four years younger than she was.

"I hope I can help you," she smiled, eyelashes batting.

"Cut the tags off this will you? I'm buying it." Will flipped out his wallet and discreetly handed the sales girl a credit card. She took the card and ran it, then came back with scissors and cut the tags off. Natalie was speechless.

"Um, I guess I should go take this off. I'm sure your aunt will—"

"Leave it on. It's yours."

"Wait. No, you can't—"

Will grinned. "If you argue with me I'm going to take these scissors and—"

He took the scissors from the sales girl and was about to cut right through the sleeve of the top when Natalie shrieked, "OKAY! I'm keeping it on, see!"

Rudy went ahead and macked on a mannequin.

The three of them descended on the food court.

"I don't know what to say," whispered Natalie, glowing in her new top.

"*Thank you* would be appropriate, but no thanks are necessary. You saved my butt the other day, I wanted to repay you, that's all."

Will knew the gift meant so much more than a simple thank you but did his best to hide the satisfaction he felt being able to buy a girl he dug something cool. Meanwhile Rudy was looking like the puppy who didn't get a bone and he repeatedly cleared his throat. Not a very subtle hint. Will couldn't help but chuckle.

"I know, I know, Rudy, you were in the cavalry, too. Lunch is on me," said Will, taking out his wallet as Rudy smiled. While Will opted for a gyro plate from Zeus's and Natalie had a chicken Caesar salad from Chillers, Rudy loaded up at the Big Apple Deli, getting two chili dogs and some screaming hot curly fries, a chocolate shake, and cheesecake. After scarfing it all down, crumbs falling in his lap, he complained about his stomach hurting. Then they heard some boisterous talking and laughter and looked over.

The sound was coming from a group of kids from school, not Duncan's crowd, but just as lean and mean, their fashions spot on, their teeth perfectly straight, their skin pale but smooth and pimple-free. There were three guys and a couple of girls and they bought frozen yogurt from Pinkberry.

Natalie was amazed at how the girls looked liked they just waltzed in off the pages of a Victoria's Secret catalog.

"I don't get it, how can they be so horribly, terribly, disgustingly, awfully . . . perfect?"

"You're only looking on the outside," said Will.

"Duh. That's what everybody does," countered Natalie.

"Not everybody," answered Will, and he looked at Natalie with his blue eyes, which were pretty perfect, too. At least as far as Natalie was concerned, even with the one slightly paler than the other.

Rudy indicated the tallest of the boys, a guy with long wavy hair, an earring, plenty of ink, and studded leather bracelets, all to complement his two-hundred-dollar jeans.

"That's Jason DeGenova," said Rudy. "He used to be such a geek. And then, like, over the summer he became this movie star. He was a klutz and now he's playing varsity basketball."

"Hormones. The teenage years can be so cruel to some and a blessing to others," said Natalie.

"Maybe it's more than hormones," said Will.

"What do you mean by that?" asked Natalie. Then she gasped. "Do you think he's—?"

"Let's not jump to any conclusions," said Will.

He looked closely at Jason. The kid had charisma for sure, he practically oozed it. He was wearing absurdly expensive jeans and shoes and on his wrist was a Rolex with too many diamonds on it. In fact all the kids in the group sported ridiculously expensive watches and jewelry and seemed more attractive, more muscular, more intense than the other kids at Harrisburg High. Will figured this clique was a good place to start. They were laughing and tossing knowing looks back and forth, acting like they owned not only the food court but the whole mall. They were the princes and princesses, and everyone else just a lowly serf. Will cocked his head and listened to the girl next to Jason tittering. Her name, Rudy said, was Janie Talooee and she was going on about last night's rave.

"It was beyond amazing, it was . . . transcendental. Rage is a two plus one. Not as bomb as you, of course, Jason, but his place is so awesome and the margaritas were locked. That guy is so dialed in it's scary."

Will knew he'd picked up the scent. Like just about everybody Will had five senses: touch, sight, smell, hearing, tasting. And like most others he also had a sixth sense, intuition. But unlike almost anyone else Will also had a unique seventh sense, a way of picking up meta-communications all around him, the unspoken, nonverbal communications that occurred between people, animals, and even plants. Minute chemicals emitted and exchanged, atmospheric alterations, and subtle but readable body language cues. And his seventh sense was picking up all kinds of things, unspoken communication between the members of this clique that said they were up to no good.

Will turned to Rudy and Natalie and spoke in a hushed tone.

"This guy Rage they're talking about, how do I meet him?"

"You don't," said Rudy, his brow furrowing.

"Don't be overly dramatic, Rudy," said Natalie. "Rage is just some skanked-out older dude who deals drugs—well, at least most kids think he does—and throws these legendary parties. Supposedly he has this ridiculously huge temper. That's why they call him 'Rage.'"

"How do I get invited to one of his parties?" asked Will.

"Duh. Not possible. Might as well try and break into Fort Knox," said Rudy.

"'Not possible' doesn't track with me," said Will. "This Jason guy, what's he into? What's he like?"

"All I know is he gets any girl he wants, drives a brand-new cherry red, tricked-out, amped-up turbocharged Mazda RX-8, and has the meanest killshot I've ever seen on *Demon Hunter*."

A small smile crossed Will's face.

"Then that's how I'll nail his ass to the wall." Will dug in his pocket and then fanned out three hundred-dollar bills. "He wins, he gets the Benjamins. I win, we party in the house of Rage."

Rudy acted as emissary, boasting to Jason and his crew that Will could kick Jason's butt on *Demon Hunter* and laying out the wager of money vs. party invite. It was a challenge that cut to the bone in Jason's ego and within minutes the kids were all jamming into a place in the mall called Rex's Game World. As Jason led his posse back to the gaming area, a small friendly looking man smiled at Will from behind the counter.

"Will Hunter? Is that you?"

Will looked at the guy. It was Rex Farmer, and he wore his usual tie-dyed T-shirt and suspenders that held up his linen pants. Rex was short and fit and had an inviting smile and bright brown eyes. He came out from behind the counter and shook Will's hand. Will smiled at him.

"Hey Rex, what'd you do, move your shop up here from Green-haven?" Will had first met Rex at his little hole-in-the-wall gamer shop in North Carolina.

"Better'n that. I'm a franchise now!" beamed Rex. "Got seven shops, all over the country. Just opened this one."

Will was surprised that Rex's business had taken off. His old place had been a dump and he always seemed on the brink of going under because Rex had a head for games but not money.

"You kids are spending more dough on games every year. You're making me a rich man!" Rex punched Will playfully on the arm.

Will gave Rex a high five and smiled at him again.

"It's cool to see you, man. You're looking great." Will wasn't just being polite. Rex had lost weight and had a tan.

"It's nice to see you, too, Will. Give 'em hell!"

Rex laughed as he patted Will affectionately on the shoulder and watched with his bright eyes as Will, Natalie, and Rudy joined Jason and his sneering posse. In seconds both Will and Jason were wired up to a couple of joysticks and huge LCD monitors. Will's three hundred-dollar bills were folded lengthwise and arranged in a triangle. The two groups of kids exchanged threatening looks. This was a total smackdown.

Jason jumped in first, and chose the gatehammer. *Excellent weapon choice*, thought Will to himself, and they watched as Jason's man kicked open a door and entered a stone-walled reception room where he was greeted by a smiling angelic young woman who offered him a mug of beverage. To drink or not drink? Jason tilted the joystick and his man kicked the legs out from underneath the false angel, who suddenly grew fangs and leathery wings and breathed fire as the goblet shattered to the floor, the liquid burning a hole that quickly spread across the room. Jason used the gatehammer to pulverize the demon girl and then pulled a cord on his jacket. As the floor fell away he parachuted down into a larger chamber.

Will had to admit Jason was good. He got all the way down to level four before being blindsided by a chameleon-like wizard demon who sprayed him with toxic wasps that quickly ate his arms off. Jason set his joystick down and stared hard at Will as if to say "Just try and top that, sucker."

Will began his turn, holding himself so casually that Rudy thought for sure he was going to get wasted by the first pack of demondogs on level two. But, using the deathfork he'd packed, Will's player dispatched the howling, snarling, biting demondogs as if they were annoying fruit flies. Jason began to sweat. He could swear he saw Will stifling a yawn as he descended down to level three via the blood tunnel, his player now arriving in some kind of crude temple or tomb where he encountered a hulking, two-headed demon armed with ax saws. Will seemed to know exactly what the demon was thinking, anticipating his every move and cutting him down with the blade of his own cache of weapons, pulling out a chaosglove to confuse the beast and then strangling him with a whipsnake until his head exploded, spewing blue brains against the walls. Then Will descended down to level four, quickly dispatching the same chameleon-like wizard demon and his toxic wasps who had offed Jason's player. Will's player then descended down to level five and Will paused the game. It had taken Will half the time to get to level five that it took Jason to get down to level four. And Will's man was still standing. The kids had never seen anything like it.

"I could go on, but what's the point?" smiled Will. "Maybe we can play some other time. After you catch up on your skills, anyway. Now about that party invite. . . ."

"There's a kickback going down this Friday night after the homecoming game," Jason said angrily. He was so livid his hands shook as he took out a pen and, grabbing Rudy's wrist, angrily scrawled an address on Rudy's arm.

"Ow! That hurts!"

"It's gonna hurt worse if you don't sit still and shut up," said Jason as he finished writing the address, cruelly adding an unnecessary exclamation point on the end that drew blood.

The reason the game was so effortless for Will could be best described by the old phrase "been there, done that." Will had actually *been* to those places, or modern versions of them, and fought those demons in the real world, and the memories of his exploits were burned so firmly in his consciousness that he could never forget even a single moment. After his first successful battle with a demon when he was fourteen, Will used his 172 IQ to design a video game and, submitting it to the top electronic gaming company in Silicon Valley, swiftly secured a long term contract to develop *Demon Hunter* and thereby assuring his and his mother's financial security for ten lifetimes.

His mother never questioned the money that came in, believing—or making the appearance of believing anyway—that the income was from "investments" that Edward had made in high tech companies on Will's behalf many years ago. Will reinvested so much of the profits that he became a major stockholder in the company and so was able to pull strings to make sure his mother's marketing job at one of the company's subsidiaries took her wherever Will decided they needed to move. As for Gerald, he was eager for any kind of cash coming into the household, so though he bitched about not having access to it, let alone control of it, he nonetheless rode the gravy train and accepted money willingly when and if it was offered.

Will was the one who controlled the approximately eighty million dollars in the accounts but he spent very little on himself, preferring instead to spend lavishly on the research, development, and manufacture of weaponry. Chasing and fighting demons was expensive. He didn't care all that much for material things anyway; all he really wanted was to put his broken family back together. To do that meant he had to find his father, and he'd gladly spend every last nickel he had—and more—in order to accomplish that goal.

Having been humiliated in front of his friends, Jason looked pissed off, but then a calm settled over him, like he was saying to himself, okay, you won this little battle, but I'm going to win the war. Smiling a sickeningly confident smile at Will, Jason waved goodbye, and then he and his crew turned on their heels and marched out of Rex's. Rudy let out a low whistle.

"Dude, you absolutely smoked him, that was so awesome!"

"I've had practice," said Will. Then Rudy danced around in that funny way of his, waving his arms in the air like an orangutan.

Will reached out and grabbed his wrist.

"No victory dances just yet, Rudy. And remember, this isn't a game, this whole thing is dangerous, more dangerous than you could ever imagine. If you should happen to see some . . . things, I guarantee it's not gonna be pretty."

Will's warning was like a blanket of gloom tossed over poor Rudy, who shut down and slumped his shoulders. Then he and Natalie followed Will out of Rex's. When they caught up to Will he spoke in a low serious voice.

"We've got an invite now. A key to a door. But I'll tell you right now it's probably not a door you want to walk through." Natalie and Rudy were about to protest but Will held up a hand. They said nothing. Will was glad he'd laid down the law. He was going to this fellow Rage's place, but for him it wasn't going to be a party. It was going to be yet another step in a long and painfully violent war.

Chapter Ten:
Party Time

The Harrisburg High School football stadium was lit up and rocking as the band played the Mustang fight song. Sharon Mitchell was conspicuously absent from her duty as head cheerleader but the fans didn't seem to mind. After all, the Mustangs were ahead 34-3 as the first half wound down. Will, Natalie, and Rudy sat high in the stands not far from the stoners and Goths, who acted like attending the game was some kind of punishment. The truth was most kids weren't there to see the game but to be seen as they strutted their designer jeans and shoes and hoodies.

Rudy was wolfing down hotdogs like they were going out of style. Will had one himself and immediately wished he'd abstained; they never agreed with him and he began to feel crappy. Natalie, too, was feeling a bit strange. She touched the side of her head, which ached. Were her ears ringing, or was it just loud in the stadium? She breathed deeply, hoping it wasn't what she feared.

At half-time the lights dimmed. After a corny skit by the drill team and some goofy members of the drama club the band played the school anthem, some lame fireworks were set off, and then a spotlight hit the new homecoming float as it entered the stadium.

Once the float had circled the stadium it came to rest in front of the student section and the P.A. announcer, his mike shrieking with feedback, proclaimed that Sharon Mitchell was the new homecoming queen. Lo and behold, there she was on the float, dressed up in a white gown looking pure and regal as she waved and batted her eyelashes and smiled, revealing her dazzlingly white teeth. She was cruelly beautiful and she knew it. She had this sly grin on her face like she knew every male from ten to eighty in the stadium wanted to jump her bones.

"I think I'm going to be sick," said Natalie.

That makes two of us, thought Will, *but it's not Sharon, it's the hot dog*. Will's stomach was doing backflips and he was starting to sweat. Sharon's eyes searched the stands until she found Will and locked in on him. She waved with the tips of her fingers as though casting a love spell. Then she used one of her white-gloved hands to blow him a kiss.

"Now I know I'm gonna be sick," said Natalie. She glared at Sharon Mitchell, then stared at Will, who was impassive, as though having homecoming queens fawn over him was an everyday occurrence.

"What is it with you and girls anyway? What is it they find so . . . irresistible?"

"I couldn't tell you," said Will. "I don't really pay attention to stuff like that."

Of course he was lying, he knew good and well the effect he had on girls, and grown women, too. Everywhere he went they checked him out with their eyes. They all sensed something, something that Will had been fighting to deny his whole life: that he had a bad boy aura about him. Everyone knew that girls dug bad boys. Except Will didn't think of himself as bad, he thought of himself as one of the good guys, a guy you could trust, a guy who would help you out if you got in a jam. What did all those women and girls know that he didn't?

Meanwhile Natalie was making little coughing sounds in her throat as the stadium lights went out and a laser light show began, dancers running onto the field and shaking their hips to a bass-heavy rap song. The laser lights played against Natalie's face and Will couldn't help but think about how pretty she was even when she was grimacing.

"Are you okay?" he asked.

"Sure, I'm fine, my throat just got really dry all of a sudden," she said.

"I'll get you something to drink."

Natalie nodded and held her fingers to her temples. No doubt about it, her ears were ringing. She wanted to tell Will but she didn't want to worry him unnecessarily. It was probably just normal tinnitus, it didn't mean anything. But just to be safe, she stopped having bad thoughts about Sharon Mitchell and forced herself to think positive things.

Will left Natalie and Rudy in the stands, then descended the stairs, waited in the interminable concession line, and bought cokes. He paid and was on his way back when he saw something that made his skin prickle. It was a guy who looked like his father, Edward, moving fast through the crowd. Will was sweating and his stomach was churning. It couldn't be his father . . . could it? He had to follow him!

He took off after the guy, but then lost him. Found him then lost him again. Was it just a hallucination? Was he just seeing what he wanted to see, what he'd been yearning to see for all these years? He whipped his head back and forth, his blue eyes searching . . . searching. There! A quick glimpse told him the man definitely looked like his father, but younger, maybe a lot younger. Will tossed the cokes in the garbage and ran after the man. But he moved preternaturally fast and in the intermittently flashing lights from the laser show it was hard to tell what was real and what wasn't. Will was about to give up when he felt something. His seventh sense had kicked in. He whirled and saw the silhouette of the man underneath the stands. Then came a voice.

"Let go, Will."

Will took a step toward the man. He couldn't see his face; surely it wasn't his father, how could it be? He had to get closer, get a better look. But the man held up a warning hand.

"Stay where you are and listen to me. I don't want you to come after me, Will. It's too dangerous!"

He knows my name! thought Will. *It is him!*

"Dad?"

"There's no time. Just heed my warning. Stay away from me, abandon your quest. Take your mother and run, just go away! Go as far as you can and don't look back!"

"But I want to help you! Let me see you!"

The laser light show guys kicked it up a notch and for a few brief seconds Will thought he saw the man's face. Maybe it *was* his father, maybe it was Edward! Will couldn't be sure.

"Dad, I can't just—"

"THERE'S NO TIME!" yelled the man. An obnoxious kid passing by blew an air horn at his friend and the ensuing movement distracted Will momentarily—and just like that the ghostly figure that might or might not have been Will's father was gone.

"Dad!" Will cried out and ran under the stands, searching. But the man had disappeared in the blink of an eye. Suddenly Will was uncertain if he'd really even been there at all. Maybe it was an apparition. It *had* to be, because why would his own father tell him to stay away?

Will searched under the stands until the stadium lights came back up and it was clear that no one was under there except him. He was nearly hyperventilating from the event and forced himself to breathe. He knew he needed to calm down. If the stranger actually was his father it could only mean one thing—that he was getting close. Close enough that they were getting desperate, trying to make him stop looking. It wouldn't work. He had questions for his father, so many questions. He hoped Edward could help him understand many of the thoughts and feelings he'd had over the years, the pain and anger he'd held inside. When he got mad the rage was like having a mad dog in a cage inside his head and he hated it. It was like a disease that was eating him alive and he was sure the answers to his questions would cure him, like a shot of some miracle drug. Because as certain as he was of his quest to rescue his father and put his fractured family back together again, Will was still plagued with uncertainties about who he really *was* inside.

Will went back, bought more cokes, and rejoined Natalie and Rudy in the stands.

"Where were you for so long?" asked Natalie.

"Talking to someone."

"Who?"

"To tell you the truth, I'm not really all that sure."

Natalie and Rudy exchanged a look. Their new friend, as was his custom, was acting hugely strange.

The halftime hoopla died down and the second half got underway. At the beginning Will kept searching the crowd for his father but he was nowhere to be found. Finally giving up, Will watched the game and noted how the Mustangs, under Coach Kellog's guidance, took cheap shots and seemed to delight in causing injuries to the opposing team. Two Gardenville Gophers were taken off the field on stretchers and when the final gun sounded the Mustangs had routed the Gophers 57-3. It was not a pretty sight.

In the parking lot Will, Natalie, and Rudy climbed into Will's Mitsubishi EVO. As Will started the car he saw Duncan arguing with Sharon Mitchell, who had changed from her homecoming gown into some tight black jeans and a black tank top and vest and wore a paisley scarf. Duncan was obviously trying to get back on her good side but she was having none of it and Duncan was getting more pissed off by the second. Then Todd Karson showed up and he and Duncan yanked Sharon into Duncan's xB. Will thought about jumping out and kicking some serious ass right then and there but Sharon looked more annoyed than scared and Will was on a mission. So he motored his Mitsubishi EVO through the post-game traffic jam and out onto Sampson Boulevard where he headed south across the river into the industrial part of town. A heavy rain began to fall but visibility wasn't an issue because Will's GPS led them directly to the address still written on Rudy's arm. Rudy was smiling as he stared at his inky badge of honor.

"I'm getting kind of used to it. I was thinking maybe I'd make it permanent, you know, have some ink laid down by Mookie Man."

In the couple of weeks since his "accident" Mookie had become quite the tattoo maven, working from his dingy basement studio. He had a crude but determined style and his designs were predominantly pagan and satanic in nature. Kids were paying major bucks for his ink.

"Stay away from Mookie," said Will.

Rudy was tempted to lip off but he kept silent and wondered for the thousandth time why everybody bossed him around. He wished that somehow he could earn some respect and longed for the day when his peers stopped dissing him. Rudy felt a stinging in his arm and looked down at where Jason had written the address. It was burning like ten bee stings.

"Uh, Will, my arm. . . ." Rudy's voice was thin and full of pain.

Will turned and looked at the affected area on Rudy's arm. It was swelling with welts where Jason had scrawled on it, and tiny drops of blood were forming on the swollen lines.

"It hurts!" said Rudy.

"Hang on," said Will as he pulled over to the curb and cut the Mitsubishi's 291-hp engine, then reached into the glove box and pulled out a leather pouch. Unzipping it he took out a small bottle and used a dropper to apply liquid to Rudy's arm, which immedi-

ately stopped bleeding. Will turned to Natalie and touched the bandana she was wearing on her wrist.

"Can I use this?"

"Of course." She took it off and watched as he tied it around Rudy's arm.

"Thanks, Will," said Rudy, relaxing. The stinging sensation had subsided and he breathed a sigh of relief.

"No problem. Just keep it wrapped up. It's dangerous to walk around with your blood exposed like that. And don't go thinking that any of the crap that Mookie or Duncan or their kind is doing is in any way, shape, or form cool, you got it? I need you to be vigilant, to stay on your toes."

Rudy nodded, and he looked like he totally meant it when he replied, "I got it, you don't have to tell me again. I'm with you man, I'm down with your way of thinking."

"Good. It might save your butt," said Will. Then he looked out the window.

"We're here."

All three gazed out. Dozens of cars both old and new lined the street and groups of kids were climbing out of them and then disappearing through a nondescript doorway halfway down the block. A couple of big older guys in tight black T-shirts stood in front of the door with their arms folded across their massive chests. Behind them the doorway was draped with a thick velour curtain. Will noticed that most of the kids entering the place were wearing black, too. *I guess black is the new black*, he thought. Then Duncan's xB pulled up and he got out with Sharon, who looked scared as he and Todd hustled her inside. *Maybe I can kill two birds with one stone tonight*, thought Will. He got out of his EVO and with Natalie and Rudy in tow he made his way down the sidewalk.

Natalie suddenly froze in her tracks, her eyes wide. She was looking at a long-haired kid wearing a huge skull necklace and the ubiquitous black. He was there one minute, then gone the next.

Will noticed Natalie's pause.

"Hey, something wrong?"

"No, I guess not. I just thought I saw somebody."

"Who?" asked Will.

"Never mind. I guess I'm just nervous," answered Natalie. "Let's go."

She didn't want to say that she couldn't have seen the person she thought she'd seen. It just wasn't *possible*. They kept moving toward the entrance.

"What if they don't let us in?" squeaked Rudy.

"Think positive, Rudy," said Will. "You are what you think, you know."

"Okay, but what if I think I'm going to piss my pants?"

"How about you don't think, and just follow," said Will, shaking his head.

He approached the doorway and didn't even pause, just walked right in past the muscle. Rudy and Natalie knew better than to make eye contact with anyone and rode Will's wake into the place.

"Note to self," said Rudy. "Always act like you belong and you can go anywhere." His face broke into a grin. "Cool."

The dimly lit hallway they passed through opened up to a large room with ceilings that soared up to open skylights. Speakers were blasting music by a heavy metal band singing about bleeding eyes and dying young. Will looked around. The scene was the antithesis of the wholesome pep rally at Harrisburg High. Booze and dope were in abundance. A half-smashed disco ball rotated rapidly, throwing helter-skelter shafts of multi-colored light throughout the space, which was thick with fetid smoke from cigarettes and weed. There were battered tables and three-legged chairs and an old neon Budweiser sign with half the letters burned out. Black leather-clad teens danced to seductive music that thumped from speakers as big as refrigerators.

Some of the kids were from Harrisburg High but many others were not. Natalie was amazed at the way the kids danced—their faces, chests, arms, and legs beaded with sweat, their eyes bloodshot, their muscles taut. The almost trance-like nature of their moves was chilling. Then she thought she saw the long-haired kid again. And as before, he was elusive, here and then gone. Natalie touched a finger to her ear. The ringing had come back.

Neither Natalie nor Rudy had ever seen anything like this bash, at least not in person. Will had seen way too much of it. Every single one of the party goers looked infected. But that was the tricky part. You could never tell until you got down to the bone whether a kid was infected, a true demonteen, or whether he or she was just another wannabe poser. Hopefully most of the kids were just mimicking what they saw on TV.

Will felt confident and in command of himself. But then the song changed, the beat becoming more and more alluring. It felt like the beat of the song was in synch with the beating of Will's own heart. It was tempting, seductive, like a siren calling out to him, and it made his blood hot. He hated the feeling and yet he craved more of it.

Natalie looked around because she thought she heard someone calling her name. And there it was again. And again. Then she realized that the voice wasn't coming from anywhere in this room, it was coming from someplace . . . else. And it was not only clear but hauntingly powerful. She couldn't resist it, could she? She had listened to the voice call her name three times. And now she began to think many different thoughts. . . .

Will was on such high alert looking for his enemies that he didn't notice anything weird about Natalie. But as the lights continued to flash and strobe and the music jacked up, suddenly Natalie looked less like the wholesome girl next door and more like a sly seductress. Will rubbed his eyes trying to rid himself of the images.

"Natalie, what's going on?" he said.

"Huh? Oh, nothing. I'm just . . . thinking. . . ."

Will looked at her eyes and followed her gaze. Kids were smiling at him, beckoning him with friendly faces, faces that said, *You're one of us!* But when Will resisted, using all his inner strength to remind himself why he was here, the faces changed, strobing back to being filled with loathing.

A kid with white face makeup, black eyeliner, a double-pierced tongue, and lowbrets danced up to Natalie and began massaging the air surrounding her in a vulgar fashion as he flicked his tongue in and out of his mouth like he thought he was some kind of snake.

Will's eyes went cold.

"Find somewhere else to be. Now."

The kid froze in his absurd dance posture, holding his breath, and for a moment looked like he might take a swing at Will. But then he exhaled and danced away, his harsh laugh sounding goat-like. Will looked at Natalie and she was her old sweet self again. That put Will back on solid ground—the incident of temptation had passed. He led Natalie and Rudy through the undulating throng toward a beat-up overstuffed chair in the corner. As they passed dancers Will shouted to be heard above the music, asking any- and everyone where he could find Rage. They acted like he'd just asked them to find Jesus or something and backed away from him as though he were suddenly emitting a noxious gas. *So much for the direct approach*, thought Will.

"Tell me again what we're doing here?" asked Rudy.

"Looking for Rage," answered Will.

"And then what?"

"And then all hell's going to break loose, maybe."

"Glad I asked."

Will scanned the room again.

"It's not safe for you two here, Rudy. Maybe you and Natalie should split, go home."

"I'm not leaving," said Natalie.

"Neither am I," added Rudy.

Will smiled but then his expression changed abruptly as he looked up and saw Sharon Mitchell two floors up on a mezzanine. She looked distressed, just like she had outside, and again Duncan appeared to be harassing her. Only this time he had Jason DeGenova with him. Will's nostrils flared as he watched Jason put his hand on Sharon's shoulders and lay a slobbery kiss on her neck. She either didn't like him or wasn't in the mood because she slapped him so hard his head snapped back. He was stunned for a long moment, and then he backhanded her. The blow brought tears to her eyes and blood from her nose. Then Jason made some kind of twirling motion with his hands. Todd Karson appeared and he and Duncan herded Sharon through a nearby doorway. She wasn't kicking or screaming, but only because they moved so fast she didn't have time to. She still seemed shocked from Jason's blow.

Will's body tensed and he looked quickly to Natalie and Rudy. Natalie looked like she was definitely getting a headache. Will locked eyes with Rudy.

"Stay here. Rudy, you *plant* yourself and watch Natalie!"

"I got it. You go rock and roll!" said Rudy.

Rudy was so amazed that no one had come up and kicked his butt out of the party that he was starting to loosen up. His head was bobbing to the music and a grin was plastered on his face. Will looked at him critically. The poor guy looked so happy to be any- where but stuck at home in his room that he failed to grasp the pre- cariousness of their position.

But Will had no time to school him. He moved across the dance floor toward the stairs. His path was continually blocked by gyrating dancers: girls grabbing him to dance and guys just plain getting in his way. In short, the whole dance floor was doing everything it could to impede him. So Will faked like he was dancing for a few seconds, which threw them off, and then jumped up and ran along an old unused bar to leap onto the stairs, taking them four at a time up one level, then two, then to the mezzanine where Sharon had been.

A hallway split off from the balcony and it was almost pitch black dark. Without thinking Will bolted down the corridor. It was an unfortunate choice; had he put some thought into his decision he might have considered scoping the hallway out more efficiently. But he did not, and therefore didn't see Todd Karson lurking in a vestibule until it was too late to prevent the tall boy from bringing a fire extinguisher down on the back of his head. As Will sank to the floor the dark hallway grew even darker.

Chapter Eleven:
Battle in the Sewer

Will's head throbbed. That was good news because it meant he was alive. He opened his eyes and the pain was so severe that when he tried to sit up he lost his balance and keeled back over. He lay on the carpeted floor another few seconds, telling himself to breathe, just breathe. The music was blasting and every downbeat felt like another spike being driven into his brain. The vocalist on the song screamed like a burn victim and Will wondered why anyone would think that was a pleasant aural experience.

He heard more screaming and quickly realized that it wasn't coming from a song; it was coming from a door down the hall. Will got to his feet and ran down the corridor, taking care this time to scope things out with his peripheral vision. The door the screaming was coming from was old and appeared to be solid oak. Will backed up and tried a full-on flying kick but only succeeded in cracking the molding. Reaching into his back pocket he extracted a small metal case and then pressed a button and with a few deft strokes sprayed a thin line of yellow foam along the door's frame. He pressed another button and the foam crackled to life and burned. Now the door came down with a shove and Will lunged into the room.

The screaming had stopped. Sharon Mitchell was waiting for him. Whoever had caused her to scream was no longer present. *Or maybe it wasn't a "who" but a "what,"* thought Will as he approached her.

"Are you okay?"

"Now that you're here I am," she said, her voice low and breathy.

"You were screaming," said Will, almost scowling at her as he scanned the room for signs of trouble. There were empty bottles of booze and cigarette butts and some dirty magazines but nothing much else except for battered furniture and tattered drapes. "What made you scream?"

"The thought that you'd never come." She smiled, licking her lips.

Her hair tousled, mascara thick, lips lush red and wet, eyes full of mischief, Sharon Mitchell suddenly looked nothing like any homecoming queen Will had ever seen. But he'd seen plenty of her new kind of persona. She reached out and grabbed his hand, then held up his palm and put her mouth to it, and her tongue. Will winced. It felt fantastic. He was a guy, after all. But he pulled his hand away. Then he grabbed her wrists and inspected both of her palms. They were sweaty but there were no mouths there.

"They got to you, didn't they." It wasn't a question; it was a statement of fact.

"I don't know what you're talking about, but I love the sound of your voice. It's so . . . hot," she purred.

"Where'd they go, Sharon?"

"Who are you talking about? Anyway, who cares now that we're alone? Here, feel my heart, it feels like a little animal trapped in my chest," she said as she grabbed his hand again and pressed it to her chest.

Will yanked his hand back.

"You're stoned. Go home and get some sleep."

He moved past her toward another door and he had almost reached it when he sensed movement. He turned around just in time to see Sharon's eyes roll back and her knees buckle out from under her as she let out a feral moan.

"Sharon!" he yelled.

He was at her side in an instant and caught her in his arms. It was either that or watch her skull crack against the black and white checkerboard tile floor.

"Sharon, what's happening?"

She opened her eyes slowly and with surprising strength wrapped her hands around Will's neck like a vise. She pulled his lips to hers and forced her tongue into his mouth. He was both repulsed and compelled by her kiss. She tasted of red wine and dirty cherries and the scent of her skin, the feel of her lips and her hips, hit him like a freight train. His whole body was tingling with pleasure while at the same time shuddering with revulsion. He managed to wrench his lips free, barely.

"What's the matter? Don't you want to hook up?" she asked innocently. It was time for Will to make a definitive statement. So when she tried to bite his cheek he dropped her and ran. As he darted through the door he heard her head smacking against the tile floor. He hoped she was out cold.

As he moved into the hallway he picked up a scent—potent, acrid, and unmistakable—and he followed it. Like a ghost from the shadows Jason darted across the hallway and through a door he slammed behind him, and Will charged forward, this time unsnapping the Mylar holster holding the Megashocker he'd strapped to his leg. He kicked the door open. Jason was standing in a shifting pool of light way across the room. An older guy was standing next to him. A single light bulb swung back and forth above them. The older guy wore snakeskin pants and boots and a tank top that exposed his sinewy upper body, which was carpeted with pagan and satanic tattoos that crawled all the way to his neck and even onto his face.

It was difficult to see what he really looked like, but Will had an uneasy feeling that he'd met the man before. It was tricky to gauge how old he was. He could have been twenty-five or thirty-five or maybe even older. But one thing was clear, his presentation was designed to let even the casual observer know one thing and one thing only: He was a badass. He was looking down at what appeared to be a bloody scarf Jason had brought to him, then he slowly raised his eyes and for a brief moment he gazed at Will. There might as well have been an electric current running between Will and this man, so strong was their mutual enmity. This had to be him. *Rage*. Will had just grasped onto that irrefutable thought when Rage reached up and crushed the hanging light bulb in his fist. The light went out.

The darkness wrapped around Will like a big gloved hand and Sharon was suddenly right in his face, smashing her lips against his and pressing her body against him. The taste of her mouth coursed through him like hot fire. He felt dizzy, legs suddenly weak, his heart pounding. He managed to shove her away.

"Why fight it, Will?" asked a deep gravelly voice from the darkness.

"Get away from me," shouted Will to Sharon, who just smiled as she gyrated, playing her part to perfection. Will was about to say something to her—he wasn't sure what, the words were still forming in his mind—when Todd Karson sprang out of the darkness with catlike quickness and slammed his fist into the side of Will's head, causing his ears to ring. Wrath swiftly rising inside him, Will dropped to the ground, felt his dermis thickening and his blood heating up as anger surged within him like a gathering storm.

The surprise attack had unleashed the beast inside Will and he spun and kicked Todd's legs out from under him. As Todd's face slammed into the floor Will thought he saw Todd's eyes flashing black with madness. Then Todd rolled over, whipped out a wicked-looking street blade, and chopped down at Will. The razor-sharp tip sank into the wood floor an inch from Will's ear. Will used his elbow to bash down on Todd's wrist and thought he heard a bone crack as

Todd howled, spittle flying from his mouth as his teeth enlarged and he squeezed his eyes shut in pain. Will leapt up and kicked the knife out of Todd's other flailing fist and felt more power surging through him, felt his blood going even hotter, as he straightened his back and then ducked into a combat crouch, his fingers curling: *Bring me all you got, sucker.*

"It feels good, doesn't it, Will. Inflicting pain," said the harsh voice from the darkness.

Will did get satisfaction from kicking the crap out of his adversaries, especially ones who'd bashed him in the head with fire extinguishers. But he didn't have time to feel bad about it now. When Todd's eyes opened this time they were the telltale liquid black. He emitted a throaty growl and the muscles expanded in his body as he jumped up. Even with one possibly broken wrist he was able to pick up a solid oak table and fling it at Will, who bent time and leapt out of the way a millisecond before the table smashed into the wall behind him, so heavy it took out a support beam. The doorway began to collapse, flooding the room with light from the hallway and, momentarily distracted, Will took his eyes off of Todd. Huge mistake, because the guy was on him like a jackal, his fingernails elongating even as he dug his massive paws into Will's neck. The pain was searing.

Time to kick it up a notch, thought Will as he reached for the Megashocker. Now it was his turn to do some damage. He activated the weapon and raked it across Todd's unsuspecting face, creaming him with a thousand volts of raw energy. Braying like a castrated bull elephant, Todd fell backward and slammed into the wood plank floor so hard that the windows shook.

When the dust began to settle Will scanned the room. Jason and Rage were gone. Giving Todd a double blast with the Megashocker to make sure he stayed down, Will ran out into the hallway. They could have gone any of four different directions. Digging into his cargo pants pocket Will whipped out some goggles, slipped them over his eyes, and activated them. With the goggles on he could catch a faint glimpse of the vapor trail that Rage and Jason had left behind. He followed it.

They were just boarding a service elevator, the mesh doors closing behind them when Will caught up to them. He ran toward them. He was almost there, almost to them, when the outer doors slammed in his face and his prey descended. Using the Megashocker he fired a current that jacked open the outer doors. Foul air from the building's lower floors swept up into Will's face as he leapt down, slamming onto the roof of the plummeting elevator car. It picked up speed and Will hoped he hadn't misjudged by jumping to begin with or he'd break both his ankles on impact. When the elevator car slammed to a halt it was jolting, but Will was in a crouch and absorbed the impact. Every muscle in his legs was screaming, but he'd suffered no breaks or sprains.

He ripped open the access hatch and dropped into the elevator car, then sprang out into the basement, but Rage and Jason were already gone. His eyes found a stairwell and he ran to it. The stairs turned to concrete after one floor and then he moved through a huge rusty portal and found himself in the sewer. *How appropriate for your kind*, he thought. He thought he heard the elevator starting up again but there was no time to investigate because the sewer tunnel he was in came alive with the sound of movement. Lots of movement. He recognized the sound they made before he saw them. Rats. By the sound of it, hundreds, maybe a thousand. He prayed that they were just normal, ordinary, filthy, disgusting plague-infested rats and not the other kind. But as soon as he saw them he knew that they weren't ordinary rats, they were demonic. Will braced himself.

They poured across the ledges surrounding the sewer river in waves, their small mouths flared, exposing nasty-looking, needle-sharp yellow teeth. Swinging the Megashocker Will dispatched the first line of them, burning their asses and quickly turning them into a smoking, heaving pile of pulp. But they kept coming and Will had to time-bend and run up the sides of the sewer walls to keep from being swarmed over. He backpedaled ten yards and watched with disgust as the creatures morphed, growing small leather-like wings and taking flight. They looked like locusts and came at him in a swarm. He dialed the Megashocker up to maximum power and sent a beam ricocheting off a pipe so it split and spread, forming a "V." The flying demon rats took the full force of the blast and were blown sideways and plunged into the sewer river. Leaping down, Will jammed the pulsing Megashocker into the river and the liquid, now charged with thousands of volts, super-heated and wiped out the whole stinking mess of them.

Will stood to the sound of someone clapping.

"Well done. Very nice. That's quite the weapon you have there, young Will." It was Rage, and both he and Jason had undergone their own metamorphoses, shedding any pretense of normalcy and allowing their true demonic shapes to emerge. They still looked more or less human—emphasis on less—but they were demons through and through: taut, muscular, their skin pale and rife with purple veins, their fingernails long and tapering to deadly looking points, their eyes liquid ebony.

Rage was clearly an older, more advanced demon and when he stood to his full height he towered a full eight inches above Jason. Will was fairly certain he'd scored big; this Rage character could very well be an Underlord.

Rage gritted his teeth and the veins on his head pulsed with anger. True to his reputation, it looked like he harbored one hell of a temper. He and Jason separated, one going left, the other right. Will knew an attack was coming and it was going to come fast. Rage and Jason began to breathe rapidly, their nostrils enlarging, chests expanding, leg and arm muscles flexing. This part, the waiting, was what Will hated the most. He just wanted to get it over with. But he willed himself to concentrate, to focus his mind on his senses, to let instinct take over and guide him into his primitive places, the places where he *felt* instead of thought and could slow the world around him down. In this way he was a superior warrior, a fighter to be feared, even by fully evolved demons.

The most likely move was for one of them to engage him head on while the other attacked his back. It was a time-honored, effective battle technique and the only way to subvert it was to forget about defense and concentrate on offense. So Will took a step backward like he was going to defend, then tore forward, rushing past Jason and forcing him to whirl and defend his flank. Jason raked at Will with his claw-like nails and just missed tearing into Will's neck and possibly opening an artery. With his other hand he made a rock-hard fist and pounded it into Will's chest, a blow so powerful that Will's heart skipped ten beats before starting up again.

Will dropped to his knees. He looked like he'd had it. But he wasn't done, not by a longshot. Using the Megashocker he slammed Jason's kneecaps and then hit him with a full-on uppercut to the crotch. The demon howled in pain—even demons hated taking a crotch shot—and then tucked into a ball and rolled across the floor and up the wall as Rage exploded with anger and flew through the air, careening into Will feet first and driving him into the wall with a punishing series of kicks, first to Will's chest and neck and then to his head. As he fought, Rage trembled with anger and screeched like an eagle. Will's skull was pounding yet he was able to spring up and grab hold of a pipe with one hand, then chin himself up and flip over so he was hanging upside down like a bat. He fought off Rage with the Megashocker while planting a fist in Jason's face.

The skirmish raged on for ten or twenty seconds that felt like forever to all three parties; pain had a way of elongating time. Fists found flesh and bone and with blow after blow Will's Megashocker sent waves of pain through his tormentors, who were so charred by the weapon they were literally smoking. He was putting the hurt on them in a big way. Rage made a move for Will but Will anticipated it, feinting one way and thrusting the other, and caught Rage by surprise, jamming the Megashocker's tip into the older demon's eye socket. Rage's head jerked violently back and forth until Will thought it was going to snap right off his body. Then he yanked the Megashocker out of Rage's eye socket as Jason's reinforcements, Duncan and Todd, arrived.

The entire sewer tunnel erupted in a flash of stench and blood as Rage totally lost it, his temper flaring, and vomited out demon bile that burst into nanoparticles, forming a cloaking cloud that enabled him to effectively vanish. And then two more demonteens arrived— ones Will didn't recognize—and started attacking Will with a vengeance. One of them was the long-haired kid Natalie had seen earlier. Using the Megashocker and a combination of martial arts kicks Will put them down. He finished one of them off by using the Megashocker to form a strangulation current that not only strangled the kicking beast but eventually beheaded him. The demonteen's body shook and vibrated with electrocution and then he exploded, parts flying everywhere and then disintegrating into sparkling microparticles. Meanwhile the long-haired demonteen lay motion-less on the floor, a victim of one of Will's time-bending Capoeira kicks.

"Good, Will, good for you," a voice echoed through the sewer, bouncing off the walls. It was *like* Rage's voice, but it wasn't him; it was deeper and had more of a rumble to it. Will searched for the ori-gin of the voice and saw nothing but a green mist hanging over the sewer. The only thing he knew for certain was that the voice was coming from below. *Way* below.

Will's hands, knuckles, elbows, and head throbbed but he ignored the soreness and fought on as Todd and Jason and Duncan mounted an attack. They got in several painful kicks before Will's anger boosted his adrenaline up a level and he lashed out, slamming Todd's head against the wall and cracking Duncan's kneecap with the heel of his boot. A few last kickass blows to these punk demons and he would boot their skanky butts all the way to purgatory. Then he could chase after Rage, maybe pick up his trail. If he was lucky, it just might lead him to the Dark Lord's lair. He raised the Megashocker to put Duncan, Jason, and Todd down for the count. Jason lunged at him and Will gave him an uppercut with the Megashocker, piercing his neck. Demon blood spurted out as Jason gurgled and toppled sideways. He grabbed for Will but Will swiped at him with the Megashocker, slicing off three of Jason's fingers. Then the long-haired kid rose up, floated up really, and made a move for Will who, with his free hand, whipped out a five-sided cutting disk and fired it at the kid, slicing off his scalp. Then Will yanked the Megashocker out of Jason's neck and was about to finish him off when he heard the clanking of the service elevator and the sound of footsteps and then Natalie's voice.

"Will?"

She'd just come down the stone steps and was walking numbly forward, her eyes unyieldingly wide as she was trying to comprehend what she was seeing. She was astounded by how Will looked, the power in his body, the fury in his eyes.

Will's heart hammered as he ran through the various probable outcomes of a human girl encountering the likes of Jason, Duncan, Todd, and the others. And in that brief moment Duncan and Todd ripped a length of pipe from the wall and flung it at Natalie like it had been shot out of a cannon. If it hit her anywhere in her upper body cavity or her head she was dead. Will bent time and ran toward her. But the pipe had been thrown too hard, and he knew that this time he wasn't fast enough.

Chapter Twelve: Infection

Call it fate or lady luck, but Natalie happened at that very moment to slip on the slick stones of the sewer and fall sideways, so instead of obliterating her skull entirely the hurling pipe only clipped her, knocking her sideways. While Will's attention was drawn to his fallen angel the demonteens retreated into the dark like bats. Will was torn. He yearned with all his being to follow them, to track them as he would a wounded animal. This might be his lucky night; he might have hurt them badly enough to slow them down and if he could follow them they might lead him right to the Lord of Darkness himself. But he couldn't leave Natalie like this. And he knew that his brief moment of hesitation had already been enough to allow the demons to escape. They had a head start and he'd be hard-pressed to catch up to them once they reached their network of catacombs. He put this failure out of his mind for the time being, holstered the Megashocker, and tended to Natalie, kneeling down beside her.

"Natalie, can you hear me?"

She lay motionless and Will's heart ached at the prospect that his error in judgment might have resulted in the death of a beautiful young woman he'd just begun to be crazy about. He silently cursed himself for telling Natalie anything, for thinking he could involve her without putting her in appalling danger.

"Natalie, it's me, Will. Can you hear me?"

She opened her eyes and her heart beat rapidly, not because she'd just witnessed something she knew to be unthinkable but because Will's face, his incredibly handsome face—with his perfect skin, his unbelievable lips—was only inches from her own. The voice in her head said, *Kiss me, just please kiss me.* But then she remembered where they were and what had just happened. She blinked and said, "I'm fine. I'm good. At least I think so."

"Let's get you out of here," he said and helped her to her feet.

In moments they were in the service elevator and rising up and away from the hellish scene of a battle Natalie still struggled to comprehend.

"Um, Will, what happened down there, exactly?" she asked. "What were those things? Were they demons?"

"Listen, Natalie, the important thing right now is to make sure you're alright."

He looked deeply into her eyes and she felt herself growing weak in the knees. But it had nothing to do with the tiny bump on her head.

She was a prisoner of his mismatched baby blues. Will held up a finger.

"Follow this with your eyes," he said, slowly moving his finger back and forth.

Natalie could see his finger perfectly fine but found her eyes wandering to Will's own: the one startling blue, the other lighter, almost gemstone blue. They pulled her in like some magic crystal ball and as she was growing faint she realized she had once again forgotten to breathe. She took a deep breath and blinked, then followed his finger back and forth.

"I'm okay. Thanks." She used one of her sleeves to wipe the sweat from her brow. "I'd be better if you'd tell me what it was I just saw back there."

"What exactly did you see?" asked Will.

"It was pretty dark," said Natalie. "But I saw enough. More than enough, I think. You cut off Jason's fingers! He's the captain of the basketball team!"

"He might have some trouble with his jump shot," said Will. At least until the fingers grew back.

"And that other kid, the one whose scalp was hanging there. . . ."

"What about him?"

"His name's Baily. Baily Winters."

"So?"

"He died in a car accident last year."

"Well, it looks like he's made a nice recovery," said Will.

As the service elevator doors opened and they stepped out into the hallway Natalie shuddered. "Will, I wasn't kidding about Baily. He was *dead*!"

"I believe you. And like I told you, the Dark Lord isn't too picky about his recruits. He must have pulled him right out of the cemetery."

"Will, those . . . things were so creepy."

"I warned you it was gonna get ugly. I should never have brought you along."

"No, you did the right thing. Those . . . creatures, those demons, they had to have taken Emily. I'm not afraid," she lied.

"They're demons, Natalie, of course you're afraid. You'd have to be nutso not to be. But fear is a funny thing. The more you resist it, the bigger and meaner it grows. So don't try and fight it, go ahead and be really, really afraid. It just means you're sane."

Natalie nodded, figuring Will must have had about as much experience with fear as anybody on the planet, and decided to take his advice to heart. She wouldn't fight her fear, she'd let it flow inside her. She'd make friends with it if she had to—whatever it took to get her twin sister back.

"So there really is such a thing as demons," muttered Natalie, mostly to herself, but of course Will felt obliged to answer her.

"For as long as mankind has existed, demons have roamed the earth."

"That sure explains a lot," said Natalie.

"Let's find Rudy and get out of here," said Will.

"Will, there's one more thing. They . . . He . . . whatever you want to call it, it tried to get to me, tried to infect me. I heard the ringing in my ears. Then He called my name, three times, just like you said."

Panic coursed through Will like venom.

"What did you do?"

"I thought of something . . . good, something wonderful."

"What?"

She just blushed. She couldn't bring herself to tell him that she held off the mind probing of the Dark Lord by thinking of him.

"Um . . . just things."

Will smiled, and touched her shoulder affectionately. She'd repelled the threat.

"Good. You did good. Come on."

Upstairs the party was in full swing, groups of kids grinding in the flashing lights to the pulsing beat. The room was even thicker with smoke than before and everyone had danced themselves into a frothy sweat. Will spotted Rudy grinning like the village idiot, one hand wrapped around a can of beer and the other resting on a plump Goth girl's bulging hip. Will hurriedly approached him.

"You were supposed to hang with Natalie," he hissed, wrenching the beer from Rudy's hand. "What the heck happened?"

"Geez, man, I'm just kickin' it a little, lighten up! I'm not your bitch!" snarled Rudy.

But Will was not about to lighten up. Anger pulsed through him. He cupped his hand around the back of Rudy's neck and squeezed, his fingers like a vise.

"When I ask you to do something, just do it, okay?" he said.

Pain shooting through his neck, Rudy gasped. He nodded.

"I'm sorry, Will. I'm cool, I just lost her for a second, then I thought for sure she'd come right back. For all I knew she was in the can or something! Take it easy, okay?"

Will let go, and when he took Natalie by the hand and led her from the hall Rudy followed like an obedient dog.

The trio was watched carefully by every pair of eyes in the place and Natalie had a sudden ugly vision that every last one of these kids was a creature like the ones she'd seen downstairs and that they would attack like a pack of coyotes and rip them to shreds. She held her breath as they made their way to the door. No one made a move to stop them. This time.

Rudy pouted and sulked the whole way home. Will didn't need to say another word; the look on his face spoke volumes. Rudy was in deep doo-doo. Any other time he might have tried to joke his way out of it but tonight was different. It wasn't just the beer he'd sipped, it was more. He felt stronger, like instead of crushing his shoulders like it usually did, the world held out wild promise for his young life. It wasn't that he didn't feel bad about not listening to Will, he just wasn't sure what the big deal was. Natalie was fine. Nothing had happened. What was Will's problem? Maybe Will wasn't as different from the rest of the meatheads at school as Rudy had thought.

He put in his iPod and listened to some Blood Eyes, a metal band whose lyrics Will would clearly disapprove of. *Well, tough beans*, thought Rudy, *Will can't hear it. Besides, I can listen to whatever I want to.* The night rushed by in a dark haze as Rudy stared out the window. When Will pulled up to his house he got out and slammed the door.

"Later, Will. See ya, Natalie."

"Rudy," Will called out.

Rudy turned around.

"Sorry I got on your case. Everybody makes mistakes," said Will.

"Yeah, sure. No worries, Will."

"I shouldn't have grabbed you like that," said Will.

"Hey, I screwed up. I would have done the same thing if I were you. It's cool."

Rudy smiled and did his little signature dance to placate Will and Natalie, then headed for the side door of his house. Will waited for Rudy to reach the door, then made a U-turn and drove toward Natalie's house.

Rudy's hand was on the doorknob and he kept it there, standing frozen like a statue, until he heard Will's car fading in the distance. Then he removed his hand, backed up, and waited in the shadows. He closed his eyes and heard a ringing in his ears. Then the voice said his name. *Rudy*. And again. *Rudy*. And again. *Rudy*. Then Rudy thought about his uncle Walter and how he'd been so angry at him for teasing him when he was younger. He imagined killing Walter with a five iron, splitting his head open like a cantaloupe. And as Rudy's heart rate increased, he reached over and wrapped his hand around the stem of one of his mother's Gold Medal roses, and a thorn sank into his thumb. He withdrew his hand. A tiny drop of ruby blood glistened. In a few moments a dark van pulled up and the Goth girl from the party stepped out and gave Rudy the finger. He was shocked, unsure what he was supposed to do. But then she smiled, revealing a huge gap between her front teeth that she'd bridged with a silver skull spacer with diamond eyes. Rudy returned the smile, ran over, and got in the van, squeezing his thumb, smiling at his drop of blood.

Will pulled up in front of Natalie's place and put his EVO in park, and Natalie reached over and turned the key, shutting the engine down. Will stared at his hands on the steering wheel.

"I guess this means you want to talk, huh?" he said.

Natalie nodded.

"You've got some explaining to do. And not about the demons. I have never in my life, except in the movies, seen anyone move as fast as you did down in that sewer, Will. And you seemed, I don't know, bigger and stronger than usual. What's up with that?"

Will stared out the window. How could he explain something he himself didn't understand? How could he tell her who he was when he asked himself that very same question every day when he got up and looked in the mirror?

"It's . . . complicated," he said.

"And you don't think I'm smart enough to understand," she bristled.

"No, that's not it. The truth is, I'm not even all that sure I understand it—what's happened to me, who I am. So trying to explain it would be futile. I will tell you two things. My puberty was . . . interesting. And I'm still . . . evolving."

Natalie nodded slowly, accepting for now Will's inability to articulate his complex existence. She knew he was different from any other boy she'd ever known. She wouldn't push. Instead she sighed as she looked out the window at her front porch where a tungsten light was blazing.

"My dad's gonna be so pissed I'm home this late. You think you could loan me that stick thing of yours you used tonight?"

"Um, I'm afraid that's impossible."

"I was kidding. You really *made* that thing?"

"Yeah. That one, and others."

"You must be some kind of genius, Will."

"I have . . . gifts."

"You certainly do."

"Natalie, I'm sorry. I should never have even thought about letting you get involved in this . . . conflict."

"But I am involved, Will. I have been since the day they took Emily. And by the looks of it we'll all be involved soon enough. You have to help me find Emily. I know she's with them. I can only hope that she hasn't . . . *become* one of them. She's not like that, she wouldn't . . . but. . . ." Natalie's voice trailed off into hopelessness.

"His power is great, Natalie. He's not easy to resist."

"But we will find her, won't we?"

Will wanted to tell her that he wasn't going to let her go any further, that he was barring her right this moment, that she'd have to watch from the sidelines—no forays into the underworld. But he knew she was so adamant about finding her sister Emily that if tonight hadn't deterred her, mere words wouldn't either. So he played it safe.

"I'll do everything I can, I promise you that," he said.

Natalie then did something that surprised and shocked them both; she leaned over and gave Will a brief gentle kiss on his cheek. It was something she did almost instinctively, just a way of saying thank you. But the currents that flowed between them were so powerful that the innocent kiss felt like so much more. Flustered, Natalie opened her door and got out. Neither of them said another word. Will watched until she was safely inside her house and then drove off, his heart singing.

As Will drove home he got down to business, replaying the evening's events in his mind. He'd made some good moves: getting invited to the party, kicking some serious ass, finding the demon they called Rage. He wasn't far from his goal, he could feel it. But he'd miscalculated by involving Natalie and Rudy. As good as it was to have real friends for a change, tonight they'd slowed him down. Having Natalie get hurt kept him from going after his goal. And Rudy was a nice goofy kid but he proved tonight he couldn't be counted on.

Will would have to give Natalie and Rudy some bogus busywork to keep them occupied while he set about finding Rage again and this time tailing the creature until he led him to the Lord of Darkness. It was critical for him to locate the Dark Lord's lair. It was his chance to discover the location of his father, for one, and possibly a clue to the location of the third power rod. He knew the Dark Lord had the second power rod, and of course he had one, so whoever got a hold of the third would have a great advantage. Will was determined to find it first. He opened the window and breathed in the night air. He felt as though the stakes in the game were steadily rising. If he didn't keep the pressure on, if he didn't make real headway soon, he feared he might be tasting defeat instead of victory.

He pulled his EVO into the garage, got out, glanced around, then went into the house. Had he been more thorough in his visual search he might have caught a glimpse of the yellow eyes peering up out of the ornamental well in his mother's garden. The creature let out a hiss, climbed out of the well, and then circled the house twice, breathing in Will's scent before departing into the dark night, as fleet as a gust of wind.

Will stood mutely, watching as his mother gently attended to Gerald. How in the world she could endure the stink was anybody's guess; Gerald had fired off a volley of slow warblers and the room was thick with his stench. He'd sucked down a six-pack of beer and fallen asleep in his La-Z-Boy while watching inane reality TV, his highly unoriginal nightly ritual. April took the remote control from his slack hand and turned off the TV, covered Gerald with an afghan, picked up his empty beer cans, and dimmed the lights. When she turned and saw Will she was jolted but calmed herself down and put a finger to her lips indicating Will should stay silent. He followed her into the kitchen where she poured him a glass of milk and offered him a cookie from the Winnie the Pooh cookie jar he'd been getting cookies from since he was a little kid.

"Thanks, Mom."

"You're welcome, Willie." Besides his dad she was the only one on the planet who got away with calling him Willie.

She tousled his hair, then put some water on to boil for her drink of choice, chamomile tea. She sat and smiled up at Will.

"How's your new school? Are you moving toward any of the goals you've set for yourself?"

"The school's okay. Good, really. The kids are just like everywhere else. And yeah, I'm getting closer to my goals every day. These cookies are great. I like it when you use chocolate chunks instead of chips."

"I know, that's why I made them that way."

They had these conversations every time they moved somewhere new. Even though Will was reasonably certain his mother had no idea what his alter ego was up to, a small part of him thought—or maybe just hoped—that perhaps she knew everything, that she was silently rooting for him in his quest, and that she only pretended otherwise because it was easier and less painful for both of them. But the softness in her eyes spoke only of love, not of worry, so how could she possibly know anything? He wondered if she still missed his father as much as he did. They'd frequently avoided talking about him for months, even years at a time, but now seemed as good a time as any to broach the subject.

"Mom, can I ask you a question?"

"You can always talk to me, Willie, you know that."

"Let's say, hypothetically, if Edward . . . if Dad were to come back. . . ."

The keening whistle of the tea kettle cut Will off and his mother stood up quickly, took the kettle off the gas, and started pouring the boiling water into her mug.

"Will, we've been over this a thousand times. It's been eight years, he's not coming back. Your father's never coming back."

"Okay, I hear you, I know what you're saying and maybe, probably I guess, you're right. But let's just say he did. . . ."

"He's not."

"Right. I get that you're totally convinced of that. But can we just do the 'what if' thing here? Can we look at the concept hypothetically?"

April let out an exasperated breath. "Whatever you want, Willie."

"Alright, then let's say, by some weird and wacky miracle he did come back. Let's say he walked right through that door right now. What would you say to him?"

April's eyes were suddenly wet from welling tears. She took a sip of her tea and then spoke in a calm soft voice.

"I would tell him he missed seeing one of the most remarkable things any father could ever see: He missed watching his boy grow into an amazing young man."

Will had a lump in his throat and couldn't help but feel his mother's pain heaped upon his own. But he pressed on because he had to know.

"Would you still love him? I mean, if he came back, would you still?"

She spoke now so softly that Will could barely hear her voice.

"I will always love your father, Willie. Until the day I die." She dabbed at the tear that had escaped the corner of her eye and Will placed a hand on her shoulder and kissed the top of her head. He hated making her upset but he had needed to know.

"Thanks. That's all I wanted to know. I gotta check on something in my darkroom."

Will went downstairs and moved through his light locks and into his secret room where everything was already powered up. He rewound the drive that captured the sensing devices he'd planted around town, and then fast-forwarded the file until he saw a large powerful signal that indicated a creature had been right outside his house. It didn't make him happy that it had been so close but it wasn't unusual.

"Bingo. Now where did you go?" whispered Will to the screen as he gripped the side of the desk so hard his knuckles went white. He watched the blip move swiftly across the screen, completely off the grid of the town of Harrisburg.

"So you're outside city limits, it appears," said Will. He watched the screen for a few more moments. When the blip didn't return, he highlighted the entire area outside the city limits and saved the image on his screen. Then he headed back upstairs. His mother was still in the kitchen and she smiled at him.

"I'm going to bed. Goodnight, Mom."

"Goodnight, Will. Sleep tight. Sweet dreams."

Climbing the stairs Will realized he was weary from the night's testosterone-charged roller coaster ride. Battles like that always wore him out physically and emotionally so he would likely sleep tight. But his dreams were rarely sweet.

In her own bed Natalie had rolled back and forth hugging her pillow, grasping at sleep and hoping she would dream of Will, not the horrible things she'd seen that night. She closed her eyes and mentally painted Will's picture on the back of her eyelids but she couldn't hold on to his image. When she did drop down into sleep the dreams she had were chaotic and frightful, invaded by hoards of flying demons, skeletons with wings, and eyes that burned with hate. She fought to release herself from their terrifying grip but as she sweated and tossed and turned she became entangled in her sheets and dreamt of being caught in a spider's web, a giant arachnid hovering over her, spinning, weaving, using its huge legs to cinch her tighter and tighter until she could hardly breathe. The dream changed abruptly and Natalie's body went slack and still.

In her new dream—Emily's dream—Natalie walked with Emily and at first it was harmonious and benign. Natalie felt that her twin was safe. But then the dream changed, as dreams always do, and they were running through a tunnel, eyes frantic, hands scraped, noses bleeding. They were running toward a dim light at the end of the tunnel; not the breathtaking light of the afterlife, but a silver sphere, a tiny light, elusive, like the light a fairy might give off while flying. The light moved and Natalie's heart pumped rapidly in her breast as she felt her sister's fear. They stumbled, fell, then scrambled up and over some rocks toward the light. Then they burst through an opening. The dream became hazy, liquid and vague, and then the light went out.

Natalie awakened and blinked, trying to hold on to the images she'd just seen in her mind's eye. But they faded. She got up and went to the window. Looking up at the full moon, she made her sister the same solemn promise she'd made so many nights before this. *I will find you. Wherever you are, I'll find you and I'll get you out of there.*

Chapter Thirteen: Saturday

Saturday morning after a hearty breakfast of pancakes, bacon, orange juice, and a banana, Will went out and mowed the front and back lawns, raked up the clippings and put them in the green rolling dumpster. He had enough money to hire a gardener for everyone in Harrisburg and beyond but he didn't mind doing manual labor; it allowed him to let his mind wander and he often got some of his best insights when he was doing something as mundane as taking out the garbage or clipping a hedge.

As he finished up the lawn and set about washing the windows Will thought about where he was on his quest. Including Harrisburg he'd been to five different towns and five different high schools in the last three years. He wondered if it meant anything, if there was any kind of pattern evolving. If there was, perhaps he could use this knowledge to get one step ahead of the Lord of Darkness instead of always feeling like he was one step behind. He made a mental note to check into the pattern thing and then climbed down off the ladder and checked the windows. They were as clean as anyone could possibly get them. He saw his own reflection and for a moment almost didn't recognize himself. His mother was right; he had grown up, he was now a young man. And as he looked at his reflected image he knew that anyone looking at him would quickly conclude that he was a *tough* young man, the kind of guy you didn't want to get into a scrape with. But he also wondered, was this young man looking back at him the kind of guy someone could really love? Someone Natalie could love? Natalie. There she was again in his thoughts. He couldn't stop thinking about her. Well, the truth was he didn't *want* to stop thinking about her.

It was noon by the time he finished all his chores and he retired to his secret chamber in the basement. He brought up a map of the USA on his main frame screen and entered all the locations where he'd done battle with the Black Spirit. A red light blinked on each of the towns, spanning the continental US: San Diego, California; Corpus Christi, Texas; Greenhaven, North Carolina; Brunswick, Vermont; and now Harrisburg, Washington. Will stared at the screen a long time but no extra insight came into his mind. So he went up into the garage and worked on his Mitsubishi EVO.

After he serviced the turbo charger and tuned the suspension he washed his ride inside and out, using a chamois cloth to make the chrome wheels shine. Then he slid the key into the ignition, fired up the kick-ass engine, and took the EVO out for a spin. He drove around Harrisburg, watching the kids playing in the street, the wives working in the garden, the husbands painting fences and fixing broken sprinkler heads. There was a plethora of dogs in Harrisburg and Will passed his neighbor Mrs. Norrington, a kindly overweight woman in her late sixties, who walked her regal little Toy Fox Terrier Scoopy every morning and afternoon. She was outgoing and friendly and waved to Will like she was running for mayor. She wore designer clothes and way too much jewelry, including a gaudy diamond ring that Will figured had to be at least five carats. Where did these people get their money?

Mrs. Norrington picked up Scoopy and kissed him, then held his paw so he "waved" at Will as well, which cracked Will up. He generally liked the people he'd encountered in Harrisburg, most of them seeming to be decent, hard-working Americans doing their best not just to get by but to lend a helping hand to those around them. There was always some charity event going on and various fund drives netted thousands to help spruce up the schools even in the crappy part of town.

Stopping at a light Will discovered that he'd inadvertently cruised back around to Natalie's street. Or maybe it wasn't so inadvertent. He smiled and thought, *What the heck, I might as well pop by since I'm this close.* He pulled up to her house. Her front yard was choked with tall weeds and the gutters on the house were sagging. He wished he could buy her a new house without drawing attention to himself. Instead he sent her a text.

"*SUP?*"

"*ZIP*"

"*I'm out frnt*"

There was a pause and Will saw the curtains in Natalie's second story bedroom move. She was peeking down at him.

"*Y?*"

"*Wanna ride?*"

In two minutes she was outside, climbing into his car.

"Hey."

"How's it goin'?"

"Cool. You?"

"I'm okay."

"Where are we going?"

"Let's let the wind decide," said Will.

Natalie smiled. Somehow, Will just always managed to bring out the happy in her.

"I'm down with that," she said, trying to act casual.

With Natalie in the passenger seat Will cooled his jets a little but he could tell by how tightly she held on to the door handle with her right hand that his driving was still fast enough to make her nervous. They cranked up some tunes and stopped by Dave's Drive On In for a couple of burgers, fries, and cokes. Then they wound their way up Davidson Road and parked at a vista pullout, where they soaked in a breathtaking view of Mount St. Emory, the volcano that had lain dormant for 600 years. Looking down at Harrisburg, Will realized how precarious the town's position was. If Mount St. Emory ever erupted again, even with only one-tenth the power of Mount St. Helens, the pastoral, bucolic town of Harrisburg would be obliterated.

As Will and Natalie kicked back with the windows down, feeling the cool breezes waft through the EVO, they skillfully managed to avoid any lingering eye contact. Swollen clouds crawled slowly across the brilliant cornflower blue sky. Neither of them was about to mention the lips-to-cheek incident from the night before but they could both still feel it. Finally, focusing on a cloud that resembled a huge pair of lips, Natalie looked at Will.

"What are you thinking about?"

Of course he was thinking about several things—one being what it would be like to really kiss her, tongue and all—but he chose not to mention that particular thought and went with a secondary idea he had rattling around in his head.

"Um, I was thinking about Rudy."

"What about him?"

"I was kinda hard on him last night. I was thinking maybe we could head over to his place and check in on him. And I had some ideas on some things you and he could do to help out. You know, for the cause."

"Um, sure. Great." Not exactly romantic, but at this point Natalie would take anything she could get.

In minutes they were in Rudy's driveway. They got out, walked up, and rang the doorbell. Rudy's mom, a haggardly thin woman with smoker's teeth, opened the door. When they inquired about

Rudy she said he had left earlier and mumbled something about getting ready for the dance tonight.

"Rudy? The dance?" said Natalie, bewildered.

"My thoughts exactly," said Rudy's mom, and then added with a smile, "You teens kill me. Always changing. A baby one day and a big shot the next. What can I say?"

They left Rudy's place after making Rudy's mother promise to have him call them the minute he came home. Natalie dialed Rudy's cell but got nothing but his goofy message: "Yo, this is Rudy Toody McGroody, leave your incredibly important message at the BEEEEEEP!" She sent him a text but he didn't reply. At this point they were starting to worry; Rudy always responded to texts. They went to the mall and checked both levels twice but there was no sign of him. He wasn't feeding his face in the food court, wasn't getting all bleary-eyed at Rex's Game World, and wasn't in any of the clothing stores checking out the chicks.

They cruised around town and hit a few of the usual hangouts: the skate park, the fast food joints, the rope swing on the Blue River landing, but Rudy was nowhere to be found. By mid-afternoon they still hadn't found him. They were left with just one more option to find Rudy but it involved venturing into territory that made Will uncomfortable in a way even sewers filled with demon rats did not.

"Um . . . I guess we better go to the dance."

"You mean the fall dance?" asked Natalie.

"Uh, yeah. Uh . . . you want to go to the dance. With me?" asked Will.

Natalie turned her head away from him and looked out the window so he wouldn't see her smile.

"Sure. Okay. Why not? I mean, if that's the only way to make sure Rudy's okay."

"I'll pick you up around seven."

• • •

A million thoughts swirled through Natalie's brain. What would she wear? How would she do her hair? What if Will tried to kiss her? What if he *didn't*?! Not that it was a real date. Unless it was. And she was still worried about Rudy. Was he mad at them about yesterday? Was he just busy? Or was there something else, something more dangerous, keeping him from getting back to them?

So she did what she usually did when she couldn't relax: she collapsed onto her bed and closed her eyes. When she was under stress or a deadline, the times when most people would have great difficulty falling asleep, Natalie nodded off like nobody's business. She simply told herself she absolutely should not fall asleep—and that almost always did the trick. This time was no exception, and she was snoozing within minutes.

After sleeping for twenty minutes without so much as a stitch of a dream, the vision images came upon her in waves. She saw faces from school, her girlfriends, and faces from her childhood. They were all frowning and many were wiping away tears because they were attending some sort of ceremony—Natalie's funeral, where she herself was in attendance, looking down at her body in an open casket. An identical casket sat next to hers and contained her twin sister Emily. Then the dream shifted as the coffins floated up into space and gathered speed.

And now Natalie was again dreaming with Emily, parallel minds in parallel universes and they were back in that same tunnel racing away from something behind them. It was a creature, a large creature, so large that when its massive feet slammed into the tunnel floor the tunnel shook and rocks rained down. A pair of clawed paws swiped at them and Natalie screamed for Emily to go, to keep going while she faced the monster down. Turning in her tracks, Natalie grabbed a large stone and was about to throw it when the creature stepped from the darkness into a pool of light and Natalie's nerves collapsed. She was so shaken by the sight of him that she dropped the rock; it was pointless to resist such a beast. It was at least eight feet tall and had mottled leathery hide, a double set of horns, and a mouth dripping with foul liquids and filled with jagged teeth. Where there should have been eyes there were nothing but hollow sockets lit from within. Natalie fell at the creature's feet and its jaws were inches from her face, ready to make her not so pretty and dead besides—when thankfully the dream shifted again and she was once again running through the tunnel, scrambling up and up and now she burst out of the mouth of the tunnel into the moonlit night.

Spinning around she saw that the tunnel opening looked like the entrance to a mine of some sort. Two enormous boulders were perched on the hillside above the tunnel opening so that the side of the mountain resembled a tormented face; the boulders were the eyes, almost glowing from the moonlight glinting off them, and the tunnel opening was the gaping mouth, open in a silent scream that was suddenly not so silent as flames shot out of it and were just about to rip into Natalie's face when she woke up.

When Will casually mentioned to his mom that he was going to the dance she tittered with excitement and not only ironed a white shirt for him but actually ran out and bought a lapel flower and wrist corsage. He wanted to tell her that it wasn't like that, he wasn't some dorky teenager going to his first dance. But he didn't want to hurt her feelings and besides, it was at least partly true. He'd never been to any kind of dance before, let alone a fall prom kind of thing. He was in uncharted waters. Gerald thought the whole thing was so funny he doubled up on his beer input, kept calling Will a "stud," and brought out several bottles of malodorous tawdry cologne for Will to sample. When Will declined the cologne Gerald grumbled and called him an ungrateful punk and stomped into the living room to rip a few in his La-Z-Boy.

April had tears in her eyes as she pinned the white rose on the lapel of his sports coat and she told him he was surely going to be the handsomest young man at the dance.

"Thanks, Mom, but I know you're only saying that because I'm your son."

"I'm saying it because it's true, Willie."

"I'll see you later, Mom," he said.

"Don't be too late." She always said that every time he left the house. But this time she added: "Never mind. You stay out as late as you want to."

She was smiling so wide Will thought her face might break and he was starting to get all emotional himself. Whether he liked it or not, whether it was planned or not, this was one of those important milestones in one's life—even if he was wearing slacks, which he loathed.

With April wiping away tears and waving, Will went out and got in his EVO and drove over to pick up Natalie. Parking his car, he honked his horn; he couldn't bear the thought of meeting her dad and enduring the ritual pre-date grilling. As Natalie came out her father, a muscular bald man with a goatee, glared out after her, no doubt wondering who this lout was who wouldn't even come to the front door. Will noted the beer already open in one hand, and a second can held in the other. *Big drinker*, Will thought. It reminded him of Gerald. Then Natalie's mother, a chunky woman wearing Capri pants and a tube top and smoking a cigarette, began arguing with Natalie's father, the two of them putting on a silent Punch-and-Judy show for nobody's benefit but their own. Will winced, but turned on a smile as Natalie got in the car. She was wearing a sleeveless white cotton dress with a tiny red rose pattern and brown leather boots, and she looked so sexy Will had a hard time keeping his eyes off her. He closed his eyes for a moment as he caught a whiff of her perfume. Lavender. It knocked his socks off. Instead of a tiny purse she had a large leather backpack slung over her shoulder and she tossed it into the backseat. Then she looked over at her bickering parents and blushed with shame.

"Sorry about that. They keep threatening to get a divorce." Natalie blinked away a tear. "Emily's disappearance . . . her kidnapping, it was really hard on them."

Will gave a slow nod of sympathy and started up the car.

"Sure. Of course. It had to be." He didn't want to get into it. He was an expert on dysfunctional families, knew the pain all too well.

"If they're going to do it, get a divorce I mean, I wish they'd just hurry up and do it. They sure don't have to stay together for my sake." Then Natalie actually looked at Will, and closed her mouth. He looked incredibly handsome, and he was blushing as he held out a corsage.

"Um, my mom went out and bought this."

"It's beautiful. And thank you. I mean, tell your mom thank you."

Natalie slipped the white rose on her wrist as they drove toward Harrisburg High. It was the first formal dance either of them had ever attended. Natalie could feel in her bones that it was going to be a night she remembered for the rest of her life. She just hoped the reason had more to do with the person sitting beside her and less to do with demons.

Chapter Fourteen: The Fall Dance

A pale silver moon hung in the sky over the high school as Will and Natalie drove up and parked. A light gray mist was rolling in off the ocean and Will awkwardly offered his arm as they walked across the parking lot and went inside. The theme of the fall dance was "Cupid's Ball," much to Will and Natalie's chagrin, and the gym was decorated with balloon bouquets and crepe paper streamers and aluminum stars, plus the mandatory dorky-looking Cupids hanging everywhere, bows drawn ready to strike with their love-poisoned arrows. The band on stage was doing a retro '80s disco thing at first—maybe to match the decorations—and then when no one was biting they slowed it down and the dance floor gradually began to fill up with couples who'd been reluctant to be the first to show off. The whole scene was as innocent as a Norman Rockwell painting—until Will looked across the dance floor and saw *them*.

Beside him, Natalie drew in a sharp breath, seeing Jason dressed to the nines in a black blazer, T-shirt, and slacks. She yanked on Will's sleeve and saw that Will was already gazing at him, too.

"Will, his neck . . . his fingers . . . I saw what you did to him, how can he even be alive, let alone walking? And look, there's not even a scar."

"They can regenerate themselves if you don't kill them properly, don't finish them off," said Will calmly.

"Okay, good to know," replied Natalie, suddenly feeling a little lightheaded.

"They can also appear perfectly normal until the Dark Lord calls upon them to do his bidding. The infection is like a dormant virus. There aren't any symptoms until it's triggered, and then it can make them really sick really fast," Will added.

Recalling what she'd seen in the sewer tunnel Natalie felt even woozier and her body swayed slightly. Will put his arm around her waist to steady her and the moment he touched her she felt hot and hyperaware of how close they were standing. Since they hadn't exactly been labeled a couple or anything they were getting plenty of looks from Natalie's girlfriends who gazed at her with outright envy.

Will could feel the awkwardness closing in around them.

"Um, do you see Rudy anywhere?" he asked and Natalie suddenly remembered that the whole reason they were at the dance was to look for Rudy, not to have fun. It wasn't like it was a real date or anything. She made herself straighten her shoulders as she scanned the faces in the gym.

"No, I . . . I've been looking but I haven't seen him since we came in."

"I hope he's alright. I should have known something was up the other night. I wasn't paying attention. I should have been paying closer attention," Will said, his face filled with guilt.

"Will, you can't watch out for everybody, be everyone's protector all the time," said Natalie.

"If I don't, then who will?"

Not for the first time, Natalie wondered what she'd gotten herself into with this New Kid. He felt like he was responsible for saving the whole world and she loved that about him, that he wanted to. But no matter how strong he was, no matter how many weird and wonderful powers he had, he couldn't save everybody. He couldn't do everything by himself.

As if he could read her mind Will looked at her a little sadly. But then he dug down and brought up a smile.

"Do you want to dance or something?" Will asked, feeling like the biggest dork in the Western Hemisphere. Duh, it was a dance, they were supposed to dance.

"I guess we probably should. To make it look good and everything," said Natalie.

He guided her onto the dance floor and they did a slow sort of shambling dance with Will leading the way. As they settled into a comfortable rhythm dancing, getting somewhat used to the electric current zapping back and forth between them, Natalie let go of her worries and focused instead on how incredible Will was. She even liked his ear lobes.

"Hey, about your parents, it's no big deal, you know," said Will after a few minutes.

"I know. Lots of kids have parents who get divorced. I hear that all the time. But you never think it will happen to you." She let him pull her a little closer. "The thing is, they've always been so . . . I don't know, distant. I don't think they ever really wanted Emily and me, that's for sure. My dad's always been way more interested in his beer and the TV than us, and my mom, she's so drugged out that half the time I don't think she even gets that we're alive. Emily and I kind of raised each other, you know?"

"That's tough. I'm sorry. I guess I know why you want to find her so badly."

"And we're going to, right?"

"Right."

Something in his voice must have made her pause because she looked up at him and said, "Will, will you promise me?"

"I promise you."

They danced a bit longer. And then Will spoke again.

"I always thought for sure my mom and dad would stay together forever. But I should have known better."

"It wasn't either of their faults that he was kidnapped by that . . . thing. If it hadn't. . . ."

"Do you believe in pre-birth dreams?" asked Will.

"After the last few days hangin' with you, I'm ready to believe anything."

"Well, you know how some people dream about past lives? I had this dream about my mother and father, about a night that happened before I was even born. It was like I was there, even though I couldn't have been, I hadn't even been conceived yet. But the dream is so real, and I keep having it, over and over. . . ."

Edward and April were living in Tucson and it was one of those nights when the desert heat lay close and mean to the ground, making everyone edgy and miserable. In Will's dream he was asleep in his bed, wearing his Scooby-Doo pajamas and sweating on his Star Wars sheets, when he heard a crash that woke him up. He rubbed the sleep out of his eyes and wandered to the stairs where he began to descend but stopped cold when he saw his mother. She looked different than he'd ever seen her. She usually had her hair up in a ponytail but tonight it hung down in long reckless curls. And instead of her usual modest earth-toned attire she was wearing a tight red dress with a plunging neckline. Young Will didn't know what a cleavage even was, he just knew he'd never seen his mom's before. She'd been drinking whiskey and she and Edward were arguing.

He was trying to get her to stop drinking but she'd have none of it and when he grabbed her elbow as she headed for the front door she whirled and slapped him across the face. The blow rocked him back on his heels and Will felt it as though it had connected with his own flesh. He saw the pain in his father's eyes and heard the door slam as his mother left in a cloud of anger. Then he heard a car start up and tires squealing.

When his father looked up at him, he scampered back to bed where he pulled the covers over his head and waited, hardly breathing, his heart beating really fast. In a few moments his father came in and without any explanation scooped Will up into his arms and carried him out to a Volvo station wagon. Will's mother had taken their other, sportier car, a Mustang. Edward strapped Will into a car seat and Will knew better than to complain; the situation was clearly grave.

They drove around town for hours, stopping intermittently at bars and taverns and dance halls, Edward searching the parking lots for the Mustang. They found plenty of Mustangs, but none the right color, and finally Edward gave up. He drove them both home and put Will to bed.

When Will awakened again it was to muffled sounds, sounds he'd never heard before and didn't recognize. He was afraid to get out of his bed but his bladder finally got the best of him. He crawled out and rushed into the bathroom and peed, then ventured slowly downstairs and saw his father asleep in the chair. The house was dark but Will could make out a large figure of a man lumbering out of his mother's bedroom. The dark shape paused and stared down at Will for a moment, then exited as swiftly as a gust of wind. Will walked down the hallway and peered into his mother's room. Her red dress was on the floor, torn and tattered. Her body was sprawled on the bed, splayed and spent, her limbs tangled in the sheets. Her eyes were bloodshot slits. She stared at the ceiling uncomprehendingly. When Will called her name she didn't budge. Tears flowed silently from her eyes. Will's father appeared and pulled him up into his arms from behind and took him upstairs and tucked him into bed.

Will dreamt that in the morning he was terrified to come down to breakfast, petrified that his childhood universe had been ripped asunder. But his mother and father had evidently worked through whatever had happened the night before because she was her usual smiling self. She rushed and swept him into her arms and hugged him and kissed him until he squirmed out of her hold and she put him back down. The family ate breakfast together. Then the dream ended with the doors and windows of the house being blasted open by a wall of flames.

"Man, that is some dream," said Natalie. When she saw the anguish on Will's face she hastened to comfort him. "It's just a dream, though. Maybe it doesn't mean anything."

"Then why do I keep having it?"

"Who knows why anybody dreams anything?" said Natalie.

"The weird thing is, some part of me is convinced that it happened. I mean, I know I wasn't there, but I also feel like, aside from that, everything in the dream was real, it all happened. Which would mean Mom—" Will broke off, in obvious pain from the dreamt incident.

"Well, even if it did, everybody makes mistakes," said Natalie.

"I know, you just don't expect it to be your own mother."

Just then Sharon Mitchell made a spectacular entrance flanked by several of her cheerleader acolytes, confused but still loyal. Gone was Sharon's freshly scrubbed girl-next-door persona, replaced now with a style sense that Natalie would have called trampy, but only if she had been feeling charitable. The other cheerleaders just looked bewildered. Natalie shook her head slowly in disgust.

Sharon went right out on the dance floor and was joined by Jason and Duncan, who sandwiched her as the music changed abruptly. Will and Natalie hadn't even noticed that the retro band had exited the stage, replaced by a hardcore-looking band of gangsta killer wannabees, a tribute band for Blood Eyes.

The drummer hammered away and the lights in the gym changed as the band erupted in a cacophony of discordant guitar and synthesizer riffs intended to rattle nerves. The lead singer was Jimmy King, the skinny captain of the volleyball team. He was a poor excuse for the real lead singer for Blood Eyes, Correl Shames, but he threw himself into the song, screeching away like a wounded bird. More and more kids like Jason, Sharon, Duncan, and Todd bled onto the dance floor and the clothing colors shifted from pastels to mostly black. Then kids Natalie had never seen before, kids obviously from other schools in the area, began to show up, all wearing similar togs: mixtures of black and leather and spiked hair and tattoos. It was no big deal, they were just crashing the dance, but it felt like an invasion.

The song grew louder and more jarring, the dancing more aggressive in tone. The speakers erupted with feedback as the microphone was dropped. Then the gym went abruptly silent, all eyes turning to the front as a figure strolled confidently onto the stage. Jimmy King picked up the mike and smiled broadly, now really feeling like a star because he was announcing something big, something totally huge.

"I give you . . . the lead singer for Blood Eyes . . . CORREL SHAMES!"

Correl was so practiced in making grand entrances that he had no problem captivating this audience of high schoolers. With a wave of his hand and the bang of a drum the lights went out. Then a solitary spotlight came on. Correl had ripped his shirt open and now held the mike and cut loose with a throat-rending scream that sent chills down the spine of every kid in the place as the band slammed into overdrive and Correl chewed his words of pain and suffering and spit them into the microphone like venom.

As Will and Natalie watched, the kids on the dance floor moved their bodies rhythmically, faster and faster, jumping and leaping to the beat until they shook like they were in a Voodoo zombie trance. Soon the entire dance floor of kids undulated and roiled in unison as though they were not separate beings but rather one living organism.

A creeping sense of alertness rose through Will as the spotlight morphed red and hit the singer full on and Will got a good long look at Correl Shames's obsidian eyes.

Aggression rose on the dance floor as though the gym were filling up, flooding, with a rising tide of poison. Kids slam-danced and some slapped each other and before long, just as Correl Shames hit his ear-splitting crescendo, a fight broke out across the gym. Will thought he recognized Rudy's whiny voice and bristled in defense. It looked like Rudy needed him again. He was probably getting thrashed by some of Duncan's posse and Will actually looked forward to bailing his little buddy out of a scrape again. It meant they had found him—and before anything too bad had happened to him.

With Natalie in tow Will moved swiftly through the throng of onlookers—they'd smelled blood and moved in for a closer look. Some kid was pounding away on a smaller guy, had him down and was hammering him pretty good.

Will shouted out, "Rudy!"

The bigger, stronger kid whirled around and stood defiant. He had fire in his eyes and blood on his knuckles. It was Rudy.

Will and Natalie stood looking at him, shell-shocked. He was wearing jet black jeans and a black tank top and his hair was gelled and spiked up and cut into a Mohawk. His formerly pimpled face was smooth and clear and he had tattoos of a skull with wings on his left bicep and a red pentagram on his right hand, his hitting hand.

Will got over the shock and pulled Rudy aside. Rudy was sweating and his pupils were huge. He pulled a bandana from his back pocket and wiped the blood off his knuckles.

"Will, my man, Natalie, how you guys doin'?"

"What the hell happened to you?" demanded Will.

"Nothing!"

"You're taller, Rudy, and you look like you're wearing Batman's Under Armour," accused Natalie.

"You never heard of a growth spurt?" growled Rudy.

"Not overnight, no," said Will. "And I see your face cleared up. They got to you, didn't they."

"You are so freakin' clueless, you don't know what you're talking about."

"Of course I do. We all do. Come with us, Rudy, maybe I can help you," pleaded Will.

With surprising strength Rudy shoved Will backward.

"Stay away from me. Both of you. And if I were you I'd watch my back."

The music flared up again and Rudy disappeared into the horde of throbbing dancers. Will pulled Natalie along as he followed Rudy and then stopped when he found him dancing with Sharon Mitchell. Rudy's wildest dream had come true.

"Looks like Rudy got his wish," said Will, then added, "Too bad he has no idea the price he'll have to pay."

"It's not your fault, Will."

"I should have paid closer attention to him, I should never have let this happen. I let you guys into my twisted life, and now Rudy's messed up." Tears welled up in Will's eyes. He'd let his friend down.

"Isn't there anything we can do? Some kind of intervention or something?" asked Natalie.

"I don't know," said Will. He'd never actually tried. He'd been developing a device, but it was as yet untested. He needed time. And looking at Rudy, he wasn't sure he had any. His funny little friend, who was now not so little and definitely not funny, was filled with prideful bliss as he gyrated with Sharon Mitchell.

Rudy turned and focused his eyes on Will and Natalie. Gone was the optimistic, friendly light. In its place was pure malevolence. It was a look that said, *I'm going to kill you, I'm going to kill you both.* Natalie shuddered as Will led her out of the gym.

Chapter Fifteen:
The Chase

The dance thumped along wildly for another ten minutes until Correl Shames made his exit and the black-clad crowd, deeming the whole affair to be suddenly very uncool, made a mass migration to the parking lot where Will and Natalie waited in Will's EVO. They slouched in their seats and watched as Jason and Jimmy and the rest climbed into cars and, yipping and yelling like ordinary teens, squealed out of the parking lot, all heading in the same direction. Rudy was one of the last to exit the gym and climbed into Duncan's xB with Sharon. Will waited a beat, then fired up his Mitsubishi and followed the pack. If Natalie was frightened by Will's driving before she was absolutely petrified now as he downshifted, laid his rice rocket out, and even had to go into a couple of corner drifts to keep up with the pack of cars screaming into the night. He had to push it; he had to keep up with his prey.

"Will, slow down!"

"If I do I'll lose them."

"No you won't, it's obvious they're staying on the highway!"

Her pleading voice got to Will so he throttled back, thinking, *Maybe she's right, they're all heading in the same direction on the highway, it won't hurt to pull back. How can I lose them?* But as they rounded the next curve the road ahead of them was clear.

"Damn!" shouted Will as he double-clutched and downshifted and stomped on the gas. The Mitsubishi rocketed forward. Natalie knew she'd just caused him to fail so she kept quiet, even as the lights along the street flew by in a blinding smear. Will pushed the EVO hard, gunning it up to a hundred and ten and still there was no sign of tail lights ahead. Then without warning the backs of Will and Natalie's head were lit up by headlights. The pack was behind them. Now *they* were the prey.

"Will, what's happening?" cried Natalie.

"Don't worry. I won't let anything happen to you."

The headlights grew closer and closer until the chase cars were right on their tail and began knocking into Will's back bumper. Natalie screamed as the EVO went into a brief sideways skid at ninety-five miles per hour but Will pulled out of it and flipped a lever. As the nitro plunged into his turbocharger the EVO jet-blasted forward in a burst of speed. But their pursuers came on relentlessly, three cars taking up the entire highway behind them. An oncoming logging truck in the left lane flashed his high beams and laid on his horn but the demonteens didn't give a crap and wouldn't yield. The guy had to swerve around them through a ditch, laying hard and long on his horn.

"What do they want?" screamed Natalie.

"Not sure yet," answered Will as calmly as he could. One of the chase cars, a jet black Nissan 350Z, roared up beside them and the smoked window on the passenger side powered down, revealing a kid with pasty white skin, gold bridgework on his teeth, and a bloody nose. He licked at the blood on his upper lip and laughed, then started to crawl out the window.

"My God, he's going to kill himself!" yelled Natalie.

"If only," said Will.

Still grinning, the kid pulled himself into a crouch and then jumped out of the speeding 350Z. But instead of falling and slamming into the pavement he went airborne, sprouting hideous pimply, fleshy wings and flying ahead of the speeding pack of cars. A hundred yards down the road he swooped up, twirled around, and then tucked into a dive and bulleted right at Will's EVO, waggling his tongue. Natalie let out a horrific scream as Will tried to swerve but the flying demonteen turned with him and smacked into their windshield face first, his teeth cutting through his tongue, which went flying. But the bulletproof glass Will had installed all around the EVO only yielded a hairline crack as the demonteen's neck was broken. His body slid off the front of the hood and Natalie winced as the EVO's tires thumped over the demonteen's body. Looking back she saw that they'd severed it in half and the remains crackled and sparked and then disintegrated.

"This is so not what I had in mind for my first dance date," said Natalie.

"Hang on!"

Two more cars hit his left flank and forced him to yank his wheel right, taking them onto a narrower roadway that snaked up the mountain. As Will fought to keep the Mitsubishi on the road the chase cars again pulled closer and then one overtook him. Now he was boxed in and to make matters worse two more flying demonteens appeared, carrying weapons. The first had a heavy chain and was swinging it, slamming it over and over against the passenger window. Number two had an iron harpoon and flew ahead, took aim and threw it. The harpoon hit the window with such force that it pierced it and lodged in the passenger seat next to Natalie.

"Okay, that's IT!" yelled Will.

He kept fighting to maintain control of the EVO as the chase cars side-banged him, trying to knock him over the edge of the road, which now skirted a massive drop-off. It was a long way down. More flying demonteens filled the air, all with primitive but deadly weapons. As they continued to attack the car, the EVO's wheels veered to the shoulder and scraped the guard rails, sending up a shower of sparks. One more bad collision and Will and Natalie would smash through the railing and plunge over the cliff.

"You've got to drive now!" shouted Will.

"Do you have a *death wish?* I can hardly back out of my own driveway!"

"You better learn quick, it's our only chance."

Still holding the wheel with one hand as they screamed up the curving mountain road, Will shifted out of his seat and with his other hand helped Natalie maneuver around the harpoon and into the driver's seat.

"I can't believe we're doing this!" she screamed as he relinquished control of the steering wheel and she replaced his foot on the gas pedal with hers.

"If you've got a better idea, let me know," shouted Will.

He hit a button and the sliding moonroof speed-retracted, revealing the star-filled sky. Then he reached around and tapped out a code on the retrieval patch on his neck. High in the sky the power rod, which was hovering at five thousand feet, hummed and shone brighter and then dropped fast.

A mace-wielding demonteen surged right at Will like a hawk and took a swing but in one smooth super-quick motion Will yanked a mini-grappling hook from his belt, hooked one end on the EVO's roof, ducked beneath the mace, and caught the demonteen's heel with the hook, bringing him down out of the air with such force that when he slammed into the pavement he was pulverized immediately. Three more flying demonteens formed a "V" and hurled themselves toward Will, who raised his hand and caught his incoming power rod. He activated it instantly and fired a salvo of flaming balls into the guts of two of them. They reacted with shocked surprise and then screamed as their bodies exploded from within. Their comrade glared at Will.

"You killed my friends!" he shouted.

"Deal with it," said Will.

And then he fired up the dual saber on the power rod and sliced the guy in half. The demonteen's scream was so loud it split open the night sky as the two halves of his body disintegrated.

The chase cars backed off momentarily, then slowed and turned on their fog lights as the mountain road wound its way into a thick bank of mist. Natalie instinctively slowed the Mitsubishi down, too, and then her face twisted into a mask of disgust as the mist seeped in through the moonroof.

"What's that smell?" she complained, almost gagging.

"It's the smell of evil," said Will. "Try not to breathe too much of it. Here." He whipped a bandana out of his pocket and handed it to Natalie, who tied it bandit-style over her nose and mouth.

Suddenly the pack of chase cars suddenly gunned their engines, raced past the EVO, and kept going on up the mountain.

"What do I do?" asked Natalie.

"Slow down, but keep going," said Will. "I don't like the feelings I'm getting."

"That makes two of us."

They kept on driving through the fetid fog, Will's eyes searching for more demonteens to waste. He was certain an ambush was imminent. But no demons appeared and in the moments that passed, the mist grew thicker and thicker and fuller of stench. With the killing behind him for the time being Will felt his heart slowing down, felt the red-hot pleasure in his battle-fueled blood begin to wane. And then he heard it. A rumbling guttural voice, like the sound of someone dragging a sack of giant bones, echoed through the night.

"You've come to enjoy the killing, haven't you, Will?"

"Show yourself!" Will shouted, his eyes darting around, catching shapes moving, glimpses of eyes in the dark, but nothing he could aim at or take a swipe at with his power rod. Something was circling him but he couldn't see it through the mist.

Natalie shrieked as a bat zipped down and flew just inches past Will's face. Then a demonteen flew out of the darkness, teeth bared, and zoomed right at Will, taking him by surprise and raking his neck with razor-sharp fingernails. Will managed to duck the brunt of the blow but he was bleeding now. He pivoted and when the demonteen swooped down, coming in for another strike, Will ducked then popped back up and struck with his power rod's dual sabers, slicing the morbid creature into pieces, its guts and bones churning out of its body as its mouth released an unholy screech of death and the severed parts crackled and dissolved into a gas that blew away in the wind. The thunderous, rancorous beast-like voice spoke again.

"That's good, Will, just a few more kills, you're almost there!"

"Almost where! Show yourself and answer me! Almost where?"

"Almost . . . home," the voice rumbled, and then as the mist cleared Will swore he heard faraway laughter.

"Give me back my father!" he shouted to the retreating figure. But he could only see the mist.

Natalie had slowed the car to a crawl and they were all alone now on the mountain road. Will holstered his power rod and sat back down.

"Stop the car."

Natalie pulled the EVO to a stop. Will got out, walked around, and yanked the harpoon out of the windshield. Then he threw it in a ditch.

"How you doing?" Will asked.

"I've been better, but I'm alright, I think," said Natalie, her hands trembling on the wheel.

"Scoot over," said Will as he got in the car. Once she was buckled in again he gunned the engine, pushing the Mitsubishi through the mist. They were on an open, clear roadway now, with occasional smaller roads forking off left and right.

"They could have gone anywhere," Will muttered. "I've got to find his lair. That's the key. I've *got* to find his lair." Will then pulled a U-turn. "But not with you. You're going home." He began driving back the way they'd come.

"I don't want to go home."

"It's not open to discussion."

"If there's a lair up here somewhere Emily's got to be there."

"I said it's not open to discussion."

They drove along in silence, winding their way back down the mountain. Natalie watched the trees go by, teeth grit furiously as she stared at the various pale shapes of the mountain. Sure, she was scared; she'd never been more scared in her whole life. But the thought of living the rest of her life without her sister was even scarier. Will couldn't do this to her. It wasn't fair. There had to be a way to convince him to let her stay. Then she remembered her dream from that afternoon, how frightened Emily had seemed as she ran through the tunnel. And Natalie sucked in a sharp breath.

"I know what it looks like!"

"You know what *what* looks like?" said Will.

"The entrance. To the lair, or whatever."

"Don't mess with me, Natalie."

"I swear, I'm not. I know, I really do know!"

"How is that possible?"

"You're not the only one who has dreams, Will. Emily and I . . . when one of us dreams, we both dream. And she dreamt about the entrance."

Will wanted to believe she was lying, that she was just trying to keep him from taking her home, but he'd seen way too much freaky paranormal stuff over the years to rule anything out. He knew from experience that nothing was impossible.

"Okay. Tell me more."

"She was . . . I mean, we were . . . in this tunnel, and we were being chased by . . . some *thing*, some really scary, really ugly thing with just empty sockets where its eyes should have been."

Will's hands tightened on the steering wheel. She was talking about the Dark Lord.

"The entrance. You said something about the entrance."

"We came running out, in the dream I mean, and when we came out I turned around and looked back. We'd just come out of this . . . it was kind of like a huge mouth, but it was an opening, an entrance to a tunnel. And there were these huge boulders on the mountain that looked like eyes."

"So it's on the mountain. . . ."

"Yes, I'm sure of that. There were pine trees everywhere. I would know this place if I saw it in real life, Will, I would recognize it, I know I would."

Will thought carefully. He'd read that it was common for twins, even when they were separated or lived far apart, to share common feelings and experiences, to have prescient knowledge of one another's lives. So sharing dreams didn't seem impossible. And Natalie's description of the Dark Lord had been spot on. How else could she have known? Will put the pedal to the metal and sped down the mountain as fast as he could.

Natalie frowned.

"You don't believe me. You don't believe a word I'm saying."

"Look in the backseat."

She did, and saw a silver metal case and another backpack on the seat next to her own.

"There's a computer in the case," said Will. "Take it out."

Natalie opened the case and pulled out the laptop just as Will wheeled his EVO into a coffee shop parking lot. He parked his car, opened the laptop, and logged onto ActiveEarth, the new real-time satellite program capable of locating a pimple on a bug's ass from space. He began typing in coordinates. Soon images of Harrisburg appeared and Will moved the cursor so that they had a clear daytime vision of Mount St. Emory. He opened another window on the laptop and brought up Web sites chronicling the history of the mining industry in Colone County. It didn't take long to dig up a map of the old silver mines on the south and east sides of Mount St. Emory.

"So you do believe me," said Natalie.

"It sounds like you were describing an entrance to a mine shaft. And according to these charts there shouldn't be more than a dozen or so of those on the mountain."

"And for sure I'll recognize it."

"Let's get going."

They drove back up the mountain and for the first hour or so their search was fruitless. The majority of the mines were totally sealed up or buried under landslides. And it became harder and harder to see because the sky was becoming crowded with dark clouds. Far away thunder rumbled. But then they had a stroke of luck. Natalie spotted a narrow roadway that eventually led them where they wanted to go and there it was, across a clearing, the tunnel entrance: the same tunnel entrance that Natalie had fled out of in her shared nightmare. About fifty yards away were a series of huge slag heaps, mountains of dirt and debris. They looked fresh.

"I thought these mines weren't active," said Will. "What's going on?"

"I have no idea," said Natalie.

They parked the EVO and got out to gaze in wonder at the mine opening. Standing there looking at the side of the mountain Natalie remembered it all too well. With the boulders and the huge dead stump and the tunnel opening, the whole thing looked like a human skull.

Chapter Sixteen: Entering the Cave

"This is soooo it." Natalie felt a chill scamper up and down her spine as she looked at the tunnel entrance. Entering it would be like walking into a huge mouth and it didn't take a whole lot of imagination to think of them as being swallowed up. Will touched her gently on the shoulder.

"I can't begin to thank you enough, Natalie. You found it. Now stay here with the car and be ready to take off if I call you on your cell or come running out with something horrible chasing me."

Will pulled a backpack from the EVO, whipped off his sports coat, and pulled on a hiking jacket with tons of pockets. He was so focused on getting ready he hardly noticed that Natalie, digging around in her own backpack on the other side of the backseat, was fast-changing her clothes, too. She pulled jeans on under her dress and turned around to put on a long-sleeved shirt.

"You know I'm coming with you," said Natalie. Will looked at her just as she finished pulling the shirt down over her stomach.

"No."

"*So* not in my vocabulary at this particular time," she said.

Will clenched his jaw, then relaxed and spoke in a calm voice.

"Be reasonable."

"We were just attacked by flying demons and you're asking me to be reasonable? Forget that. I'm going in." She shut the car door firmly to underscore her determination.

"Natalie—"

"The only way you're going to keep me out of there is if you kill me right here on the spot. Barring you slicing me in half with that thing of yours, there's nothing you can do to stop me."

Will took a deep breath and looked at the mountain and then at Natalie.

"Okay, rule number one. Keep up with me and don't ask questions about what I'm doing. Rule number two. When I say run, you don't hesitate, you don't stop and think about it, you just run. Got it?"

"Got it."

Will un-holstered his power rod and did a quick check on it, watching the luminescent blades closely as they cut through the quiet night. Satisfied, he put the weapon away as Natalie shook her head.

"I feel safe with you. Especially when you have that thing."

"Well, that's a mistake. You should never, ever feel safe when there are demons around. Don't ever let your guard down."

"Right. Okay. I get it."

"You know when people say things like 'I'm not trying to scare you'? Well, I *am* trying to scare you. I want you to be totally scared, so scared it's like you're walking on the edge of a razor. That way you'll be alert. Don't let fear be your enemy, Nat. Fear can be your friend, it can keep you alive."

She blew out a breath. "I understand." Then she smiled. "You called me 'Nat.'"

"Sorry."

"No, that's okay. I like it."

Will looked at Natalie and she could tell he was clearly mulling something over. She wondered if he was actually considering offing her on the spot just to be done with it. But then he reached into his backpack, dug around, and pulled out the bolt-driver, the same wicked weapon she'd seen Rudy mistakenly fire in Will's basement.

"Here, take this. You may need it."

He handed it to her and she took it. It felt more than just heavy, it felt like she was holding a compressed Volkswagen in the palm of her hand. He slid a lever on the boltdriver, which exposed several cartridges.

"It's pre-loaded. All you have to do is cock it like this," he showed her, "and fire."

Natalie gulped at the thought of firing the thing and put a hand to her chest. "Don't mind me, I'm just having a heart attack."

"Hey, if you don't think you can—" Will stopped in mid-sentence as Natalie suddenly gripped the weapon tightly and aimed it right at his forehead.

"You don't get it do you?" she said, her voice firm now, all traces of her timidity gone.

"Apparently not—if you're going to waste me with that thing."

"Emily's my sister. My twin sister. I can't rest until I know she's safe. And nothing's going to stand in my way. I just . . . had a moment of hesitation, that's all. I'm good to go now." She lowered the boltdriver and clipped it securely to the sequined belt in her jeans.

Will smiled thinly and patted her on the shoulder.

"Okay then, Lara Croft, let's move it."

He flipped on a halogen light and they approached the tunnel opening. Though the timbers that supported the tunnel were rotted and looked like they might collapse at any second, the tracks for the old mining cars were smooth, the metal shiny.

"Look at the tracks," said Natalie. "This mine closed forty years ago, there's no silver left in this mountain, but it looks like someone's been using them. I wonder what they're taking out?"

"By the looks of those piles out front someone's been taking out plenty. Searching for something or maybe making room for something," said Will pensively.

"Yeah, but what?" asked Natalie.

"Hopefully we'll find out," said Will. "Whatever it is, it's not going to be particularly fun, that I can guarantee."

Will paused and then turned to Natalie and held up a hand.

"Okay, this is strictly a recon mission, we're not going to engage."

"In English, please?"

"We're just going to go in and have a look around. We're not here to kick ass. I can't risk anything . . . happening to you."

"Gotcha. Strictly recon. No engaging. Roger that, Captain."

"And don't call me captain."

"Yes, sir. And Will?"

"Yeah?"

"My little moment of bravado back there? It was really more for me than for you, you know? I mean, sometimes I have to psych myself up. I wasn't going to shoot you."

"Thanks for that."

"To tell you the truth, I'm petrified."

"I know. Me, too."

"Oh, great," said Natalie.

As they entered the black-walled tunnel they fell silent. Will's halogen torchlight danced along the walls and illuminated the path in front of them. The rocks inside were moist and they could hear the sound of creatures scuttling about. But the sounds weren't coming from the ground, they came from above. When Will and Natalie reached a larger, more open area, Will shone his light up and they saw dozens of bats clinging to the ceiling.

"Should I be afraid of them?" asked Natalie in a whisper.

"No, they're just regular old bats, they won't hurt you. And didn't I say no questions?" Will shot her a look and moved forward. As instructed, Natalie kept close.

They moved farther down the tunnel in a gradual descent. The place smelled of mold, the air stale and fetid. Will dug into his backpack, took out a small device, and gently tapped it into a crevice in the side of the tunnel. After another twenty yards or so he repeated the process.

"What are those?"

Will turned and looked at her, his eyebrows arched.

"Sorry, that was a question, wasn't it?"

"Yes, it was. And these are micronic ultra-high frequency speakers. They send out high-pitched sound waves that demons can't tolerate. In case we have to retreat, I want a way to dissuade them from following."

"And you trigger them by. . . ."

"Using this switch," said Will, holding up a device that looked like a small flashlight with a red button on top. "We need to keep moving."

"Will, stop for a second," said Natalie. "If I'm going to be any help to you, I need to know what I'm looking for. You want to find information about your father, but what else?"

Will knew she was right. This just wasn't the best place to have this conversation. He pulled her to the side of the tunnel, so at least their backs were protected.

"You know the weapon I've been using tonight, the power rod? And how there are three of them?"

Natalie nodded.

"The Dark Lord is trying to get his hands on all three, to create the ultimate weapon. I know he has one power rod. I have another. I have to stop him from finding the third. Because if he found the third, and was somehow able to get his hands on mine, then he could use the Triad to get a hold of the key to a portal."

"I'm guessing this portal isn't to Disneyland."

"I don't think you really want to know the details."

"I've come this far, go ahead and humor me," said Natalie.

"The key, if there is such a thing, is supposed to open the portal to the Infinite Caves of Suffering Demons. That's where all demons go when their earthly bodies have been destroyed."

"So they're not exactly happy campers."

"Right. If they were to somehow be set free, given a pathway to re-enter earth. . . ."

"Then all of mankind would pretty much be doomed."

"Uh-huh."

"Will?"

"Yeah?"

"You were right. I didn't want to know the details."

"Just, if you see or hear anything about a rod, or a key, tell me. Okay?"

"Okay."

Natalie looked pale and Will frowned.

"Do you need a minute?"

"No." She shook her head. "I'm as ready as I'm going to get. Let's go."

They kept moving through the mine shaft, silent again. They could hear the thunder and even though they were far from the entrance the cave still strobed with flashes from the lightning. Then the thunder stopped and they listened as rain began to pound the earth.

Concerned about getting caught down in the mine in a flash flood, they picked up the pace. Then Will stopped and shined his light at the roof of the cave they'd hiked into. The ceiling was covered with stalactites and water dripped down from a fissure, some kind of opening that was blocked by debris. The dripping was quickly becoming a steady stream—and then the debris was knocked free by the force of the water and the water came down as though a god above them had spilled a giant goblet. Will grabbed Natalie's arm.

"Come on!" he yelled as he pulled her back the way they'd come.

They rounded a corner and were immediately swept off their feet by a wave of water as the entire tunnel flooded, water surging up the sides and swiftly washing them deeper into the bowels of the cave. They fought against the current but it was far too swift and powerful and as Natalie was pulled into a smaller tunnel, sucked away from Will, her head smacked into a rock and she sank beneath the water.

"Natalie!" shouted Will, his arms tearing into the water as he swam toward her. Then the flood abated as quickly as it had begun and Will was able to crawl to his dropped light and then to Natalie. She lay on her back and didn't appear to be breathing. Will knelt and his lips were an inch from hers when she opened her eyes.

"Um, Will . . . ?"

"I thought you might need resuscitating."

Natalie sat up rubbing her head, too dazed to feel embarrassed.

"Are you alright?" asked Will. "You hit your skull pretty good back there."

"I'm fine. I'll have a headache, but it's no biggie."

"I shouldn't have let you come. I knew you'd get hurt."

"Get over yourself. I said I'm okay. Let's keep going."

Natalie stood and for a few seconds her vision was blurred but it soon cleared and she smiled bravely. Shaking his head Will trained the light ahead of them and they forged onward.

They came to a small divide and as Will paused Natalie saw something out of the corner of her eye. It looked like the figure of a girl, flitting through the shadows.

"Will—over there. *Emily.*"

Will grabbed her arm. "Wait, Nat, we don't know that's her."

"But what if it is?"

Natalie's heart was racing as she yanked out of his grasp and ran after the shadow.

"Natalie, come back here!" shouted Will as he chased after her. She was going to get them killed.

He caught her at another junction. There were freshly dug tunnels everywhere, tunnels that crisscrossed the original mining tunnels.

"It's like some big underground freeway interchange," said Natalie.

"Many demons live and travel from place to place underground. It doesn't take them long to dig a tunnel, I'll tell you that," said Will. Then he grabbed her arm again. "You can't run off like that."

"I thought I saw her. I thought I saw Emily."

"We've got to stick together."

"Fine. But she went this way," said Natalie. She pulled him down another dark corridor and Will had no choice but to shine the light ahead so she wouldn't just bang into a rock wall and break her nose.

"Are you sure it was Emily?"

"I'm not sure of anything. Just that I saw *something*." They took a few more steps and then they heard laughter.

"This way. It's coming from down here," said Will, and Natalie followed him.

They crouched down to pass through a long low catacomb leading to a large cavern that, they saw as they reached it, was filled with demonteens. They were lounging around, drinking and smoking. Some hung from the ceiling like bats. Others seemed to be awakening as they rose effortlessly up out of the dirt. They spoke in a terrifying throaty language not of this world. Will and Natalie didn't recognize any of them from school. Jason, Todd, and Duncan were nowhere to be seen. Their laughter grew louder. It was the result of a little torture play unfolding as a young demon girl was having her neck pierced with studs. She clearly disliked the pain and the other demonteens thought her cries were amusing. Moving closer and seeing them more clearly now Natalie sucked in a fearful breath. Their eyes. One yellow, one green.

"It's them," she said to Will in a hoarse whisper. "They were . . . at the river the night . . . they're the ones who took her, they took Emily!"

A couple of the demonteens, one with a silver Mohawk, worked up wads of phlegm and spit at the girl. Their spit missed the girl but hit the wall and where it landed it burned the rocks. *Great*, thought Will, *just what we need, toxic loogies*. But then the laughter stopped as the lot of them heard, and then turned and saw, Will and Natalie. They bared their teeth like vampires and some of them hissed like vipers.

"What have you done with her?" said Natalie. "What have you done with my sister?"

The demonteens hissed and spit some more and moved in unison toward Will and Natalie. Will tightened and stepped in front of Natalie.

"Stay behind me," he said to her. Then he offered boldly, "I'm looking for Rage."

The demonteens glared at him without saying a word. Then Mohawk spit directly at Will who used the sleeve of his coat to deflect the toxic missile. His coat smoldered.

"You've come to the right place."

The voice echoed off the slick walls and bounced around the cave. Will turned and saw the silhouette of a creature perched in a catacomb opening just above them. It was Rage. Again Will had the feeling that he'd met this creature before. Perhaps in battle, perhaps only in a dream. But he was familiar.

The demonteens in the cave assembled, picking up an assortment of lethal-looking warrior weapons. A couple of them, including Silver Mohawk, hocked toxic spit onto the ground in front of Will.

Rage whirled on them. His eyes glowed red and his nostrils flared and he belched out a horrific roar.

"Leave him to me!"

The demonteens backed off and stood trembling, just itching to get in on the kill. As silent as a ghost Rage floated down and landed in front of Will and Natalie.

"You're either very brave or very foolish. A little of both, I suspect," he snarled. "Why have you come here? This is hallowed ground, not fit for the likes of you."

Will's blood began to heat up and he saw hints of red everywhere. His hatred of this creature was something he could taste. And yet he felt something else, too, something he couldn't articulate. His anger rose and swelled within him.

"You know why I'm here, I'm looking for my father!"

At the mention of Will's father, Rage seemed to fold into himself with pain, as though some invisible being had lanced him in his gut. But he recovered swiftly and when he opened his mouth a thousand black moths with glowing scarlet eyes poured out and swarmed around Will and Natalie. They backed up as Natalie shrieked and swatted at the moths, feeling like her heart was going to burst from fear. The demonteens laughed and howled and began spitting on the floor of the cave, over and over, encircling Will and Natalie with spittle so toxic it began to sear through the ground.

"You have come to meet your death!" shouted Rage, his head expanding. He pulled a small switchblade from the back pocket of his leather pants and the blade and handle both grew quickly; suddenly the demon was holding a shimmering sword. Will had anticipated the move and whipped his power rod out and activated his dual blades. Rage thrust his sword at Will, who deflected the blow, and as their respective weapons met in a spray of sparks it created a crashing sound like giant cymbals colliding. Rage moved with inhuman speed. He was on Will's left, then suddenly in front of him, then abruptly on his right, moving like the otherworldly creature that he was.

"Your father is no longer of this earth!" he shouted.

"You're lying!" shouted Will, fearing the worst and hoping his words would somehow ring true, that Rage *was* lying, that his father wasn't dead but alive and captive. He had to be!

Will saw a demonteen moving to his left and did a backward somersault, landing between the demonteen and Natalie seconds before the beast lunged at her. Will rewarded the creep with a whirligig slice-and-dice move and the attacker howled as he watched himself being cut into four pieces. Will's body thrummed with pleasure at the kill.

"I said he's mine!" bellowed Rage as the other demonteens stopped spitting and retreated and the cave went silent.

"There. That's better. Now," he said to Will, "will you kindly oblige me?"

"Oblige you how?"

What Will hadn't noticed was that the circle of toxic spittle the demonteens had laid down was now complete and had eaten through the floor of the cave. At that precise moment the floor gave way and Will and Natalie dropped through it. Rage smiled as he gazed down after them, watching them fall.

"Thank you so much," he laughed, then jumped into the hole after them.

Chapter Seventeen:
Meeting the Dark Lord

Will and Natalie were lying in a crumpled heap. Water dripped down from stalactites hanging above them. The air was thin with silence; all they could hear was each other's labored breathing.

Natalie opened her eyes and blinked. Maybe this was just a bad dream. A really, really bad dream. But she knew better. The cave they were in was honeycombed with tunnel entrances and a half-dozen burning torches were sunk in the ground in no discernable pattern, their flames licking upward. She heard a loud THUMP and saw the shadow of a figure landing in a nearby catacomb. Dark figures began dropping into nearly all of them. The dream was getting worse.

Will had rolled over at the sound of the first figure dropping and now was crouched next to her.

"Natalie, any broken bones?"

"I don't think so." Her knees and elbows and ankles hurt like hell from the fall though.

Will helped her to her feet and then looked down at his empty hand. Crippling panic gripped him like an iron glove. Where was his power rod? There! In the corner, glowing. Will held out the palm of his hand and the power rod flew up and slapped into it. *Good boy,* thought Will. Red and yellow and green eyes glowed from all the surrounding tunnel entrances. Except for one. In one there lurked the whites of human eyes. A torch burned nearby, sending flickering slivers of light that illuminated the human's face. Will knew he'd probably sustained a head injury in the fall and was seeing things— because slumped against the wall of the tunnel opening was the very man he'd been searching for all these years. Edward.

"Dad?"

The human figure who appeared to be Edward just shook his head back and forth slowly. Will took two steps toward him and he put up a hand. Will stopped. Then the human figure spoke in a child's whisper.

"I did the best I could."

"Dad . . . Edward! Let me come closer! I have to know this is you!"

But again the human figure held up a hand, waving Will off in no uncertain terms. He appeared to be sobbing silently and his voice, when he spoke, was raw with emotion.

"But I failed. At the end of the day I simply . . . failed. I couldn't protect you, and now this is happening."

"Silence!" Another voice rang out in the cavern. The voice of Rage. But where was it coming from? Will looked around but couldn't see him. He was no doubt hiding in a shadow, ready to pounce in a surprise attack.

The human figure resembling Edward tore at his own face with his fingernails and cried out in agony.

"I failed you!"

"Dad, don't!" yelled Will.

The tunnel entrance where Edward appeared to be suddenly dimmed as the torch illuminating it was blown out by a gust of wind. And then it flared back to life and went out again, over and over, creating a strobe effect. And then Will thought he saw *two* figures in the tunnel entrance: Edward and another, larger figure. It looked like they were grappling, like some hideous two-headed beast. The other figure had to be Rage and he was going to hurt Will's father.

"Dad!" shouted Will as he lunged toward them. But the move left Natalie unprotected and all at once the demonteens who'd dropped down swarmed into the cave, swirling around her and brandishing weapons. Will's protective instincts went into overdrive. He backpedaled and launched a furious counter-attack, leaping and kicking and wielding his power rod, firing away with fireballs.

"Stay away from her!"

A fireball slammed into Silver Mohawk's face and the force sent him blasting backward into the wall of the cave where he shrieked in pain until his head fell off. Another demonteen attacked and Will twist-kicked him so hard he slammed upward and was impaled on a stalactite. Will saw the fear on Natalie's face and yelled at her.

"Natalie, run! Get out of here!"

But she stood as still as a statue. If she wasn't going to run. . . .

"Use the boltdriver!" shouted Will.

She was in a trance, paralyzed with fear, but when a flying demonteen zipped by and raked at her with a four-fingered claw and sliced off a lock of her hair she was jolted into action, grabbing the boltdriver from her belt and cocking it. Her hands shook but she held the weapon steady and fired. The shot hit the offending demonteen square on the side of the head and took it cleanly off, leaving his body to drop to the ground where it wriggled, headless, until it disintegrated in an explosion of tiny bloody sparks.

"Good shot!" yelled Will.

They were making progress against the swarming demonteens. Torches flickered and again Will saw his father Edward in the tunnel opening, his eyes looking sad, as though he knew his future held nothing but tragedy. The tunnel entrance went dark and then suddenly there stood Rage, blood dripping from his scalp.

"What have you done?" yelled Will.

"Your destiny is sealed!" screamed Rage. The lights flickered and Edward appeared in another, different tunnel opening. And Rage was gone, surely in pursuit, perhaps to finish Edward off, to kill him for good.

"Dad! You're coming with me!" shouted Will to Edward.

But then the tunnels and the cave filled with a horrible keening sound, the sound of a beast being sacrificed, slaughtered, and disemboweled. And it was growing louder as the creature, whatever it was, came closer.

Rage closed his eyes and used his huge strong hands to crack his own neck like a chiropractor would. He appeared to be in pain, as though he was harboring inner, conflicting demons, demons who were telling him to do two different things.

"Run, Will! Get out of here!" shouted Rage.

Will's brain flooded with confusion. Why was Rage urging him to flee? It didn't make sense. One minute the guy's trying to kill him and the next he's yelling at him to vacate the premises? But there was no time to figure out what was going on. Will heard thundering footsteps that might as well have come from Godzilla's big brother, they were so deafening. A lull, and then something unseen blew into the cave. It was a feeling more than a being or spirit and it surrounded Will and Natalie, gently caressing their skin. Suddenly, Natalie was ten years old. Her grandmother, who was in poor health, was sleeping on her parents' couch. Young Natalie entered the room and went to the old woman's purse. She took folded money from it and went out and bought candy at the 7-Eleven on the corner. Later that day she saw how her grandmother had fixed her broken glasses using a bandage and felt a surge of guilt rise up in her, a feeling that worsened when her grandmother opened her purse and, instead of becoming angry at the missing money, took the coins that remained and gifted them to Natalie. Natalie flushed with humiliation at the memory and her thoughts went dark as she wondered what kind of human being she really was inside.

While she was raking herself over the coals, Will, too, was led into a shameful corner of his memory. He was six years old and his older neighbor had just gotten a new Labrador puppy. Inside Will was so jealous he could hardly contain himself and begged to tag along when the boy took the puppy for a walk. The older boy agreed. Will longed for the puppy, wanted it so much for his very own. He felt laughter inside as he watched the young gangly dog lope around foolishly, full of the simple joy of being alive. Will became angry that he himself had no puppy. All he could think about were ways to make the puppy his; surely he deserved the puppy more than his neighbor, who came from a large family whose father was a banker and bought his children lavish gifts. As Will and the older boy reached the highway Will heard the car and lunged for the puppy with fingers outstretched. Was he trying to save the dog? He told himself he was. But his motion frightened the young pup, herding him into the street where the driver of the car tried to veer but could not. The car's front bumper connected with the puppy, sending it skyward for thirty feet, and then it landed in the ditch where it drew a few last breaths. Even though it was an accident Will had never truly forgiven himself.

Will pressed a finger into his temple, trying to urge the bad memories and feelings of hopelessness out of his mind. Why was he thinking such things now of all times? And then he understood. The Black Spirit was present. This was his doing. He fed on fear and shame and hopelessness. The massive footfalls started up again and the cave shook until the sound was so loud Will and Natalie had to cover their ears.

And then a section of the cave wall collapsed and in the middle of a swirling cloud of fog there stood a ten-foot-tall monster. With so much fog and debris swirling in the air Will couldn't see the creature clearly. But he knew perfectly well who it was. The Dark Lord. The beast howled. The walls vibrated. The remaining demonteens launched one more attack and Will feinted and dodged and used his power rod's double saber to cut them to ribbons. The walls of the caves soon splashed with their shimmering droplets of blood, but the Dark Lord just stood calmly and watched, his powerful chest heaving, his glowing eye holes narrowing with every death.

"Killing is in your blood," said the beast. "A few more kills and you shall be free of your earthly curse."

"Give me my father!" shouted Will.

"And . . . Emily. . . ." said Natalie bravely.

"Your . . . father. . . ." muttered the beast. He looked like he'd just swallowed something that disagreed with him and he belched a sulfuric cloud that smelled of rotten eggs. Will and Natalie's stomachs turned and they instinctively covered their mouths. But Will didn't back down.

"Release my father! SHOW him to me NOW!" shouted Will.

The anger swelled inside him until he felt he might burst from it. He shot a fireball that sank into the creature's neck and then bounced around inside. It exploded and buckets of the Dark Lord's monster blood and guts splattered all over the cave walls. But he seemed almost amused by Will's blatant attack as his wounded areas swiftly regenerated.

The Dark Lord said, "Your eyes have seen what you so desperately seek! Believe them!"

"I have seen nothing of what I wish to see!" countered Will.

He was about to switch his power rod over to double saber mode again when the massive beast flew forward and bowled him over. Will tumbled backward as though he'd been slung out of a catapult and the back of his head cracked into the cave wall. He was losing consciousness but was still alert enough to plunge the tip of his power rod saber into an oncoming demonteen, eviscerating him.

"Excellent!" cried the beast.

Another demonteen leapt upon Will and they rolled across the cave floor, the creature's claws scraping Will's back and drawing blood. With a snarl the demonteen sunk its teeth into Will's arm.

Pain shot through him like a thousand volts of electricity and Will dropped his power rod. Another demonteen banged into Natalie, knocking her over, and the boltdriver skidded across the floor of the cave. Will rolled over, grabbed it, and fired two shots, hitting Natalie's attacker in the gut and the other in the forehead. Both beasts wailed in agony and disintegrated.

"Death comes easy to you!" howled the Lord of Darkness. "You have achieved greatness!"

The beast's fetid breath warmed the cave. Will wasn't sure if he was seeing things correctly but it sure seemed like the huge demonic monster was smiling.

"You'll never find the third power rod!" screamed Will. "And you will release my father!" To punctuate his words Will shot a volley of fireballs at the creature, who was hit by a couple and deflected the others, his anger growing swiftly.

"Do not try my patience, boy!" shouted the beast.

"If you don't hand over my father I'll kill you!" Will shouted back.

The creature absorbed Will's threat and closed its eyes. And as it breathed in it grew another two feet, expanding, its hide becoming thicker, barbs forming on its shoulders and face. And then it opened its eyes.

"Just one more kill, William, just one more," rattled the beast.

"What are you talking about? Explain yourself!" cried Will.

"Your destiny will become clear to you! Soon I shall own all who are dear to your heart and then you shall bow down to me as it is written!" yelled the beast.

"I bow to no demon!" shouted Will.

He grabbed and fired up his power rod and attacked but the beast was swift and strong and not only eluded Will's masterful strokes but dealt a few punishing blows to him in the process. Now Will's swipes with the power rod were defensive as the beast raked at him with massive claws and kept on coming. No matter how smart and fast and strong Will was, the fiend was relentless. Will tried to anticipate the creature's next move but guessed wrong and Natalie screamed as she saw the beast's claws tear into Will's chest and neck. He was losing blood and his arm grew weak, his strikes with the power rod lame and unsteady.

"Give the rod to me!" shouted the beast.

Knowing he was falling off the ledge Will did the only thing he could: he used his last bit of strength to throw his power rod as hard as he could up the tunnel they'd come down. The rod sang through the air and disappeared in the darkness, eventually finding its way out of the catacombs and soaring up into the sky to hover until called upon again. Then Will keeled over, his face hitting the dirt hard, tiny pebbles imbedding themselves into his forehead. The Dark Lord advanced on Will, snorting, muscles tensing, ready to deliver the death blow.

Natalie found Will's backpack and dug around inside for something—anything to use in their defense. As a slew of fresh deadly demonteens flooded into the cavern, Will's mind started going soft, his world getting fuzzy. All he saw were vague shapes, and the sounds he heard were garbled like a tape played at half speed. He and Natalie were surrounded, outnumbered, doomed. And then the cave exploded into the whitest radiance Will could imagine and he was dead certain he was going into the light for the final time.

Chapter Eighteen:
A Life Saved

Natalie had her arm around Will's waist and his arm pulled over her shoulder and she was stumbling up a tunnel with every ounce of energy her body had to give. She pulled another incendiary flare ball from the backpack and threw it behind her. It exploded on impact and saturated the tunnel with a blinding phosphorescent light that held for six seconds before dissipating, buying her a few more precious moments in which to flee with her wounded warrior. She looked at Will and her heart ached; he'd already lost way too much blood and was looking pale.

"Hang in there, Will, I'm going to get you home."

Will could hear her but could not summon the strength to speak. He wanted to tell her to just leave him, to go on and save herself, that his own life was not worth it since he'd failed so utterly. But his eyes wouldn't open, his lips wouldn't move. He was halfway to the land of corpses. Even with the head start created by her brilliant diversion Natalie was in danger of losing the race because with Will's weight holding her back she could only shamble along like some awkward ape, not the kind of creature that had any hope of outrunning superhuman flying demonteens. And onward they came.

Natalie could see the light of the tunnel entrance even as she heard the demonteens' shrill keening echoing off the slick tunnel walls as they moved in for the kill. With their talon-like claws extended and their mouths agape thirsting for blood they were almost upon them when Natalie's hand in Will's backpack found the trigger switch for the micronic ultra-high frequency speakers Will had hammered into the walls on their way in. She pushed the button to activate it.

The tunnel vibrated with supersonic sound waves and the demonteens went berserk, their brains spinning in their heads, synapses exploding as they flew defiant in their final throes and then dropped like moths aflame. They retreated in a wounded pack back into the darkness as Natalie exploded from the tunnel opening with Will. Wasting no time she loaded him into the EVO and sped off into the black night. Will had just enough strength and consciousness to smile up at her from where he was flopped on his seat. He shook his head slowly.

"Okay, so I broke a few rules," said Natalie.

Will closed his eyes and sank into the inky darkness.

Natalie pulled the EVO into Will's driveway and helped him out of the car. He clung to her like a child as she half-dragged him into his house through the kitchen door. In the living room April and Gerald had a card table set up and were playing Trivial Pursuit with their neighbors Fred and Belinda Halvorson, a portly and pleasant-looking couple who appeared to favor wine over Gerald's homemade beer. Natalie did her best to keep quiet but under Will's weight her foot hit a stool and alerted April.

"Will, is that you?" she asked.

Natalie looked at Will with panic in her eyes, but he'd passed out again. What should she do? She tried her best to impersonate him and answered with a raspy voice that she hoped just sounded tired.

"Yeah. G'night . . ."

April cocked her head quizzically.

"Sweetie, are you okay?"

Natalie shook Will, who opened his eyes as he briefly regained consciousness and swiftly took stock of the situation.

"I'm fine. Just going to bed," he croaked.

Will motioned to the stairs leading to the basement and Natalie nodded and helped him through the doorway. What neither of them realized was that all four adults could see their reflection in the mirror and got a panoramic view of Will, looking out of it, with his arm around Natalie's shoulders.

April gasped and started to get up.

"Oh my God!"

But Gerald put a hand on her shoulder and pulled her back down into her seat as they watched Natalie and Will disappear down the stairs.

"April, they're teenagers, the kid obviously tied one on, leave him to his misery," said Gerald, chuckling while Fred and Belinda Halvorson exchanged knowing glances.

"It's about time he started to grow up. At least he's with a girl, that's progress," he added.

Though she returned to the game and socializing with the Halvorsons, April remained worried. Her instincts told her that Will wasn't just suffering from some ill-advised teenage dalliance; she knew there was something wrong with her son. But each time she looked at the stairs Gerald grasped her hand firmly and she didn't argue.

Down in the secret chamber Will moaned with pain as Natalie helped him onto the futon and unbuttoned his shirt. This was really not the way she'd imagined first taking a boy's shirt off. She lifted the defensive "skin" Will had worn underneath and assessed the damage. He was wounded badly, with long gashes across his neck and chest.

"Where do you keep that magic goop of yours?"

"Locker . . . over there. . . ."

Will's hand shook as he pointed to a foot locker underneath one of the computer stations. Natalie dragged it out and examined the myriad of bottles inside.

"Which one?" she pleaded.

"Yellow label," said Will weakly.

In moments Natalie was smearing the potion over Will's wounds, just as she had after the so-called "hazing" incident. Only this time it was much worse and she was terrified that he might not make it. He grimaced and gritted his teeth as it stung his flesh. His whole body was on fire and he felt freezing cold at the same time. Natalie found a first-aid kit and dressed the wounds expertly. As Will looked at her with questioning eyes she smiled faintly.

"My aunt's a vet in Yakima. I used to help her at her clinic over the summer."

Will wanted to smile; he wanted to sit up and tell Natalie what a great job she'd done and how brave she'd been and how proud he was of her. But all he could do was suck in a long deep breath and then his body's natural instincts took over and shut down his mind, pulling him into a bottomless sleep.

For the next four hours Natalie prayed and made deals with any and every deity she could think of to not let him die, to just please, please save Will's life. She never once took her eyes off him. She was dreaming with her eyes open, conjuring a life lived with this brave and magical boy who'd arrived in a storm of danger. She imagined just walking together hand in hand, no demons and no danger, doing nothing but breathing each other in, talking and pausing every few strides to turn and kiss. Finally, after telling herself no a thousand times, she gave in to desire and slowly and gently pressed her lips to his. She told herself that this kiss, this miraculous stolen kiss, was not the fulfillment of a desire but a means of saving him. She would kiss him back to life.

. . .

When Will awakened he thought for a moment he'd died and gone to heaven. Her lips were so soft, her kiss so gentle. At that moment Natalie's eyes blinked open and she blushed, withdrawing into embarrassment, her face hot, her heart thudding.

"You made it," she stammered.

"Kinda looks that way. Were you just—?"

"I . . . thought you might need resuscitating," she offered, echoing Will's words from the tunnel earlier. *Lame, so very lame*, she thought to herself.

Will was blushing now, too.

"I do. I mean, I did. Thanks."

"You're welcome."

"Back in the cave. What exactly did you do to get us out of there?"

Natalie felt so giddy at his recovery that she grinned.

"Oh, a little of this, a little of that. You were right about fear, it can be a friend. Although I have to say, I wouldn't exactly want it as a BFF or anything."

"You're the most incredible girl I've ever known," said Will as he sat up.

He removed the dressing and saw that already his wounds were well on their way to healing. He looked again at Natalie and felt a pang in his heart. As sure as his heart was beating he knew he'd fallen for her and wished that somehow things could be different, that they could be leading different lives, normal lives, and not have to be battling the most destructive creature the world had ever known. He was filled with doubts and questions about what had happened in the cave. Why was the Dark Lord spurring him on to kill? Why had Rage been so schizo? Was he just insane or was there something more going on that Will needed to figure out? Why did Rage warn him to get out? And was that really his father in there? Or was it all an illusion created by the Dark Lord? Will was convinced of only one thing: that he needed time to think, to concentrate, to slow things down so he could see the big picture more clearly.

He sent Natalie home, making her promise to get some much-needed sleep and assured her he would call her the moment anything came up. She looked like she might not believe him but agreed to go. She walked home and then texted to let him know she was safe in her bed.

Once he knew Natalie had gotten home safely, Will opened the *Demon Hunter* game-building program and set about updating the game. Working like this helped him relax and when he was a little laid back he tended to think better. Not necessarily more clearly or more concisely but with more freedom, and right now freedom was what he needed if he had any hope of untangling the web of questions that gripped his mind. Using previously built tunnel and catacomb templates (he'd been in so many that the number of pre-constructed images was nearly infinite), he re-enacted the battle in the silver mine. It took him hours but he went into a zone as his fingers flew across the keyboard and caressed the mouse, dragging and dropping, building, coloring, adding sound and effects. When he was done he rechecked his work and "played" the game. Then he saw the number. The kill number in the upper left hand corner of the game. He'd kicked some serious ass in the tunnels tonight, dispatching with nearly two dozen demons. But the number, his tally, was ominous. He was up to 665 kills. The Dark Lord had urged him on. *Just one more kill, William. One more.* Will's backbone tingled as he stared at the number. One more kill and he'd have 666.

His heart racing Will logged on to his mainframe and brought up the map again, the map of where he'd lived for the past several years while he'd been relentlessly hunting the Dark Lord. San Diego, California; Corpus Christi, Texas; Greenhaven, North Carolina; Brunswick, Vermont; Harrisburg, Washington. Each city was still marked by a small red circle of light and he touched the monitor, using a screen tool to draw a line from city to city to city, connecting the dots. When he was done he stared at the hauntingly simple image. It was a pentagram with two points up, the very way that those who worshipped the Dark Lord drew them. The last point on the symbol was the dot for Harrisburg, right where Will was now, right where he'd been led to. And it occurred to Will that perhaps all these years it had not been he who had been hunting the Lord of Darkness but the other way around.

Will suddenly felt like a pawn in the Dark Lord's vile game. What game the cold-hearted fiend was playing was something Will didn't know but was sure to find out. He was positive that the answer would not only be painful for him personally but disastrous for mankind as well. He didn't know how or when but he knew deep in his gut that a very bad rain was about to fall.

Will was exhausted and after checking his town grid for any demonic movement he laid down on the futon and shut his eyes, telling himself it would only be for a moment, he would just rest, not sleep. He didn't dare fall off the edge of consciousness. No, he would merely give his eyes a break, a few precious minutes to recoup his energy. His body ached from head to toe but lying down allowed his muscles to relax and within minutes sleep overcame him like a balmy ocean wave, pulling him under, softening his world, gently ushering him to a place with no light or sound. He was out like a light and began to snore. And as he snored someone peered into the room and watched him very closely.

Chapter Nineteen:
A Gathering Storm

The tempest began with a whimper the next day, leaves on the trees swaying, moisture gathering in the air. Will's house trembled ever so slightly as thunder rumbled across the mountains. In the basement Will was still fast asleep on the futon when he woke up in a cold sweat. He felt lightheaded and unsteady, the bones of his body disturbed by a momentum he could feel gathering some distance away and growing closer by the second. The house shook again lightly, the screen door rattling in breezes that huffed out of the nearby woods. Will went to his monitors and scanned them for demonic activity but the grids were clear. He checked the weather and saw all indicators pointing to a relatively calm night ahead. But he knew better. He knew the kind of storm that was brewing would be not only a meteorological event but a metaphysical one as well. Some things you hear. Some things you see. And some things you feel in the depths of your soul. This was one of those.

Will moved quickly through his lab and up the stairs. He peered out the window and saw a sight that he'd prayed all his life he'd never see again: purple clouds forming, bunching together, and pushing across the mountains toward his home. It wouldn't be long before the entire house was surrounded. His wrist watch beeped a distress signal and lit up and he raced back down the stairs. The program monitoring demonic movement was coming alive, red dots glowing faintly and then more brightly, now more forming, now the whole lot of them on the move. In his direction.

They're coming, Will thought to himself, and he recalled the raspy words of the Dark Lord: *Soon I shall own all who are dear to your heart and then you shall bow down to me as it is written!* Will's stomach tightened as he came to a horrifying conclusion and spoke out loud to himself.

"Mom!"

He ran to the stairs and took them three at a time. He burst into the kitchen calling out for her.

"Mom!"

They were coming for *her*! As sure as he know there was evil on this earth Will knew this was what was happening. The Dark Lord was coming for April like he'd come for Edward. He planned to make Will an orphan. Will made a move to go upstairs but he was assaulted by a horrible smell and as he turned his head slightly he caught sight of a figure in his peripheral vision. It was Gerald, sitting in the dark in his La-Z-Boy drinking his stinking homemade beer. Except he didn't just have a little; the cretin was surrounded by a dozen or more pitchers of the stuff.

He croaked out to Will: "There's nothing you can do to stop the inevitable."

Gerald cut loose with a belch so loud it shook a nearby frame holding a photograph of Will hugging his mother after a victorious soccer game. Then Gerald released an overpowering batch of gas bombs and drank again deeply, emptying an entire pitcher. As Will's eyes adjusted to the darkness he could see that Gerald was bloated, his corpulent body swelling as he sucked down more of his homemade grog. And then Will saw his eyes. They weren't Gerald's usual brown and bloodshot but a watery black. And then he saw that Gerald's left palm held a mouth that was drinking out of its own bucket of beer.

Will shook his head to make certain he wasn't dreaming. He wasn't. It was all real and as Gerald continued greedily sucking down the beer he kept swelling up more and more, bloating grotesquely now, becoming so distended and swollen that when he stood the La-Z-Boy was wedged onto his fat ass.

His skin morphed now, flushing from pink to ruddy red to purple and then to a blue-green. He spit and the slobber landed on the carpet, immediately burning it. Will made a move for the upstairs doorway but in a flash the fat beast was in front of him, blocking his path, his lower jaw disconnecting like a python's as he lunged at Will. A horrible truth dawned on Will as he sidestepped the gaping maw. He'd been living with a demon for years.

"All this time," said Will, staring at Gerald in disbelief. "You've been waiting, biding your time. Why?"

"Let's just say I've been a kind of chaperone, Willie," replied the Gerald beast. Will hated anyone but his mom calling him Willie and Gerald knew it. As Will's anger rose within him Gerald sensed the impending conflict and a hideous tentacle erupted from his armpit, snaking out toward Will. The thing was covered with slime and had a barbed tip—poisonous, no doubt. Will ducked, then tapped a code into the retrieval patch on the back of his neck. He dove and tucked and rolled into the darkness of the living room to buy himself the four or five seconds he needed.

Will spoke from behind the sofa.

"I always knew you were a monster, Gerald, I just didn't think you were one literally!"

"You won't be so hard on me when the scales fall from your eyes, Willie," burped Gerald as he detonated a volley of farts, fouling the air with a toxic mini-fog bank.

"So you *knew* all along—what I was doing, who I was hunting," said Will. Silence. Then the fat Gerald thing stomped into the living room and with one mighty puke of rancid beer toxin set the couch Will was hiding behind on fire.

"You thought you were soooo sneaky!" bellowed Gerald as the power rod crashed through the picture window and obediently snapped into the palm of Will's outstretched hand.

"Why didn't you try to kill me?" demanded Will.

"Maybe I did," bleated Gerald. "You've always been a slippery little scumbag."

"Don't give me that," said Will. "You've had a thousand opportunities to put me in my grave. I don't understand. You're one of *them*. Why didn't you kill me? Why have you been bird-dogging me all these years?"

"Like I told you, I've been chaperoning you. Making sure things went according to plan." Gerald was growing carbuncles and boils and they festered rapidly and emitted a stench so strong Will had to partially cover his mouth.

"Whose plan?"

"Oh, I think you know whose freakin' plan I'm talking about, Willie."

There it was again, that name Will detested. The power rod glowed and pulsed with force as Will stood up and squared off against the creature who had been his stepfather, which now sprouted a dozen more slithering tentacles from his armpits, neck, and belly. Will heard his mother calling from upstairs.

"Will? Gerald? What's going on down there?"

"We're fine, Mom," said Will. "Just stay there and I'll be up in a minute."

"I don't think that's going to happen," burped Gerald.

Will activated the double saber on the power rod and twirled it as he advanced on the creature.

"Go ahead and cut me. I won't mind," blurted the corpulent beast as he moved to the doorway leading to upstairs and wedged his massive buttocks into it, purposefully blocking Will from getting to April.

"I think you'll mind when I cut you in half, Gerald."

Will's eyebrows furrowed as he took measure of this strange fat ugly brute in front of him. He'd always disliked Gerald, but now, knowing that he was going to have to kill him, he almost felt sorry for him. Emphasis on the *almost*. He thought about this creature touching April, and his blood boiled.

"I'm sorry I've been so harsh with you all these years, Willie," said Gerald, who, in an impossibly odd turn of events now appeared almost tearful. His tentacles shot out and whipped around but he wasn't trying to kill Will, merely keep him at bay. Will sidestepped a tentacle and then hacked it off. It spurted a goopy kiwi-colored blood that clotted instantly and turned solid, pulsing and then cracking and exploding.

"I've only wanted what's best for you, boy," wailed Gerald. "Because what's best for you is best for all of us."

Tears were running down his cheeks now and Gerald's nose was running like a toddler's as he sniffed and burbled and cried. He looked genuinely remorseful.

"For years I've had to hide my true feelings and act aloof and distant," Gerald warbled.

This is an act, thought Will. *He's mocking me, taunting me.* But another tiny voice in Will's head told him that Gerald's performance wasn't a performance at all but an expression of genuine emotion. But where was it coming from?

"I shouldn't be saying this," said Gerald, "but I've always cared so very deeply for your welfare. Every time you came home from . . . doing what you do . . . I always thought to myself, I don't know how I'll cope if anything happens to young Willie."

Things were getting way beyond weird, and it occurred to Will that the creature might be purposefully trying to mind warp him, so he shouted loudly, "Enough of this crap!"

Will charged forward and used the arctic gust on his power rod to freeze and incapacitate two more of Gerald's tentacles before kicking them to bits. Gerald bled more lime gunk and dropped to his knees, which made a squishing sound as they hit the floor due to the abundance of protruding boils.

"Tell me what's really going on!" demanded Will.

"I have done what's been asked of me," stammered Gerald as he half-heartedly swiped at Will with more tentacles. In a flash of swift, anger-fueled energy Will spun and used the double-edged lightning sword to cut off six more of Gerald's maddening tentacles, which fell to the floor and writhed like cleaved snakes. Gerald moaned in pain but he was smiling wistfully as his decaying life's blood spilled from him, as though he felt he was bound for a better place. He moaned as his massive body began to expand even more and Will glanced out the window at the purple clouds now angrily crowding the house.

Will heard his mother whimpering and wrenched his gaze from the window and looked up at her. She was at the top of the stairs looking numb, shell-shocked, paralyzed with terror as a thousand questions pinballed through her brain. She was staring at what was left of Gerald's monstrously mangled body. It was difficult, to say the least, for April to comprehend, let alone process, the image she now confronted: the burbling backside of the man she'd lived with for years, swelling with such force that the Dockers she'd bought him were all but ripped off. And the tentacles . . . so many tentacles. April felt faint.

"Stay where you are, Mom! I'll come to you!" shouted Will.

Gerald made one more weak lunge at Will who, with a mighty swing, slashed what was left of his stepfather into quadrants, silencing him forever. Gerald's remains, like those of all demons, hissed

and sparked but didn't just disintegrate. But because of Gerald's perpetual gaseous state his remains went up in a horrific explosion.
Gagging, Will rushed up the stairs and held his mother tightly. The
house shook with the force of an earthquake and lightning blasted
down out of the sky and Will heard the sound of the Dark Lord's
laughter ringing in his ears.

He felt a ribbon of panic wrapping around his ribs as he realized
something he knew was of no small importance. By dispatching Gerald, *he'd just made kill number 666!* Will looked down at his hands,
wondering if the kill had changed him, if he was now going to go
through some metamorphosis. But he was the same. Wasn't he? He
felt angry and apprehensive, felt his blood heating up, but that was
normal in these circumstances, wasn't it? The ground rumbled and
the sky opened up and rain poured down. But it wasn't an ordinary
rain. Will dashed to the window. Hundreds of thousands of tadpoles
were falling from the sky. It was as if the Dark Lord had scooped up
the dregs of a lake and was dumping them down on Harrisburg. Will
looked at his reflection in the mirror. He was still himself, 666 kills
or not. He was going to get through this thing if it killed him.

Then he looked at his mother. She was still in shock, still staring
at the last remains of the creature she knew as Gerald rapidly decom-
posing in fiery sparks.

"Will, I . . . I . . . what . . . how . . . ?" Her thoughts were jumbled
and confused. She began to speak not in English but in some incom-
prehensible tongue and Will knew she'd gone even deeper into shock.

"Don't try and think about it right now, Mom, don't think about
anything except how much I love you. I'm going to take care of you;
I'm not going to let them get you. I'm not going to let anything happen to you!"

April's knees buckled as the sights and sounds of the previous
sixty seconds overwhelmed her and she lost consciousness. Will
scooped her up into his arms. His wrist watch began emitting emer-
gency signals again and he hurried down the stairs and set his

mother down on a chaise lounge in the living room. Then he went to the coat closet and yanked open the door. Turning on the light he quickly tapped a code on the wall and a hidden panel whisked open, revealing a bank of switches that Will began activating. He was putting the house into lockdown mode. The infrastructure of the house came to life and one-inch thick steel shutters rolled down over the doors and windows. All those weeks ago when they'd moved in the workmen had done their job.

Will picked his mom back up and moved them downstairs and into his secret chamber, where he lay her down carefully on the futon. With wide eyes he watched his monitors. The red dots were still coming, more and more of them, the Dark Lord's army. It was a blizzard of malice and Will switched a couple of the monitors over to exterior real-image surveillance. He began to sweat. His heart was stampeding in his chest as he watched the approaching purple clouds, clouds that brought with them the most painful memory of Will's life. The clouds roiled and grew darker and more menacing and Will braced himself mentally for the onslaught, running through various defense strategies in his mind.

But then something unexpected happened. The clouds kept on moving, right past his house. Will checked the infrared monitors. The red demon dots were shifting now, too, still coming, but converging and turning left on the screen, away from Will's house. And then it hit him. They weren't coming to his house, they were converging on another house in the neighborhood. He felt an awful pang of dread in his chest as he realized where they were going. They were going for Natalie.

Soon I shall own all who are dear to your heart and then you shall bow down to me as it is written! The Lord of Darkness had been talking about *Natalie*.

Will cursed himself. He should have known! He had to save her. He'd made probably the biggest mistake of his life and now he had to make it right. He raced to a huge aluminum crate and, dialing the combination, unlocked it and extracted a futuristic-looking weapon resembling a small bazooka. It was a weapon of his own design of course, a high-powered electroflayer, a gun that fired bolts of electricity capable of chopping a good-sized oak tree in half. He returned to the futon, where April was just struggling to sit up.

"Mom, I want you to hold this."

April was still mind numb but enough of the shock had worn off that she could comprehend what Will was saying. She took the weapon into her arms.

"Here's the trigger," said Will as he placed her finger on it. "Can you feel it?"

April nodded.

"Good," said Will. "I have to go. . . ." He searched for words that would not alarm his mother further and decided to keep things as vague as possible. "I have to run an errand."

His mother's eyes grew large with fear and Will took her face in his hands and kissed her forehead.

"Don't worry, I'll be back. If anyone, or *anything*, comes through that door besides me, don't even think about it, don't try and figure out what it is, just shoot it. And keep on shooting until. . . ." Will's voice trailed off as he imagined the unthinkable. "Don't worry, I'll be back. I won't ever leave you, I promise."

Then Will ran to another aluminum locker and took out one of his newest weapons, the VB2, a high-powered medium-range voltage bombardier. It was always good to be prepared.

Chapter Twenty: A Love Lost

Will ran out the front door and felt the earth shaking beneath his feet. A short but powerful jolt, maybe a 5.0 earthquake. He glanced up at Mount St. Emory and saw a thin tendril of smoke snaking up from its peak. The mountain was coming alive. Time was running out. He used his remote to open the door of the Mitsubishi and set the voltage bombardier down in the passenger seat. He'd only run a couple of field tests on the weapon but felt confident it was battle-worthy. The VB2 shot balls of packed electro-charges that swarmed around the target and then exploded, creating a net of doom. Will hoped he wouldn't need it but had a feeling he would.

Will pulled backward out of the driveway, the wide-rimmed racing tires on the EVO smoking on the pavement. He flew down Maple Street and passed what looked like a nasty domestic disturbance. A short bald man with a goatee had his wife on the front lawn and was pulling her hair as she screamed and slapped at him. Will didn't have time to stop and play cop with these two freaks so he simply swerved across the street and clipped a fire hydrant, popping off the stop cap so a sideways geyser of water blasted the scrapping couple and knocked the bald guy clear back to his porch.

At the first stop sign Will saw another sad disturbance. Hefty Mrs. Norrington had little Scoopy tied off to a stop sign with his leash and was cruelly swacking at him with a stick, an evil gleam in her eye; the old broad actually seemed to be enjoying it! Will put down his window and used a short throwing blade to slice through Scoopy's leash, setting the little dog free. He dashed off down the street as Mrs. Norrington cut loose with a string of expletives aimed at Will that would have made a dock worker blush.

Will pressed the EVO hard and was circling around to Natalie's street when he saw that it was blocked off by city workers from the gas company and some police who'd erected a barrier. He rolled his window back down and caught the tail end of a cop's explanation to an irate driver, telling him that due to the recent earth movement they suspected a break in the main gas line and workers were on their way to try to locate and repair it.

Will yanked hard on the wheel, cut through an alley, and gunned the EVO through side streets so he could approach Natalie's house through the back way. It was a circuitous route but if he was lucky he could take the Dark Lord's assault team—if they hadn't struck already—by surprise. His route took him past Harrisburg High where he paused at an ugly sight. There were demonteens in abundance but they weren't wielding weapons, they were holding paint brushes and rollers and were just finishing up slathering the school with paint. They'd painted the whole school a terrifying shade of blood red. The outline of the Mustang had been obliterated and in its place they'd painted a huge black pentagram with a goat's head in the middle. *Terrific*, thought Will. *What a fitting mascot.* He made a note to himself to wipe the school off the face of the earth when he had more time.

He screamed around the high school and down Holmes Point Road and that led him to N.E. 32nd Street, the back road to Natalie's place. He tore down it, skidded to a halt, and stared at Natalie's house through the backyard. The entire structure was cloaked in the ominous, roiling purple clouds, which gave off tiny lightning bolts that had already wilted the landscaping. A posse of demonteens circled the house in the clouds. Will checked his power rod in its holster and then whipped out the voltage bombardier. He crossed the backyard lawn and knelt down where Natalie's parents lay prone. He quickly checked for pulses. They were gone.

He had no time to feel sorry for them or for Natalie because he heard a blood-curdling scream. Everything seemed to go into slow motion like a movie. The house shook as though being slammed by a giant fist. Will cocked the voltage bombardier just as a hole was blown in the roof from the inside of the house and the Dark Lord rose up through it, carrying Natalie. Her screams of fear cut through him like a knife and he ached to kill the Dark Lord on the spot. But he held his fire. He couldn't risk it, not when the beast had one of his massive gnarled claws wrapped around Natalie's neck. No, he would have to lay low and not strike until the moment was just right.

Will heard the neighing of horses—not regular horses but some disturbing hellish creatures who brayed as though being flayed by whips of molten cables. The purple clouds expanded and filled the sky, darkening it even more. Then the heavens cleaved open as thunder rumbled. Shards of lightning sliced down and an opening in the clouds formed. A team of black horses spilled down through it, galloping in the sky and hauling a hearse carriage with no wheels. Demonteens flew around and opened the back of the hearse and Will's heart thudded as he watched them slide out a coffin and open the lid. The coffin was lined not with satin but with a breathing, pulsing membrane of sickly flesh. Will's skin crawled as he watched the Dark Lord sweep up with Natalie in his arms and force her into the coffin.

"NOOOOO!" Will bolted up from his position and fired the voltage bombardier. The weapon erupted with a thunderous blast and shot dozens of glowing ordnances into the sky where they exploded *en masse*, taking out six of the demonteens and cutting into the back of the Dark Lord's thick hide. The beast whirled and puked a stream of his toxic acid at Will, who dove out of the way in the nick of time as the toxins hit the storage shed. Will glimpsed the propane tanks stacked on the side of the shed and covered his head with his arms just before the whole shed blew. The blast nonetheless knocked him fifty feet into the air and slammed him against Natalie's chimney. He thought for sure he heard bones cracking. He slumped to the ground, inert, convinced by his screaming pain receptors that every bone in his body had been shattered. He watched with the one eye that wasn't swollen shut as the horse-drawn hearse was swallowed up by the purple cloud bank and the sound of the thundering horse hooves faded into the night.

The Dark Lord laughed and flew after his prey as Will was surrounded by demonteens. He was lying flat on the patio, one side of his face against the cold stones. The demonteens all held lances with fiery red-hot tips and were ready to skewer Will like a shrimp on the barbie. Images churned in Will's brain as he rolled onto on his back and stared up at his assailants. He saw Natalie screaming, her eyes pleading, reaching out to him, her arms flailing for help he was unable to give. The leaden sense of failure held him down far more surely than any planetary gravity could. What was the point of moving, of rising up and attacking? He knew he was outnumbered and more than that knew he had failed to such a miserable degree that he deserved to die.

Then he thought of his mother, April, all alone in the basement of their house and he was galvanized. He might have let Natalie down but he wasn't going to give up yet. He would make sure his mother was safe and then . . . perhaps he could atone for not blasting through the police blockades in the first place and getting to Natalie before the Dark Lord and his murderous band of followers could. He leapt to his feet despite the pain still pulsing through his body.

"If you're going to kill me then let's get on with it!"

He whipped out both his power rod and Megashocker. But the demonteens didn't advance, no; instead they backed off, staring at him with their ugly wet-black soulless eyes and then turned and flew away into the sky leaving Will to wonder what had just happened. But there was no time to ponder. He jumped into his EVO and floored it across town to his own house where he yelled as he entered the front door.

"MOM!"

Down the stairs he went and through the light lock and into his sanctum where he rounded the corner to his lab and heard the resounding BOOM-BOOM-BOOM! of the electroflayer as his mother's finger repeatedly squeezed the trigger. Bolts of electricity blasted through the walls of his sanctum and April was in danger of literally bringing the house down around them when Will reached her, pried the electroflayer from her trembling hands, and held her tight.

"I told you I'd be back. It's okay now, Mom, everything's going to be okay."

April was weeping, her chest heaving, her eyes bloodshot and strained wide with fear.

"Come on, let's get you out of here," said Will as he picked her up and carried her up the stairs to her room. He set her on the bed and she watched blankly as Will packed one of her suitcases and spoke calmly to her, telling her he was going take care of everything and that they would be together again soon. He only hoped his words were truth.

As Will drove away from Harrisburg on his way to take his mother to the airport he checked his rearview mirror. As far as he could tell they weren't being followed. The thin tendril of smoke emanating from Mount St. Emory had grown into a thick plume now and every few minutes the ground shook with more intensity.

All the way to the airport Will kept glancing over at his mother, who had a deep sadness in her eyes. They were almost there when she spoke, softly and with regret.

"I never wanted any of this for you, Willie."

"It's okay, Mom. I'm going to take care of everything."

"I'm not sure you can. I'm not sure anyone can."

Will felt his stomach tighten. She didn't sound like she was in shock anymore; in fact she sounded almost like she'd been expecting something like this to happen. Fear coursed through Will's body. What did she know? Had she known about Edward's family business? He had so many questions and so little time.

"Did you know about Gerald? I mean, what he was?"

April was quiet for a long time before she spoke.

"Do you ever look at the world around you and wonder if any of it is real? Sometimes I do that, Willie, and I don't always know what the answer is."

"What's real is how much I love you, Mom, and that I'm going to make sure nothing bad ever happens to you."

"Do you even know what you're fighting?"

"It doesn't matter what I'm up against. What matters is that I have a duty to protect you and I will do that. No one . . . nothing is going to stop me."

April smiled at Will's bravado but then sighed heavily and nervously smoothed out the wrinkles in her pants. She was trembling and it hurt Will to see her like this. He vowed he would nail the son of a bitch that caused it. But he couldn't let his mom see his anger so he put on a brave face.

"I think a part of me did know what Gerald was," confessed April.

"Then why . . . how could you live with him?"

"Edward came to me one night. . . ."

"Dad came home?"

"Yes, Edward came home. It might have been in a dream, but he spoke to me very clearly. He said I should allow Gerald into my life, that it was *necessary*."

Confusion swirled in Will's head.

"Necessary for what?"

"He didn't say. He just said not to try and resist Gerald, that it would be better for me. And for you, Willie."

"Dad . . . Edward said this to you? In a dream?"

"I said it *might* have been a dream. It felt so real. But of course he's long gone so it had to have been a dream. Right?" April's eyes drifted far away as she sought refuge from the terrible reality confronting them.

Will's head was still spinning. Why would Edward have told his mom to stay with a hideous creature like Gerald? He could not for the life of him come up with an answer. And he had precious little time to think because they had arrived at the airport now and it was hectic with activity. People looked scared and heated arguments were breaking out all over. He double-parked his EVO in the passenger loading zone, got out, and ran around and opened the door for his mother. He helped her out of the car, grabbed her carry-on bag, and they went inside. Will pushed by several people to get to the counter only to find out that almost every flight had been delayed because an Airbus A-320 had crashed en route to Harrisburg. Making matters worse, Mount St. Emory's rumblings were discharging smoke and ash into the air so it didn't look good for any departures.

Will knew he had to be aggressive. He herded April back out and helped her into his car, then sped out of the departures area of the airport and circled back around to the entrance. He made a U-turn onto the road leading to the air freight and private plane terminals and spotted a seven passenger Falcon 10 private jet taxiing out of a hangar. He cut it off with his EVO.

"What are we doing?" asked April.

"Just sit tight," said Will.

He got out, popped the trunk, and ran around to the back of the car. Opening the jack compartment, he pulled out two thick stacks of one-hundred-dollar bills tightly wrapped in plastic. It was always good to have a little spending money handy for emergencies—and by "a little," he meant two hundred thousand dollars. He opened April's door and as she watched he stuffed half the money into her large purse, then pulled her toward the Falcon. The pilot was already eyeing the cash and it wasn't hard to convince him to take April aboard. *Nothing speaks quite like money*, thought Will. They got on the plane. Only two other seats were filled, with guys in expensive-looking suits. Will paid them no attention as they scowled their disdain.

As he buckled his mom in her seat he saw the panic in her eyes and gave her a hug.

"Look at me. Everything's going to be okay. Find somewhere safe."

"I will," she said.

"Don't tell me where you're going and don't try and call me. Phones won't be secure. When you get settled in I want you to send me a postcard, just some touristy kind of thing. Send it to this address." He handed her a piece of paper with an address on it. "I'll come to you." Then he gave her another hug.

The pilot's door was open and he shouted back to them as the jet's engines whined and the plane vibrated.

"If you're getting off make your move now, kid. I'm going up."

"I gotta go now, Mom." April was crying silent tears and it broke Will's heart. She held his hand and didn't want to let go, fearing that if she did it would be the last time she ever touched her son. He gently lifted her fingers from his and then kissed her on the forehead. There was nothing more for him to say. He'd given her the best instructions he could. He turned to leave but stopped when he heard her voice.

"Will, whatever happens, know that I love you."

"I love you, too, Mom."

"And Will. I'm sorry."

They both let those last two words hang there. Will wanted to know what she meant; what was she sorry for? But there was no time to ask. Will could only offer a temporary emotional salve he hoped would make his mother feel okay.

"Whatever it is you're sorry for, I forgive you," he said. And then he got off the plane.

April looked down at her son as he ran to his EVO, jumped in, and sped off. She shook her head.

"You can't possibly forgive me," she whispered. "Nobody can."

The jet taxied out to the runway and without pausing for the perfunctory safety messages from the pilot the Falcon 10 screamed down the runway and lifted up into the sky. April prayed with all her might.

Chapter Twenty-One: Lock and Load

Back home Will tore through his sanctum, arming himself. He knew this was it. This was going to be the battle that defined his entire life. He stripped off his usual clothes and opened a cabinet that held a remarkable suit that had just arrived by FedEx the previous day. Like all his weaponry and tech gear the suit was of his own design, though he'd had to employ six different tailors around the globe to have the garment crafted. It was woven from a bonded metallic-like fabric, a composite of Nomex, Kevlar, and threads of a metal Will had invented in one of his chemistry classes while the other kids were testing the electrolysis of water and determining the density of a potato. The fabric was nearly impossible to tear and provided maximum protection against even the sharpest titanium blades. It was Will's for-real Under Armour. Just like the commercials only better. After he pulled himself into the skintight suit he zipped himself into his leather combat jacket and pulled on a pair of high-capacity cargo jeans with enough pockets that he could load up for a twenty-four-hour battle if need be.

Next he pre-soaked some self-adhesive patches with the healing balm, and then sealed them in individual packets and slipped them into a sleeve pocket for easy access. When he was a kid and fell off his skateboard or out of a tree or something and scraped himself up, his mom would come to his aid with what she called a "magic band-age," guaranteed to make his "owie" stop hurting. He had some magic bandages for real now but he knew the pain he'd experience that night wasn't going to be taken care of so easily. These "owies" were much more likely to be the permanent kind. But he didn't care about getting banged up or scarred; as long as he made it out alive he'd be thankful. He calculated his chances of surviving the upcom-ing battle at somewhere between five and twelve percent. What the heck, he always rooted for the underdog; maybe someone would be rooting for him.

He opened several more aluminum travel cases and checked and loaded the Rapid-Fire Terra Blazer, the Death Hacker, the Long-Range Blinder, a couple of mini-bot drone searchers, and finally an invention that he'd never even had the time or opportunity to test, a tube-shaped contraption called the Demon Trapper. All the weapons were loaded and cocked. Only a couple more items to go. He opened a cabinet filled with goggles and glasses and contact lenses and took out a container. Then he looked under the futon and pulled out an old metal Batman lunch box and rummaged around inside. He took out a small plastic packet and pocketed it.

Standing now in front of the mirror he checked himself out. The image he saw was not that of a sixteen-year-old boy. No, what he saw in his reflection was a one-man wrecking crew ready to wage war. It was time to settle the score.

High in the bowels of Mount St. Emory Natalie lay in darkness, her mind deadened, her throat numb from screaming. When the Lord of Darkness had first touched her after invading her house and tossing her parents aside like rag dolls, she was so shocked she could barely move. His hands, his arms, were so strong that as long he held her she knew from the depths of her being that she was powerless against him. Then he had blown a hole in the roof—with his breath!—and flown up and placed her in the coffin and she had fought and screamed. She'd lashed out with her fingernails and pounded with her fists but he shut the lid anyway and then her world went into the dark and she continued to claw at the unspeakably horrid thing that surrounded her. It was like a hideous grown-up version of a womb. She raked her fingernails across it but the living thing, whatever it was, recoiled like it was in pain and though Natalie couldn't hear the being scream she knew it had felt the effects of her attacks upon it. She stopped fighting. The coffin did not appear to be attempting to injure her, so she lay still. And the membrane relaxed. Natalie wasn't sure how, but she understood the creature, the *thing* lining the coffin, sensed it more than anything else and what she sensed told her it wouldn't hurt her. So they rode together and Natalie gradually got her wits about her. The membrane had to be a creature of some sort who was being punished by the Dark Lord, she concluded, and this in turn steered her toward thoughts of her own probable fate. She shuddered and her heart beat so fast she thought it was going to jump out of her chest. She took long deep breaths and tried to think of anything except about what was really happening.

She felt the being around her tighten as the temperature inside the coffin soared and they swayed back and forth. Then it felt as though the box was lifted out of the hearse and carried somewhere, and dropped. Natalie's head hit the coffin's roof and the being inside it with her flinched. Then all was quiet. The top of the coffin flew off and smashed against a wall.

Natalie wasted no time climbing out. She looked around for an escape but the darkness surrounding her was so utterly complete she could only see the images she manifested in her mind's eye. Sparkles of light. Faces of her family and friends. They all floated around like orbiting celestial bodies. Overcome by the trauma of her journey, Natalie sat on the ground, then slumped over and sank into a sleep that bordered on unconsciousness. It was a dreamless sleep that could have lasted an hour or a day but when she woke up she did so because she realized, in a rush, that she was no longer alone. And the presence she felt, it felt *familiar*.

"Emily?"

Something stirred in the darkness. It might have been a rat or a cockroach. Or a demon ready to pounce. But she didn't think it was any of those things. She moved toward the sound.

"Em? Is that you?"

She heard a whimper. It was but a tiny noise, really, hardly a sound at all. Then a handful of rocks tumbled down from somewhere high on the wall. A dim shaft of light found its way into the cave and illuminated a human figure several yards away. After a few seconds Natalie's eyes adjusted to the faint glow and she saw what she had been praying to see for all these months: her twin sister Emily.

"Emily! Oh God, Em, it's you!"

Natalie rushed across the cave to where her twin sister was standing. Because of the angle of the light she could only see Emily's face but she praised the good forces of the universe because Emily was okay, she was alive! She moved to hug her but Emily shook her head and bared her teeth like an animal. She was breathing rapidly, sucking the air in greedily and then blowing it out in anger. Then Natalie saw her sister's eyes. They were bloodshot and had deep dark circles under them. They were full of pain and terror, the eyes of someone who's seen so much they can never be brought back. In Emily's eyes Natalie saw the sum of the Dark Lord's terror.

"Oh my God, Emily. . . ." said Natalie as she reached for her sister again.

Emily's eyes widened and she hissed, "Stay away from me! I'll kill you!"

Natalie obeyed though it took all her willpower.

"Emily, it's me! It's Natalie, your sister!"

"Emily, it's me! It's Natalie, your sister!"

Emily's eyes narrowed and she shook her head from side to side.

"I don't believe you . . . no more tricks . . . stay out of my head!"

Emily emitted a low, nearly inhuman growl from deep in her throat and turned her face to the side, refusing to look at Natalie. Natalie wanted so badly to hug her twin, to feel for herself that Emily was alive and whole, but she had to establish trust first.

"It's me, Em. Natalie."

Emily again growled and shook her head.

"Remember our ninth birthday party? The one where dad hired that ridiculous cowboy clown? Remember? He was so drunk he could hardly make the balloon animals? Remember how you cried, and I told you it didn't matter, that it was still our birthday, we were nine years old and nobody could ever take that away from us. And . . . and the cake . . . the angel food cake with strawberry frosting? Remember, Em? Please. . . ."

Emily stopped shaking her head back and forth and grew quiet. Her breathing slowed down. She softened. And then her eyes found Natalie's and she whispered, "Natalie? Is it really you?"

"Yes!" said Natalie, barely able to contain her joy. She'd broken through. "I knew you were alive! I could feel it! You were talking to me all along, weren't you, in your dreams!"

"Yes," said Emily, her voice full of anguish and despair.

"I never gave up hope, Em, I always knew I'd find you!"

Again Natalie reached for her sister and again Emily barked out the warning in a mean and nasty tone, shocking Natalie.

"I told you to stay back!"

"Are you . . . infected?" asked Natalie.

And now Emily's jaw tightened as she thought of all the hours, the days, the weeks she'd been subjected to the demonteens' onslaught of evils. And yet she'd held on to hope, held on to goodness. More tears poured forth from her bloodshot eyes.

"No. I . . . I wouldn't let them."

Natalie flushed with pride. She knew her kooky, free-spirited sister was good inside, that she had a pure heart.

"I'm so proud of you, Emily. You beat them, you wouldn't let them get you."

"No . . . I . . . I didn't. . . ."

Emily actually allowed the smallest of proud smiles to form on her face. But then her brief moment of bravado passed and Natalie watched with despair as the gleam went out of her sister's eyes as she sank back down into a deep depression.

"They only kept me alive to . . . to hurt me," whispered Emily. "They would let me escape . . . and then hunt me down, over and over. . . ."

"That was the dream . . . I was with you in the dream."

"I know, I felt you."

"We're going to get you out of here. We're going to stop all this and get you out of here," said Natalie.

Emily closed her eyes as sadness engulfed her.

"No . . . there's nothing we can do to stop them. He's too strong. He's taking over. It is written."

"What do you mean?"

"You'll find out. We'll all find out," said Emily.

More light spilled into the cave and Natalie began to slowly piece together the image in front of her, her mind resisting, not wanting to acknowledge the horror. Emily wasn't standing of her own accord, she was being held up, her limbs outstretched, lashed in place by thousands of tiny thin red things that looked like filaments. Natalie choked back her screams as she realized that Emily was caught in a huge web made of blood vessels. Then she felt dozens of those same vessels swiftly wrapping around her arms and legs.

"Natalie, run!" screamed Emily.

But the veins already had too strong a hold on her.

"What ARE these things?" she yelled.

"They used to be . . . humans," answered Emily. "The beast transformed them."

Then Emily saw her twin pulling a key from the coin pocket in her jeans.

"NO! Don't try and cut them!" she warned.

But it was too late. Flooded with panic, Natalie tried to saw away at the creeping veins with the teeth of the key. The veins cut and bled but for every one she severed two more sprouted in its place and they took hold of her so quickly she knew that she wasn't going anywhere for a very long time. At the sight of her twin sister now entrapped alongside her Emily began to weep uncontrollably, her keening cries echoing through the dark caves.

Driving through Harrisburg in his EVO Will couldn't help but notice how docile the town suddenly appeared. There were no fights breaking out on the front lawns, no elderly women beating their dogs, no one behaving poorly as far as the eye could see. In fact there were few people anywhere; it was as if the whole town were on vacation, which was weird because the volcano in Mount St. Emory was rumbling and storm clouds kept rolling in, thickening the sky. It wasn't as if people were leaving in droves as he thought they might be, either; an active volcano is nothing to sneeze at and Will wouldn't blame anyone for ditching their digs in Harrisburg, packing up the family and getting the heck out of town. They were just . . . quiet.

He shook off his thoughts and concentrated instead on Phase One of his plan, which meant returning to the place where he'd almost met his maker—the opening to the mine shaft. He double-clutched and geared down to roar past a grocery van and then took the turn that led him up the side of Mount St. Emory. When he came to the wooden barriers that the U.S. Forest Service had erected to keep traffic off the mountain he didn't hesitate but just blasted right through them. He'd learned that lesson already. He sent out silent prayers to Natalie as he sped up the winding road. *Please be okay. Don't be afraid. I'm coming to get you and nothing is going to stop me.*

He pulled the EVO onto the road leading to the mine tunnel entrance but stopped short. Opening the trunk he lifted out the mini-bot, activated it, and placed it on the ground then put the car in reverse and backtracked. The mini-bot, which looked like a pimped-up miniature Mars Rover, blinked and whirred and its wheels churned in the damp soil as it trekked forward.

Will parked his car and, using the Death Hacker, the weapon whose blade changed shapes depending on what needed to be hacked to death, he covered his car with branches. Because even demons knew how to use ActiveEarth. He hiked up to a ridge and then flipped open his mini-laptop and powered it up, quickly loading images broadcast from the mini-bot, which was awaiting instructions from its position at the mine tunnel entrance.

"Okay little fella, let's take a look around, shall we? And by the way, sorry about having to throw you under a bus like this."

The mini-bot blinked and chirped and rotated its little camera as if to say, *Sorry about what?* Then it rolled forward and lit up the mine tunnel with its tiny halogen headlights. As he looked at the images broadcast by the mini-bot Will wondered if he'd guessed wrong, wondered if maybe he should have taken the direct approach and ripped right into the mountain through the mine tunnel. He was about to change his whole battle plan when the mini-bot's lights found a nest of demonteens lying in wait, armed to the teeth. They hissed and snarled at the tiny robot and rushed to attack it, realizing only too late that it had a cube of concentrated C-4 strapped to its back. Will pressed the detonator and the C-4 ignited and rocked the tunnel with a massive explosion that toasted the whole clutch of demonteens.

Watching the explosion from his vantage point on the ridge Will felt sorry—for the mini-bot. Even though they weren't sentient creatures he still felt they had little personalities and he always disliked sacrificing them. As for the demonteens, most of them were way beyond redemption. So as far as Will was concerned the whole lot of them could go straight to hell. In fact that was his whole plan: Send them all to Hell.

At any rate Phase One was completed. It was time to move on to Phase Two, entry. He re-checked his equipment and began climbing the side of the not-so-dormant volcano.

The Dark Lord turned and faced Rage. His almond-shaped eye sockets glowed from orange to red and then quieted down to shimmering saffron. Rage was sweating, bound to a huge wooden triangle by the same creeping blood vessels that held Natalie and Emily. His face was twisted in agony, partly because he was overcome with guilt, but also because the Dark Lord, wielding a power rod, was slowly drawing the lightning saber back and forth across his thigh. Even demons bled, and the power rod's molten blade felt like a branding iron. Smiling with enjoyment the Dark Lord paused in his torture of Rage and slipped the power rod into his tunic.

Then he walked slowly across the cavern and touched an ancient book. The pages were made of cabretta leather, the back cover of marble. It was the second half of the book from Will's basement. The Dark Lord had been looking for the first half when he'd traumatized young Will those many years ago.

Rage spoke up: "You mustn't continue with this madness."

The fiend gazed over at Rage and shook his head.

"Your negative attitude is discomforting. This is a day for great celebration."

"I have nothing to celebrate," said Rage. The Dark Lord sneered and the veins tightened around Rage's neck, beginning to choke him.

"You know I cannot tolerate your disrespect!"

Minute particles ignited in mid-air as the Dark Lord spoke harshly, his anger causing them to ignite and pop like tiny firecrackers.

"It is written in the book, and so it shall be!" bellowed the Dark Lord.

Rage spit back at him, "Mortals wrote the book!"

"They were given celestial inspiration! Therefore they were no mere mortals, but dwelled in between the earth and . . . our places. The prophecy *will* be fulfilled, there is no question to be raised. It is, as they say today, a done deal."

Rage struggled against his bonds. But the veins only tightened on him. He shouted at the Dark Lord: "Immortals can defy the prophecy. YOU can defy the prophecy."

"But why would I?"

"Because even you, in all your supposed ancient wisdom, have no concept of what will be unleashed."

"Oh, I have every concept. I have *thirsted* for this since my earliest days. And you will be silent!" shouted the Dark Lord.

Clenching his fist/claw he conjured a sphere of shimmering white light and slammed it into the side of Rage's head. Rage's scalp bled and he cried out in pain. He moaned and then his breath went still. The Dark Lord conjured another sphere of pain but when he leaned close and listened to Rage's feeble breathing he tossed the sphere against the wall where it exploded into a thousand fragments. The Dark Lord then left the chamber.

Rage opened his eyes. He'd always been good at playing possum. When you're under the thumb of the most terrifying monster the world has ever known you learn ways to survive. He'd been forced to kill and steal and lie and cheat, to bend the minds of teens to his will and infect them with evil. At times he'd found himself enjoying the thrills that came along with corrupt and sinful behavior but other times the deeds he carried out saddled him with agonizing guilt that paralyzed him with migraines for days. He was a creature conflicted, driven by necessity into the dark corners of his mind but sometimes able to magically connect with his core, which he told himself was good. He'd been coerced into spreading evil each and every place the Dark Lord had led them and now he knew he'd reached the end of the line. He would welcome death, but only after he'd done one last deed, accomplished one final goal worthy of praise. Not praise from the Lord of Darkness but from what few good forces still remained in the universe.

Rage looked at the ancient book on the pedestal. He was all too familiar with it. He knew the first part that young Will had read told only half the story. The other half was here, and within it lay humankind's destiny. It had only to be played out—unless Rage could find a way to stop it.

Chapter Twenty-Two:
The Assault

Confident that the mini-bot's diversion had bought him at least a little time, Will proceeded farther up the side of the mountain, passing the skeleton of a rusted-out truck and an old wooden shack leaning against the wind. He reached a meadow thick with hickory and wildflowers and surveyed the land ahead of him. After blowing up the mine entrance he now had two choices. He could either enter through the smoldering cone of the volcano or he could spelunk down through an adjacent fissure, the choice he'd opted for ahead of time, deducing that at hundreds of degrees the temperatures inside the cone itself were downright inhospitable. He'd done his research and downloaded and scoured the topographical and geological maps of the mountain and knew there were vertical cave entrances near the bluff where he was now climbing. Using a portable density reader he was able to locate an area where openings were likely to occur near a small verdant gorge about three-quarters of the way up the mountain.

He tapped a code on the back of his neck and in two seconds his trusty power rod came sailing down out of the sky and landed in the palm of his hand. He activated the temperature function and sent a wide spray across the gorge as though he was shining a flashlight with a broad beam. The leaves on trees froze, as well as a few dozen hapless insects, and he immediately found what he was looking for. Steam. The hot air rising from a vertical cave opening combined with the freezing temperature from the power rod and created a plume of steam. Here was his opening. He tossed the power rod skyward to its nesting place once again, not wanting the Dark Lord to get his hands on it. He made a silent vow he would only call upon the power rod as a last resort.

Using the boltdriver he was able to blast a series of titanium pitons into the rock surrounding the fissure. To them he attached a top-quality climbing rope capable of handling high-impact force. He knew the Dark Lord's minions would be sifting through the rubble at the main tunnel entrance and concluding that the explosion was merely a diversion. So time was ticking down. But as always, Will was super-prepared. In under a minute he had the pitons in place and the rope secured and had slipped into the climbing harness. Hoisting his weapons backpack onto his shoulders he dropped down into the dark cave like an expert spelunker. He was descending into the very heart of doom but he felt confident. Feeling anything else would have slowed his progress and he couldn't let Natalie down again. He had to save her. If it was the last thing he ever did, he knew he had to save her. The Dark Lord wouldn't care about her if it wasn't for him and he would not allow his careless love to cause her any more pain.

Thirty feet into his descent he switched on his halogen light and scoped out his position. He was moving down a good-sized cave that was growing wider the deeper he dropped down so he increased his speed. He had to hurry. If he had any hope of reaching Natalie and rescuing his father once and for all he needed to have the element of surprise. So he zoomed faster down into the darkness. He closed his eyes and felt his way for fifty yards but then got a prickly feeling and forced himself to a sudden jerking stop, his gloves growing so hot from the friction that he thought they might burst into flames.

Flashing his light below he saw that he'd just barely averted being impaled by a series of crystal-like stalagmites jutting up out of the darkness. He once again thanked his intuition for literally saving his ass and pushed the images of how he might have been skewered out of his mind. He impelled off the side of the funnel cave and found purchase on a ledge, where he fired a couple of pitons into the rock sides and tied himself off, bringing the rope from above down to his current position. His heart rate increased as he looked around for another avenue and he breathed a sigh of relief when he saw that he could now go horizontal; there was a cave opening only a few yards below him. He swung down and crawled into it. It was a tight fit, and crawling along on all fours he suddenly knew what it felt like to be a mole.

He could feel himself getting closer to the core of the mountain as the temperature increased rapidly. He began to sweat, not only because it was so incredibly hot but because he couldn't help thinking about what would happen if he was too late. What if the Dark Spirit had already infected Natalie, or worse, had decided she was expendable and killed her? Will redoubled his efforts crawling through the narrow tunnel until it broadened out and he was able to stand upright. On two feet now he moved as swiftly as he could through the cave, taking care to make as little sound as humanly possible.

When the Dark Lord came for him, Rage appeared totally spent, his body slack, his skin even more pallid and mealy than usual. But inside he was coiled and ready to strike the millisecond he was freed from his bonds.

"It's show time, as they love to say," rumbled the Lord of Darkness.

With a wave of his clawed hand the blood vessel vines that had been enveloping Rage shrank away like so many tiny scolded snakes, retreating into a disgusting placenta-like heap on the floor. And just like that Rage was free. He followed six paces behind the Dark Lord as was required by demon law as they exited one cavern and moved through a tunnel into a smaller one. Rage's hand trembled as he reached into his snakeskin pants for the small bone shiv he'd been hiding there for days. The Dark Lord immediately sensed Rage's nervousness, whirled, and with astonishing speed moved behind him and placed a tight hand on his shoulder. Rage began to babble to cover his fear.

"Your Lord, I was just about to say that I'm—"

"Nervous?" said the Dark Lord as he now walked beside Rage, his clawed nails digging into Rage's shoulder.

"Y-yes," stammered Rage. He tried to force the pictures out of his mind, the images of what he was planning on doing because he knew the Black Spirit could crawl into his thoughts at any time. So he made his move, pulling the shiv out and swinging it as hard and fast as he could. He had meant to blind the Master Demon by stabbing him through his eye sockets to lance his brain. But the Dark Lord was way ahead of him and not only twisted the shiv out of Rage's hand but used the weapon against him, plunging it into his left arm. Rage cried out in pain. The Dark Lord laughed.

"I often know what you're thinking even before the thoughts begin to form in your brain, Rage," said the Dark Lord.

As they were adjacent to a deep soal of stagnant water the Dark Lord took advantage of the opportunity and with a flick of his fingers raised a dozen leeches out of the scum pond and into the air. They hovered and Rage's skin crawled as he foresaw what was coming. The slimy black creatures metamorphosed into shark leeches with rows of tiny jagged saw-like teeth.

"Please, no. . . ."

"I'm afraid the time for clemency is long gone," said the Dark Lord.

And then with the slightest of gestures he commanded the shark leeches to sail through the air and slap against the side of Rage's head. He smiled as the muculent creatures crawled rapidly into Rage's ears.

"This will be the mother of all migraines I should think," chuckled the Dark Lord. "Now come, we have much to do."

Rage had no choice but to follow and obey, so great was the pain that was building in his head as the shark leeches snaked in through his outer ear canal, chewed their way past his ear drums, and slithered down into his Eustachian tubes.

As the tunnel Will was trekking through widened into a broad expansive cave he stopped and realized his breathing was raspy and uneven. He checked his pulse. It was high. Cursing his stupidity he took out a small bag of Gatorade and sucked it down in three long gulps. It would be a huge waste of his young life if he were to pass out from dehydration and die at the hands of the Lord of Darkness in such an undignified manner. No, if he was going to go out, if this was his time, then he would go down swinging, that was for sure. Hopefully the Gatorade he just sucked down would last him for the duration of his subterranean journey. He tossed the bag down on the floor of the cave—littering was the least of his worries at the moment—then shook his head. He was hearing faint music and he was unsure if it was for real or just his imagination.

He moved forward and with each step the music grew louder. It was a familiar piece, one of the many thumping pagan-like choruses he'd heard a zillion times before. He saw a light at the end of the tunnel he was traversing and knew he had no recourse but to head straight for it. But first he stopped and knelt down and waited. He couldn't afford to be anything but doubly careful; you never knew when they would spring a trap on you. When no attack was forthcoming Will moved onward. Reaching the opening, he stood and stared at a sight he would remember forever.

Down below in a monstrously huge cavern were hundreds of the infected. And not just demonteens, but other people he recognized from Harrisburg, as well as the five other towns where he'd lived while pursuing the Dark Lord. They all wore black leather and scarlet clothing and their eyes were a stomach-turning gooey black. Rex Farmer from Rex's Game World was there, his shaved head sporting an Iron Cross tattoo. He was smiling and moving to the music alongside a wheelchair-bound woman dressed like a biker with a "Hell on Wheels" tattoo on her flabby arm. No wonder Rex's business was booming. He'd sold out. Too bad he wasn't going to live to enjoy the spoils. Mrs. Norrington was there, too, and though her manner of dress was comparatively modest, she wore a demented expression that told Will the old woman had plenty of sick thoughts rattling around in her contaminated brain. And she'd evidently found and infected poor little Scoopy because the tiny dog was drooling as it chewed the head off a dead rat and its eyes were as black as lumps of coal.

His mother and Gerald's card-playing neighbors the Halvorsons were there, Fred wearing a studded dog collar and Belinda holding the leash. Correl Shames was there, looking mean and cocky. Faculty from Harrisburg High gyrated alongside pupils and Will recognized teachers and students who'd come from far away, schools he'd attended in California, Texas, North Carolina, and Vermont. This was some kind of gathering, a huge celebration. There was something big going on and Will had a feeling he was going to figure in the proceedings in a major way.

As his gaze swept across the vast cavern he saw dozens more demons dancing and sitting in tunnel entrances; the entire place was honeycombed with them and they led in almost every possible direction. *The entire mountain must be filled with tunnels*, thought Will, *and not just from the silver mine*. It looked as though some creatures had been hard at work for a very long time digging the complex series of interlocking burrows and catacombs.

The music was coming from a huge, state-of-the-art stereo system, the tunes supplied by a crazed-looking DJ who bobbed his head wildly, the plethora of piercings though his lips, ears, eyebrows, nose, and even his forehead jangling like wind chimes.

Will froze as, all at once, the demons in the cavern cast their collective gaze upon him. But instead of anger or malice their expressions spoke of adoration, even a kind of reverence. It was as if they felt great affection for him. He wondered how they would feel as he was killing them one by one.

Then Will saw Rudy. He was dancing to the diabolical beat, body-rubbing with Sharon Mitchell, their eyes trancelike, high on some kind of drug or perhaps just the adrenaline they were feeling, some twisted rush of pleasure from being ghastly. Duncan and Todd and Jason were there, too, and Mookie in his wheelchair. Will was about to call out to Rudy when he saw Coach Kellog emerge from a tunnel, smiling and giving him a thumbs-up gesture like he'd just scored a freakin' touchdown or something.

"I knew you'd join the team, Will!" he shouted. He was decked out in a black wife beater, slick leather pants he was way too fat for, and absurd-looking steel-toed boots. He looked so stupid Will wanted to puke.

Rudy stopped dancing with Sharon and looked up at Will. For the briefest moment Will thought he saw the old Rudy as he did his funny little wacko dance and his eyes looked almost human. But he wasn't, of course. Will remembered the Demon Trapper in his backpack and hoped it would work.

"I'm going to get you out of here, Rudy," he told him.

Rudy shook his head and quickly reverted to his demonic self.

"Nobody's going anywhere, Will. Most of all you."

Sharon suddenly leapt up like an animal, bounding from rock to rock until she reached him. She wrapped her arms around Will and made a move to kiss him, her tongue snaking a good six inches out of her mouth. It was barbed and slimy. Will backed up and grabbed one of her wrists. He checked her palm. She had a small nasty-looking mouth with sharp teeth in the middle of it.

"Don't be such a prick, Will. Give us a kiss," hissed Sharon.

Now she had three tongues wagging at him, one out her mouth and one coming out of each hand. Will whipped out a small knife and cut off the tongue on her right hand. The mouth there squealed in pain. Sharon's eyes narrowed and she lunged again. Will caught her with a breast-kick that sent her sprawling backward. She whirled and vomited at him. He ducked but some hit his hair and it burned. Will swatted it out.

The chamber erupted with laughter. Again Will's eyes swept across the crowd of lost souls. It seemed like the whole of the town of Harrisburg was there. They'd all made deals with the Black Prince, sold away their souls for gratifications of the flesh. *I want to be taller, thinner, richer, luckier. I want to be stronger, to rule men, to get back at my ex-wife. I want to torment those who have hurt me. I want to live forever.* They all had wants and desires, and satisfying those desires meant paying the ultimate price. Though they didn't know it, they had joined an army that would never stop marching. They began yipping and screeching and Will wanted to unload his weapons and waste the whole lot of them then and there. He was sorely tempted. And then he saw Rage.

The rat bastard demon was standing in one of the catacomb entrances, his head twitching like there was something crawling around inside it. His gaze was strange—sad yet somehow beckoning. Will's blood began to boil when he saw what was dangling from a chain Rage held in one hand. It was Edward's railroad pocket watch: bait, for Will. Will's heart punched against his ribcage and as the red curtain drew across his mind's eye he lost all sense of reason and anger overcame him. He raced across the chamber in pursuit of Rage, who fled down a tunnel while the demons below chattered like rats in a box. Their shrieking din rose up around him as he charged down tunnel after tunnel. The army of demons followed eagerly like coyotes on the scent of blood and as Will ran after Rage their cries grew louder and more obscene. They could sense that the game, the hunt, was nearing its conclusion and no one wanted to miss a delicious moment. Will the New Kid, the demon hunter, would soon be confronted with the surprise of his life.

Chapter Twenty-Three: The Killing Caves

Will kept chasing the elusive demon, driven by a powerful feeling that by confronting and defeating Rage he would finally find his father. Surging with a burst of speed he ran like a super-halfback, dodging through stalagmites and leaping across a chasm to tackle Rage. The two tumbled in the dirt and Rage's sharp nails clawed at Will, ripping through the sleeve of his leather jacket but failing to puncture the body armor suit Will wore beneath. Then they both sprang to their feet like jungle cats and squared off. Will attacked with a series of Savate kicks but Rage deflected them, kicking and punching and clawing back.

For a brief moment Will thought he might be losing his mind because he was certain he saw a blood-covered leech fly out of one of Rage's ears. But Will *wasn't* seeing things. Rage clawed at the ear like a dog, clearly going mad from the creatures inside his head. Will seized the moment and finally caught Rage under the chin with a kick that sent the demon sprawling backward. Rage's head smacked into a boulder, stunning him, and Will took the opportunity to leap forward, pin him against the rocks, and get right in his face.

"Where is he?" demanded Will. "Where's my father?"

"You're so close . . . so very close. . . ." said Rage, a tinge of sadness and defeat in his voice.

"Why doesn't anybody speak English down here!" shouted Will. "It's a simple question! Where's my father? Where's the Dark Lord keeping him?"

Rage looked like he was going to answer but instead clutched the sides of his head and began laughing and crying at the same time as his head shook back and forth. His head was shaking so fast it looked like Rage's head might fly right off his neck. Then, as suddenly as the spell had come upon Rage, it left. He took out the railroad pocket watch.

"This belongs to you," said Rage.

Will snatched it from the demon's grasp and held it. It was like a talisman; holding it infused Will with power and energy. He felt like he could conquer the world.

"Where is he?" he again demanded.

"You have an appointment. Look at the time," said Rage.

Will glanced at the pocket watch. It was 7:06. Or if you ignored the usual way time was told and interpreted the numbers differently it would have been 6:66. Will's grip on the demon had momentarily relaxed and Rage broke free and disappeared into the darkness. Will chased after him but stumbled. For one long moment in the black Will felt utterly and completely alone. And then just as suddenly as this terrible feeling had come upon him he was visited by another one. This time he felt a closeness to his father, a closeness he had not felt in years. He cried out to him.

"Dad!"

Will heard no reply, save for the warm winds whooshing through the shadowy catacombs. He ran blindly forward and came blasting out of a tunnel into a large cavern. Rage could have gone in any one of several directions, could have ducked into any number of tunnels. Will chose one but was met by a pack of demons. Some were demonteens and some were older demons and they all rushed him.

He whipped out his Megashocker and zapped three of them but there were too many of them. Two got close and ripped at him with their claws but his suit of under armor held and again he avoided serious injury. *Thank God for science class*, thought Will. Then a huge old mature demon, a mechanic from North Carolina who had once worked on his mom's car, came in low, squatting like a sumo wrestler, his arms ropey with muscles.

"You're a long way from Greenhaven, Buck," said Will.

Big Buck smiled.

"The trip was worth it just to see you, Will," snorted Buck.

Buck made his move and Will sidestepped him and brought the Megashocker down on his neck, raking it through his scalene muscles. Blood gushed out like Buck's neck had sprouted a fountain. But if he was fazed he didn't show it. He just grunted and whirled and swiped with one of his massive ham hands and his blade-like claw nails sliced Will's left hand, drawing three thick lines of blood. The wound was deep and Will knew he'd have to act quickly. Summoning his time-bending speed he circled Buck in a blur, jamming the Megashocker into both his eyes and then stabbing him directly in his chest. Buck went down hard, dead before his head hit the ground, and he sparked and dematerialized like so many fireflies.

Backing into a small cave Will yanked a healing patch out of a sleeve pocket and slapped it on his hand. The bleeding stopped almost immediately and Will knew the wound would be healed in minutes. But he couldn't wait, he had to keep moving. He raced out of the cave, chose another tunnel, and double-timed it, ripping along until he came to a Y-junction. Again he chose and again another pack of ghoulish demons cut him off. At the head of the pack were Duncan, Todd, and Jason. Duncan held a rusty saber with jagged edges.

"I would soooo like to cut your arms off," he snarled.

"The feeling's mutual," replied Will. "Bring it on!"

Todd and Jason held Duncan back and shrieked some unintelligible demon words in his ear. Duncan's whole demeanor changed as he nodded. Then the trio of Harrisburg juniors zoomed up while other demonteens swooped down. This group was a total freak show. Will was suddenly surrounded by demons that looked like they wanted to devour him and they were starting to really get on his nerves. He armed himself with the Rapid-Fire Terra Blazer.

"Hungry, are we?" said Will. "How about chowin' down on this!"

He fired off staccato shots, blowing the heads off seven of the creatures while the survivors, including Duncan, Todd, and Jason, shrieked and swooped up into the darkness above. The funny thing was they didn't seem all that alarmed that Will had just toasted their buddies.

Then Will caught sight of Rage and gave chase again, thinking to cut him off. But then another gigantic pack of demons dropped down from above out of a huge fissure, claws outstretched.

"If you freaks keep this up somebody's gonna get hurt," said Will.

Then he calmly used his Long-Range Blinder and zapped them with a light explosion that blew out their eye sockets completely. They just kept flying around, bashing into the walls and falling to the ground like dead birds, where Will scorched them with the Rapid-Fire Terra Blazer and their bodies squirmed and crackled and dissolved.

"Nobody listens," said Will.

Another wave of demonteens, undaunted by the fate of their comrades, attacked. One got through, slamming into Will head-on and knocking him back against a jagged boulder that cut through his armor and pierced his skin. It was just a flesh wound but Will decided it best to temporarily retreat. He backed quickly into a low dark chamber and was reaching for another healing patch when he felt a sudden searing pain in his shoulder. Turning around he saw Principal Steadman gripping the other end of the spear embedded in

Will's shoulder. Steadman smiled and jammed it farther in before he let go. Standing next to Steadman were Duncan, Todd, and Jason. Steadman's forearm crutches were gone. The principal smiled.

"There's no going back now, Will. We've all come too far for you to leave the party."

Duncan and Todd and Jason were jabbering in demonspeak amongst themselves and then Duncan belched and smiled at Will.

"Look at it this way. You're no longer the New Kid," said Duncan.

"You're so much more," added Todd.

Will wondered what the hell they were talking about but was still in shock, his eyes wide with disbelief as he pulled the lance out and stared at Principal Steadman.

"They got to you?"

"Yes, they got to even me," said Steadman. He did a little dance like that old black and white movie star guy Fred Astaire. "Look at me. I can dance! Don't you see, it's so much simpler this way. This way we're all on the same page."

"I'll never be on the same page with you as long as I live," said Will.

"That's what you thi—"

Steadman was going to say "think," but Will had whipped out a silver throwing blade from his boot and flung it at the principal. The scalpel-like blade sunk into his forehead and he toppled over but he still had a smile on his face. His feet kept on dancing until his body exploded in a shower of sparks.

Duncan, Todd, and Jason fled but other demons swooped down and looked plenty ready to rumble. Using his left hand Will yanked out the spear and threw it with enough force that it skewered an advancing demonteen, killing it on the spot.

Unlike the wound on his hand, the one inflicted by Principal Steadman was real bad. Will had to buy himself some time. Blood poured from his back as he changed his position, squatting down to charge and fire his weapon again and giving a pair of flying monkey boys a double blast that not only blew the eyes out of their sockets but flamed their wings, too. They nose-dived like planes shot out of the sky. More shrieks of gleeful bloodlust bounced off the cavern walls as Will kept wasting them. They were like crazed religious fanatics, proud to meet their demise on the field of battle, certain some twisted nirvana awaited them on the other side. The Terra Blazer was out of juice and Will tossed it aside as he fled into another of the myriad stone coves. He yanked out two healing patches, reached back, and applied them to the gaping wound on his back. The bleeding took almost a full minute to stop and Will sat gasping for breath, listening to the demons caterwauling as they flew through the chambers, trying to pick up the scent of his blood.

As he pushed onward down another tunnel it occurred to Will that the demons attacking him weren't just sacrificing themselves, they were also *herding* him, manipulating him, guiding him. He was a pawn in some sort of game and he had no idea what the rules were. He couldn't think clearly; he kept seeing Rage and could not help himself. He pursued the demon with every ounce of strength he had, and yet Rage continued to dance just out of his reach.

At an expansive stone juncture Will looked up and saw that his cat and mouse game with Rage was being observed from high above by the Dark Lord himself. What was going on? What kind of psychotic sport was he engaged in? Where was Natalie and where was his father? As much as Will wanted to climb the sides of the walls and hack off the Black Prince's head, he felt bound to pursue Rage. He sensed—no, he *knew*—Rage had answers and he wanted them so badly he could taste them. He could feel the truth coming within his reach.

Will charged onward through a maze of tunnels but stopped when he heard the one sound that was like a dagger in his heart, sapping his strength and willpower: the sound of crying. He stepped through a pool of light into a stone vestibule and when his eyes adjusted to the low light he could make out two forms that appeared to be part of a piece of fabric that covered the entire wall. Firing up a light stick Will was able to see the entire horrifying scene clearly. The forms were female, and they were woven into a huge net of pulsing crimson veins, a living breathing creature that held them in its throbbing grasp.

"Natalie?"

Natalie's eyes opened and though she was trying to be brave she could not hide her terror. Her sister wept and whimpered beside her. Will unsheathed his Death Hacker.

"Hold still, I'm getting you out of here."

Natalie could still move her mouth and whispered a warning as she shook her head from side to side.

"Cut one and two grow back, Will."

He understood. He would have to bend time and slice and dice faster than he ever had before or the sisters would be engulfed entirely by this living web. He rapidly took stock of how they were being held and was measuring where his first cuts would land when he saw something in Natalie's eyes and felt a brush of wind behind him that made him duck. And it was a good thing, because two demonteens had just swooped in, double swords drawn, and the blade that one of them swung would have surely lopped Will's head off. Spinning around as he wielded the Death Hacker Will deflected their blows, fighting off their onslaught.

Because his Death Hacker's blade could change shape in mid-swing he had a mighty advantage and though they fought with cunning he still managed to slash the punks to shreds. Then he turned and took a deep breath. In a series of rapid-fire swipes with his Death Hacker he cut both Natalie and Emily free. The vein web creature wailed in pain and agony and the sliced arteries spurted blood and whipped around like fallen power lines.

Will helped Natalie and Emily hustle down a tunnel. Natalie's eyes were still wild with fright, blood staining the night clothes she'd been wearing when she was kidnapped, and she looked to Will.

"We've . . . got to get out of here. . . ." she stammered.

"We will. Right after I find my father," said Will.

No sooner had the words spilled from his mouth than he again saw Rage just up ahead, racing toward a massive cavern entrance filled with a bright light.

"Just stay behind me," said Will, unwilling to send them on without him or to let this opportunity fall through his fingers when he was so close.

In seconds they were at the entrance. They stood in awe and surveyed what was before them. Natalie's voice was hoarse as she croaked out three simple foreboding words.

"Oh my God. . . ."

This was no ordinary cavern they were looking at. It was as huge as an indoor stadium, a massive underground structure that had been excavated and built up and adorned with carvings and drawings. *That's what the slag heaps were all about*, thought Will. The demons had been busy little suckers; this wasn't just a hole in the ground, it was an underground dome. Dominating the room was a set of colossal marble thrones. They were unique because it appeared that you stood inside them rather than sat on them, and they were part of some gigantic elaborate locking mechanism. The whole thing was intricately carved from stone and surrounded by a myriad of symbols chiseled into the circular floor, which was also made of marble and appeared as though it was capable of rotating. Off to one side was a marble sarcophagus.

Will's stomach turned. This wasn't just some meeting place. For these heinous, dreadful creatures it was a place of worship. It was nothing less than a cathedral. He knew that one of the thrones was for the Dark Lord. But who was the other one for? And who was the sarcophagus for? He knew deep in his gut he was about to find out.

Chapter Twenty-Four: The Prophecy

R age was standing next to a burbling dome, a lava clot in the center of the cathedral. Bursts of steam and globs of molten lava kept blasting up out of the clot. A tiny bit of lava landed on Rage's cheek and burned his flesh and he barely flinched, just motioned with his fingers, mocking Will, entreating him, taunting him. Will stepped into the open space carefully, speaking softly to Natalie and Emily.

"Stay here. It's going to be okay."

How it could possibly be okay was something neither girl could fathom but Natalie nonetheless nodded her assent and tugged Emily down with her into a crouch to watch, just out of sight of a nearby demonteen wearing red face makeup. Will walked forward, his eyes darting back and forth between the Dark Lord and Rage and the dozens upon dozens of demons who had gathered to watch the proceedings. It was like walking into the arena at the Colosseum in Rome, and Will knew one thing for sure. In the drama that was about to play out he wouldn't be a lion but a Christian. He turned and leveled his best tough-guy gaze up at the Black Prince.

"What do you want?"

"It is not a matter of what I desire," said the Dark Lord.

He dropped down from above, snarled, and then calmly floated to one of the thrones and stood. He picked up a human skull and fondled it like one would a household pet. Seeing the creature responsible for her months of torment, Emily tensed and began to tremble. Natalie wrapped a comforting arm around her sister but her body still shook from fear. Natalie stole a glance at the red-faced demonteen perched above them. If he noticed them they'd be in big trouble.

The Dark Lord now shouted: "What we desire is of no consequence! It is what is *written*."

As these words flowed from the Dark Lord's mouth the entire congregation of demons in attendance began chattering and shrieking and clattering their weapons. They were ready for a really big show, and Will knew he was part of it. He just hoped he wouldn't have to call upon his power rod because if the Dark Lord somehow got his grubby paws on it he would be two-thirds of the way to attaining the ultimate power. Will promised himself again that he would do anything to prevent that from happening. He would have to win this battle without his power rod. The Dark Lord spoke in low murderous tones, his voice rising in timbre as he jabbered in demonspeak. It was a horrendous sound but the crowd seemed to love it because they began to echo his words. The air was thick with tension and Will was in danger of succumbing to a pervasive feeling of inevitability, as though he was losing his free will and could only play along in whatever game they all had in mind. He knew he had to shake things up.

"Hey, crow face! You got something to say, speak human!"

The Lord of Darkness cocked his head as though he wasn't sure he'd heard Will right. He crushed the skull he was holding and it crumbled into a fine dust. Natalie held Emily tighter, wondering why Will was deliberately provoking the beast. It would have been a great time right then for one of his brilliant heroic plans.

"Yeah, I'm talking to you! The one who got beat with an ugly stick!"

The Dark Lord grumbled and snarled and vomited a stream of toxic puke that splattered on the floor of the cave.

"Wow. That's really cool," said Will. "Man, I sure wouldn't want to see you with diarrhea!"

The Dark Lord stood up abruptly and with his right hand sent a string of power zapping toward Will, who saw it coming and deflected it with one of his metallic elbow pads. He wasn't so lucky with the sphere of pain that followed; it glanced off his ear and hurt like hell. But nonetheless he put on a cocky brave face.

"Give it up, Jerk of Darkness. If you free my father now I will consider sparing you. Otherwise. . . ." Will made a throat-slicing gesture and gurgled an appropriate sound effect. He was terrified inside but strangely calm at the same time. It was somehow easier to be blatantly dissing the monster than trying to reason with him or play his game of fear.

The Dark Lord raised a claw like he was going to hurl another attack at Will but suddenly seemed to change his mind. Smiling through his ragged yellow teeth and narrowing his glowing yellow eyes he hissed at Will, "Your attempts at humorous bravado are amusing, but we have an agenda, young Will."

The Dark Lord made a motion with his fingers that caused Rage to convulse as he held his head, the shark leeches still inside digging deeper into his brain. Rage screamed at the top of his lungs.

"WILL! If you want your father you must come through meeeee!!!!"

Then Rage pulled out a sword and charged at Will, swinging the weapon wildly, blood flying from his ears as his head bobbed back and forth. Will used the Death Hacker to deflect Rage's blows. It was a classic blade-on-blade fight and the demons above screeched so loudly the cathedral shook. They spoke demonspeak but soon Will could decipher their simple chants.

"Kill! Kill! Kill!"

Will knew Rage meant to kill him and he fought with every bit of skill and dexterity he'd developed in all his years of training and of hunting and wasting demons. Rage was good, but Will was better and he used expert footwork, adapting, flexing, evading, nearly dancing as they fought on and on, Will's Death Hacker performing flawlessly, morphing, changing shapes, growing longer or shorter, bending into a loop or becoming straight as an arrow as necessary. He was beating Rage down, wearing him out. The mature demon was sweating and was in obvious agony due not only to Will's blows but the shark leeches as well. And as he grew weak he left an opening and Will seized the moment, thrusting the Death Hacker downward and cutting off Rage's pinkie finger. The demon bellowed in pain.

For a brief moment Will felt something very strange for the demon: pity. It was enough to make him pause and Rage looked shocked but still ripped a strip of cloth from his shirt and began cinching it around the pinkie stump to staunch the flow of blood.

As the demon was attending to himself Will glanced down at the lava clot and saw that he could actually see *into* it. He blinked because he could hardly believe what his eyes were telling him was below. It was unlike anything he'd ever seen or even imagined before. It was a version of Hell that made the paintings of Dante's Inferno he'd seen in art books look like a teddy bears' picnic. He was staring down into the Infinite Caves of Suffering Demons.

The massive underground space wasn't just a cave, it was another world, another dimension. It was the true underworld. In it were untold scores of demons, millions of them stretching down as far as the eye could see, all the demons that had ever been toasted throughout the ages. And more were arriving every moment, demons, ghosts, and ghouls from all over the world coming in on streams of liquid light, freeways for the damned, all so very eager to be first in line to burst forth from the portal once the key had opened it.

But where is the key? wondered Will. If the Dark Lord had this whole space set up, it must mean that he had it, or was close to obtaining it, and Will had to prevent him from using it. He recognized a few of the demons that he'd sent there personally and imagined they would not exactly be filled with joy should they have the opportunity to meet him again. The whole lot of them was slathering and writhing in agony, lusting to be set free from their torment, eager to spill up in a flood, regenerate, and overtake the earth like a plague with their unforgiving evil. But without the key, they couldn't be set free.

Will's battle with Rage resumed. The Dark Lord, the true Demon Master, watched, his eye sockets narrowed into saffron slits, his mutated face twisted into an ugly sneer. He seemed to take great pleasure in the fight, even though Will was clearly gaining the upper hand. When a hapless demonteen made the unfortunate mistake of flying down to get a better look at the fight and blocked the Black Prince's line of sight he paid the ultimate price when the Dark Lord—in a shockingly sudden burst of anger—flew out and skewered the demonteen on his outstretched claw and then flung him backward into a corner. The demonteen's body slammed into the rocks just above Natalie and Emily and his body flopped down, lifeless now, and degenerated. His weapon, a tri-blade sword, clattered on the rocks. Natalie eyed it, her heart beating fast. The red-faced demonteen nearby sniffed the air, his nostrils growing huge, and Natalie's muscles tightened. Could he smell them? Would she be able to get to the tri-blade sword in time if he found them?

As Will continued to pound away at Rage with his Death Hacker, Rage grew weary, and Will pounced on him like any predator would their wounded prey. He formed the Death Hacker into a three-pronged fork and stuck Rage deep in the shoulder. The wound must have been severe; Rage began a metamorphosis, losing his demon skin and becoming more and more human-like, his face going all rubbery as it changed and transformed, as though a greater power was molding him into what he was supposed to be.

Will heard a commanding growl and out of the corner of his eye caught sight of the Dark Lord leaping down from his throne and landing between the two combatants, his strength and weight bringing such force to bear that the solid granite beneath them cracked asunder.

"Though the irony of the situation pleases me, I feel we should do this together, Will," croaked the Dark Lord. And then he drew a power rod from inside his leathery chest. It was nearly identical to Will's, except it had no retrieval sleeve on it. The Dark Lord activated the lightning saber and, with a move so blinding swift that Will barely saw it, stabbed Rage full on in the stomach.

Rage moaned, his features still morphing, and doubled over. The power rod blade had passed entirely through him and he was writhing in agony. The lance had impaled against a boulder and the lightning saber continued to sizzle his flesh. The shark leeches flopped harmlessly from his ear canals and a cloud of gas formed around him. His demon self seemed to be gone now and as he lifted his head up the small hairs on Will's neck rose and a chill raced up and down his spine.

"Dad. . . ? EDWARD?"

Rage was Edward. Will had very nearly killed his own father!

"NOOOOOOO!" shouted Will, tears spilling from his eyes.

The Dark Lord's own glowing pus-colored eye sockets opened wide as he delighted in the misery he was causing and Rage, now almost completely transformed back into Edward, looked at Will with such agony that it nearly broke Will's heart.

"I'm sorry, Willie."

"Oh God, Dad. . . ."

Edward's voice was a ragged series of gasps as he spilled the facts.

"He . . . infected me when I was sixteen. Your grandfather developed an antidote, so I was safe as I raised you. But . . . when he kidnapped me I . . . succumbed. It's up to you, now, Will. . . ."

The Dark Lord withdrew his power rod from Edward's stomach and swiped the air to shake the blood from the pulsing blade. Edward staggered, precariously near a ledge overlooking an apparently bottomless chasm, one of the many vent holes leading farther down into the bowels of the volcano. Will slashed at the beast with his Death Hacker, trying to get to Edward, but the Dark Prince was deft and deflected the blows while Edward clutched at his stomach, trying to stop the flow of blood. Will could not watch his father die. No matter what the cost, he could not stand by and just watch Edward—who had raised him and nurtured him and loved him and shared the family secrets and destiny—collapse into death.

Will felt the red curtain in his mind's eye go deep scarlet with rage as he transformed into a whirling dervish, twisting and leaping and attacking the Dark Lord with his Death Hacker, the blade changing shape as he swung it with all his might. But it was for naught. The Lord of Darkness was not only massive in height and girth but preternaturally strong as well. So Will broke all his oaths and reached behind his neck, tapping the code on his patch and summoning his Excalibur, his power rod. It swooped down out of the sky, racing down through tunnels and catacombs and landed in Will's outstretched hand to the cheers of those assembled. But Will was too focused on killing the Dark Lord to notice.

"Excellent!" bellowed the Dark Beast as he shifted his weight between his two massive feet and attacked Will full-on, swinging his own power rod. The lightning blades clashed in a shower of sparks as the cathedral erupted in a cacophony of demon cheers. The crowd wanted blood.

The monster was twice Will's size and far stronger and no doubt more cunning; he'd lived a thousand years, killed and tortured untold legions of humans. But Will would not let his fear show. He knew the Dark Lord was crafty and could crawl into your brain without warning. So when terrifying images of his own death raced through Will's mind he knew it was the monster's doing and he conjured up images of his own, mental pictures of him defeating the Black Beast with a series of artery-severing power rod strikes. The battle raged on two fronts: in their minds and bodies.

Then Will tried something he'd never tried before: *He* made an attempt to invade the *Dark Lord*'s consciousness. His fury was so great he just lashed out—and in a flash he was there, he was in! To say his host's mind was filled with disgusting and corrupt thoughts was the ultimate understatement. The Dark Prince's brain was a roiling cauldron of suffering and destruction: whole cities going up in flames, Dresden, Pompeii; scores of innocents suffering and dying in Auschwitz and Hiroshima. The beast thrived on human torment and agony, feeding on mass starvation and genocide. The images swirled and assaulted Will and he shrank back, out of the Dark Lord's brain.

"You are learning so fast," muttered the Dark Lord, puffing up his chest.

Will lunged and thrust his power rod saber at the Dark Lord, surprising him, forcing him to use his inner arm to shield the blow, and the hot blade sizzled as it seared his leathery flesh. The beast cut loose with a terrifying howl that shook the cathedral walls and the gathering of demons gasped and chattered in demonspeak. Will took a deep breath, inwardly proud of the minor victory. But, galvanized by Will's aggression, the Dark Lord spun and kicked and feinted left then brought his other fist, the one not holding the power rod, rocketing up in an uppercut that caught Will full on the chin and lifted him off his feet. While Will was in mid-air the Dark Lord swung his saber blade and even though Will sucked in his stomach, the tip still caught him, slicing through the under armor (no substance on earth was strong enough to offer protection from the power rod's saber blades)—and connecting ever so barely with Will's skin. Another gasp from the gallery as everyone looked at Will. Had blood been drawn? No. Though bruised, Will's skin held. Watching from above, Natalie breathed a sigh of relief.

"Your hubris is your weakness," said the Black Prince.

Will risked a glance at Edward and saw that he was growing pale. Will had to do something and he had to do it now! He lunged like he was going for another frontal assault then kick-stepped off a nearby boulder and cartwheeled over the Dark Lord. When he was directly above him he stabbed down with his power rod and caught the monster in the back of his neck. Sickening phlegm-colored globs of blood shot up as the beast bellowed in pain. Will landed behind him and swung his power rod saber again, only to meet one of the beast's wrist shields. The Dark Lord had turned and was smiling. *What is wrong with him?* thought Will. It was as if he was *happy* that Will was so incredibly skilled.

"You have shown me much, young one," growled the Dark Lord.

He spit in the palm of his clawed hand and the toxic loogie burbled. He slapped it on his neck wound and it ceased spouting blood. It seemed the Dark Lord had his own healing patches.

Now the battle shifted into a higher gear, the lightning-hot power rod sabers colliding again and again and sending cascades of sparks in every direction while the demons howled with glee. The red-faced demonteen leapt down to cheer and saw Natalie and Emily hiding by the wall. He growled, baring his teeth and Emily let out a muffled shriek. Wasting no time Natalie dove for the tri-blade sword just as the demonteen flew at her. She brought the weapon up and plunged the three blades upward with all her might. They sank into the demonteen's chest, neck, and throat. Luckily his death howl was drowned out by the cheering throngs.

Will used his power rod to send a volley of fireballs at the Dark Lord's face. He deflected them and returned a half-dozen force field orbs that slammed into Will's body, knocking the wind out of him.

Will's whole body ached. He had to retreat and he started to run backward but noticed the floor was slick with the Dark Lord's gunky blood. So he turned and ran directly back at the towering monster instead, dropping down onto his knees and sliding right at him, hoping to surprise the fiend and open his belly from below. But the

Dark Lord was waiting for him and he slammed one of his huge elbows into the side of Will's head. Will's body went flying sideways and his power rod flew out of his hand, skittered across the floor, and banged into a rock. Will hit a stalagmite, then immediately leapt to his feet and lunged for his power rod. But it was too late. The Dark Lord had his huge hand wrapped around the coveted rod. Now he had two.

Will stood on shaky feet. The Dark Lord smiled. The crowd of demons cheered. Will sought solace in one very powerful notion that he hoped was true, it had to be true.

"You'll never get the third rod of power!" he yelled at the Dark Lord.

The huge beast appeared sad and hung his head, then threw it back and laughed a mocking laugh, joined by a chorus of laughter from the crowd of demons.

"But don't you see, Will, *I just did!*"

The next sight caused a wave of hopelessness to wash through Will's body, for the Dark Lord produced, from beneath his tunic, *the third power rod.*

"Yes, Will. I had the second one all along. Killed a Shaman in Tunisia for it four hundred years ago. YOURS was the third."

Will's mind momentarily went blank. He was trying to calculate the ramifications of what had just transpired and his brain was overloaded with the dreadful possibilities, all of them catastrophic. He searched for hope and found none. He looked at the faces surrounding him: Rudy, Sharon, Duncan, Jason, Todd, Mrs. and Mrs. Halvorson, Mrs. Norrington, Rex Farmer. They were demonic to be sure, but they were smiling and happy as well. Will could only watch as the Dark Lord took all three power rods and joined them, tips to tips, forming the infamous Triad of Power. The cathedral rumbled. The ground quaked. Massive blinding bursts of light shot out in every direction from the triangle. The yelling and chanting and incessant demonspeak coming from the assemblage rose into a deafening roar. Will could think of only one slim ray of hope.

"But . . . you don't have the key!" he shouted above the din.

But again the Mighty Leader of All Demons smiled confidently. His arms shook from holding the Triad of ultimate power and as he turned it slightly the power within ebbed and the triangle calmed down. All eyes were upon the Dark Lord. He motioned to the dual thrones.

"On the contrary. It's right here! The key is right here before all of us!"

The crowd roared its approval. Natalie pulled Emily to her feet and then farther back into the shadows of the tunnel entrance where they were hiding. Whatever the Dark Lord meant, it couldn't be good. Where was this key he was boasting about? Natalie looked around the cathedral and saw no sign of any key, just the Dark Lord and Will, the thrones, and the demon throng surrounding them. The Dark Lord stepped closer to Will, holding the Triad. Confusion was written all over Will's face.

"You're lying!"

"Come now, boy, you're smarter than that! Don't you understand yet? Will, YOU are the key." The Dark Lord motioned to the thrones.

Will was dumfounded. He stared at them. What could it possibly mean?

"The two of us. Side by side. As it is written," said the Dark Lord.

"No!" shouted Edward from where he'd collapsed on the ground, still bleeding and barely holding on to life. "You can defy the prophecy!"

Fists clenched with rage the Dark Lord sent a force beam of pain at Edward, who moaned in agony.

"Tell him, Rage, tell him the truth!"

"Leave him alone!" shouted Will as he drew his Death Hacker.

In a movement too swift to be seen by the human eye, still holding the Triad, the Dark Lord snatched the Death Hacker from Will and used it to inflict Edward with a mortal wound.

Edward's last gasping words to Will were these: "Will, I'm not your father."

And then he toppled over the ledge into the chasm. Will was in shock. He raced over. His foot caught a rock. He reached out for Edward—for the man he'd always believed to be his father—and fell into the chasm after him.

Chapter Twenty-Five: Resolution

Will was on his back, falling through darkness. Time slowed down as his mind raced back to his extraordinary pre-birth dream of that fateful night so many years ago. His mother had gotten a fever itch and gone out looking for trouble and she'd found it in a big way. He remembered driving around with Edward looking for her, and then falling asleep. He remembered waking up, having to go to the bathroom, walking down the hall . . . and the man, the tall dark figure leaving his mother's bedroom, his mother splayed on the bed as though used and discarded like so much trash. He remembered the man turning and looking at him now. And he recalled a significant detail from the dream that he could never remember before, a detail so horrifying that he'd been blocking it all these years: the man's face was that of a creature, and the place where his eyes should have been burned ochre bright, yellow like the sun. Will now understood. The dark pre-birth dream all made perfect sense now. It was real. It *did* happen. He'd been given the dream to warn him. It explained his extraordinary abilities, his inner conflicts, his dual nature—the war that raged within him between good and evil. It was the Lord of Darkness who had taken his mother, and impregnated her. Edward *wasn't* his father! The creature that had just killed him was. And this of course led to one inescapable and horrifying conclusion: *Will was the son of the Devil*.

As he kept falling he heard Edward's voice: "You have to let go, Will." And Will thought for a moment he understood. Why shouldn't he let go of the whole damn rotten deal? Why shouldn't he just forget about vengeance? If this was his fate, his destiny, his birthright, why shouldn't he take his rightful place? He imagined the surge of power he would feel if he chose to become not just one of them, but a leader amongst them, a warrior prince. The world would bow down to him. Who could resist that?

"All hail Will Hunter!"

"Your word is our command, Will!"

"To you we pledge our allegiance!"

"You will rule forever, Will!"

His whole teenage life he'd been an outsider, the outcast, the New Kid, the kid who nobody ever warmed up to or made friends with.

"Who do you think you are?"

"You don't belong here."

"Nobody knows you."

"Nobody likes you."

Now he had the opportunity to be befriended, hell, *worshipped* by everyone he met! He could stop worrying about caring for people. He could have all the girls he ever wanted.

"You're so handsome, Will!"

"And so strong!"

"You're the coolest boy I've ever known!"

"Take me, Will, please?"

"I'll do anything you want."

Will's world shifted into the red, scarlet seeping through him, the ruby curtains falling now over the last act—or was it the *first* act? Yes, this was just the beginning! The first delicious taste of his new life as the earth's unquestioned ruler! Everyone who had ever done him wrong would pay! Will was coming close, he was going to cross the line. But then again he heard Edward's voice echo through the tunnel: "You must learn to let go."

And suddenly it hit Will what Edward meant. It was time to let go of his hate, his lust for revenge. If he was going to survive he would have to release his attachment to the hatred he felt for the beast and replace it with something more pure. He would have to cease being motivated by anger and retribution—by rage. He would have to say goodbye to the red curtain that fell across his eyes as he amped himself up for battle. He would have to *love*. He thought of Natalie. And he thought of his mother. But he wasn't sure he had the strength.

He remembered his original plan, which now seemed lame and unworkable, and he reached for the pocket on his jacket sleeve. Then he heard someone calling his name and knew exactly who it was. *Will. Will. Will.* The voice came from above and it burrowed so far into Will's head he thought it would never come out. The attempt at infection had begun. Will had a choice to make.

Natalie watched as the Dark Lord held the pulsating Triad of Power. His eyes narrowed as he stared at the pit his sole heir had fallen into and mind-spoke to him, to his son, calling out his name, setting the infection in motion. Then he held his breath and listened to his heart—yes, even *he* had a heart, of a sort—pounding as the cathedral's walls echoed with the chants of his disciples. "He will rise!" they shouted, again and again, as if their pleading would cause the prophecy to come true. The Dark Lord knew better. He knew no machinations by mere beings, mortal or otherwise, could guide the unpredictable hands of fate. Fate was in the boy's hands now. If he died, then so be it. His body would be placed in the sarcophagus. But if he lived, then he *was* the key, and he and he alone could ascend to the throne. Together they would combine their regal blood—the father's blood on one throne, the son's on the other—and the lock would open and the portal would explode and a new time on earth would begin.

"He will rise!" the demon mob shouted. "He will rise!"

The Dark Lord thought he saw movement and raised a mighty claw, silencing the bloodthirsty hordes. And then every single creature watching held its breath. There . . . rising up from the hole in the ground . . . the tip of a head . . . a boy's head! It was Will, climbing out of the hole. He stood, his eyes closed, his breath labored. Blood trickled from his mouth and the crowd gasped. There was blood! The crowd began to chant with unbridled glee.

"Blood! Blood! Blood! Blood!"

Then Will opened his eyes. Even demons can shed tears and thousands were shed in that moment because young Will's eyes shone the telltale glistening black! He was infected! The cathedral erupted with a cheer so loud it could be heard for miles. Their prince had come!

As Natalie looked down at Will her stomach clenched into a knot. She was dead. Her sister was dead. They were going to die because their last hope had been turned inside out and offered up like some maniacal practical joke. The boy she thought she loved, their only hope of survival, had given himself over to evil. She put her arm around Emily's shaking shoulders and pulled her sister's face into her shoulder, away from the scene unfolding in front of them. There was no need for her sister to witness more. The battle had ended badly. *Sometimes you just lose, that's all*, she thought. She tightened her fingers around the handle of the tri-blade sword. She wasn't going to go down without a fight. But she was a realist and she knew how that fight was going to turn out.

"Take your place, my son!" shouted the Dark Lord, indicating the throne. The huge creature stepped over, ready to enter his own standing throne as his minions cheered their throats raw.

Will spoke up, his voice raspy.

"Yes, Father."

Natalie's pain was unbearable as she watched Will obediently walk over to the Dark Lord. Then father and son took their places in the standing thrones, the Dark Lord smiling proudly and still holding the Triad of Power. The thrones pulsed with crimson light and began to rotate and the lava clot rumbled, the portal to the underworld trembling, eager to be opened by the key, the prophecy! Will smiled at his father. The Dark Lord smiled back. All that he'd worked for had come true.

"Father?"

"Yes, my son?"

"May I hold it?"

The Dark Lord looked down at the Triad of Power in his clutches.

"There will be time for that later."

"I . . . want to feel the power . . . please, father?"

As demons have tears, they have emotions, and as they have emotions, they are subject to the same vulnerabilities as mortals. Pride. Hubris. The Black Prince had an uneasy feeling but yet . . . *this was his son.* What harm could come from letting his own flesh and blood taste the energy of the holy Triad? The boy had chosen to be infected. He deserved a reward. But still the Dark Lord hesitated.

"Please, father?" Will asked again.

The Dark Lord looked at Will. He'd waited so long for Will to join him, for this moment to come! The boy held out his hands. And the Dark Lord couldn't help himself. He extended the Triad of Power to his son.

Will allowed the energy of the Triad to pulse through his body and up into his mind. He locked eyes with the Dark Lord, his nemesis, his father, and pushed into the creature's mind. He was in again and again he was inundated with horrific images of human pain and agony, souls leeched of their goodness and sullied with malice. Experiencing these torments was both painful and strangely euphoric, as though the very natures of Will's own soul were at war with one another. He knew that to survive he must quell the hatred and anger rising within him and call upon all the good and honorable and unspoiled thoughts and feelings he could muster. He remembered birthdays and Christmas mornings spent with Edward and his mother. He remembered Natalie's gentle kiss. He grew stronger and as his own healthy loving thoughts collided with the Dark Lord's thoughts of evil it created an explosion, a maelstrom of conflict. The pure and good thoughts Will had brought with him caused immeasurable pain in the Dark Lord's mind. Never before had he endured such agony.

The Dark Lord roared and in a millisecond Will was out of the beast's mind and back in his own. The realization that something was about to go horribly wrong dawned on the Dark Lord just as Will, still holding the Triad of Power, stepped out of his throne and with the Triad created a swirling lance of astonishingly pure power, the mightiest sword the world had ever seen, and with one powerful swipe whacked off the top of his father's throne—with the Dark Lord's head still in it. The cathedral erupted into chaos. The giant unlocking mechanism grounded to a halt.

Unbelievably, the Dark Lord's body fought on. When Will turned the Dark Lord struck out, sightless, and caught Will with a blow hard enough to draw blood. The Dark Lord's headless body careened into Will, a claw finding Will's wound and sinking in. Will used his foot to kick the Dark Lord's headless body backward and it toppled in the corner.

The cathedral exploded with even more chaos, the demons eager for revenge. Will used the Triad to cut a bloody swath through the dumbstruck horde of panicking demons that swarmed toward him. He sliced through Duncan, cutting him in half. He lanced Todd's head clean through. He chopped Jason into quarters and did the same to Correl Shames. He cut down Mrs. Norrington and Sharon Mitchell. He was methodically toasting each and every one of them, sending them down below to the Infinite Caves of Suffering Demons.

But then something Will hadn't planned on happened. During the melee, the bloodbath that Will hoped would be the ending of all the demons in the cathedral, the Dark Lord's body had risen and found its head. Instead of joining the fight, the wily Devil had picked up his head and placed it on Will's throne, using the claw he'd dug into Will's body to wipe Will's own blood on his cheek, and then with his headless body stood in his own. By some perverted, wicked twist of fate the unlocking mechanism once again began to operate, the massive ring rotating slowly, the howls of the underworld seeping up, the dark souls below bursting at the seams.

Will had to move fast. He looked around for Rudy and when their eyes met Rudy came flying at him, fangs and claws bared. Whipping out the untested Demon Trapper, Will activated it, firing a blast that caught Rudy in mid-air and then sucked him into the trap where he went silent and frozen. If they made it out, maybe he'd have the time he needed to turn him back. If Will's grandfather had been able to create an antidote, so could Will.

A demonteen screeched to his left and Will looked over to see Natalie shielding Emily with her body and using the tri-blade to flail away at demons like a true warrior princess. But her three attackers were closing in and she wouldn't be able to hold them off for long.

"BEHOLD!" shouted Will, his voice ringing through the cave.

He held up the Triad of Power, the three power rods joined together. Hundreds of demons froze in shock, unsure what to do. Their prince held the Triad of Power. What would he do? Will knew exactly what he was going to do. He had a plan. He just hoped it worked.

"This portal to Hell? I have some bad news. I am hereby closing it. FOREVER!" While the stunned assembly watched, with all his might Will threw the Triad into the lava clot, into the portal to Hell. The ensuing explosion was reported as far north as Alaska and as far south as Los Angeles; an earthquake, they said, one of the worst on record. The force of the impact of the Triad striking the portal to the underworld was such that it created not only a gigantic blast, but a tremendous implosion, a detonation so strong that the portal, instead of being blown open, was melded shut. A maelstrom of fire blew through the underworld, burning the souls below into extinction. Those who survived the initial gusts of fire fled, only to be swept up in a back draft and singed into nothing but smoke. And then the lava clot burst and the volcano erupted.

Will grabbed Natalie by the arm just as the Devil was refitting his badly scarred head back upon his massive body. He was blown upward by a blast of hot steam and lava and the walls around them erupted with similar geysers of lava and water, creating an instant steam bath. A dense mixture of ash and gas was filling the cathedral, pressurizing it as the demons wailed with grief. Natalie pulled back, stiff with fear, unable to trust Will.

"Natalie, come on!"

"You . . . your eyes. . . ."

Will blinked and let go of her arm to quickly pull off the black contact lenses. Then he spit out the gelatin fake blood caplet.

"It's me, Natalie, it's Will."

Natalie flushed with relief and hugged him tight. He let himself hold on to her for a moment, then pulled her and Emily toward the sarcophagus.

"Get in here!" He pushed them and the Demon Trapper in, climbed in himself, and then pulled the heavy lid over them, shielding them from the earth's wrath as the massive cavern filled with erupting lava and boiling water and mud and debris. Will kept an arm around Natalie, who squeezed her eyes shut, held Emily's hand, and tried not to think about her last trip in a flying coffin as they rode the eruption up and up through the volcano's opening, shooting upward like a rocket. Bombs and blocks of magma traveling at ballistic trajectories ripped past them.

People observing the Plinian eruption of Mount St. Emory saw the usual things they expected: the eruption column rising out of the volcano's convective thrust region, the huge plume billowing out and up into the umbrella region, the clouds of smoke and ash drifting quickly with the prevailing winds. And then came a whopper of a fireworks display, not only smoke and ash but blasts of red hot lava spearing into the sky like spikes thrust up by Satan himself. Those observing would not be able to identify the Triad of Power as it blasted up and out of the cone and split, the three pieces soaring off into three totally disparate regions. Nor would they be able to identify, even upon studying video of the eruption, the rectangular-shaped object that came blasting up and sailed all the way out to Lake George where it landed smack in the middle, creating a massive geyser.

An airtight compartment, even one bearing great weight, will often float, providing the air trapped inside provides sufficient buoyancy. And float the sarcophagus did, sealed as it was by the incendiary blast. It floated until the winds from the north pulled at the currents and the marble coffin tipped over and a corner hit land. That's when Will used his boltdriver, still safe in a pocket, to blow the lid off the thing so the three of them—four if you counted Rudy in the Demon Trapper—were able to stumble out into shallow water, gasping for air and rejoicing that they had somehow done the impossible and cheated the Devil.

Natalie looked at Will, at the unique blue of his eyes.

"I thought . . . I thought you'd. . . ." She couldn't finish.

"I know. It was just a disguise. Contacts and a stupid fake blood pill from Halloween when I was a kid."

They began laughing and laughed so loud and long that even Emily couldn't help smiling. It was incredibly cathartic, releasing the tension, letting the strain and stress float out of their minds and bodies. No drug or libation could ever rival the feeling of emerging from such an ordeal to find they were still alive. Every cell in their body was in full celebration mode. It was one kick-ass feeling. The last thought that Natalie had when the eruption had started was that she was sorry she would never be able to kiss Will again. Now she wasn't about to waste any time. She wrapped her arms around him and their lips met.

"Thank you," she said, when she finally pulled away. "For helping me find Emily and getting us out of there. And, you know, saving the world."

"You were incredible," Emily added softly.

It made Natalie's heart ache, how quiet Emily had become from her experiences. But her sister was alive, away from those terrible creatures who had kidnapped her. She had her life back. She wasn't going to be able to forget what had happened anytime soon, but she could learn to live with it. She had to. They would learn to live with it together.

Will just nodded, and blushed from the praise. He was, after all, just a kid. Not an ordinary kid of course, because a kid who was half mortal and half demon could never by any stretch of the imagination be considered normal. But maybe normal was overrated.

Exhausted, they lay on the grassy slope by the side of the lake and watched as the sun slid slowly down out of the sky and the eruption of Mount St. Emory waned. It made for one heck of a sunset and lying there holding Natalie's hand Will felt more alive than he ever had in his whole life. When the stars came out they gathered up the few belongings they had left, including the Demon Trap with Rudy ensnared inside, and walked down into Harrisburg.

The town would never be the same. Much of it had been decimated by the blast, including the high school, which had been totally obliterated. Moreover, the moral corruption that had swept through the town courtesy of the Black Prince had left such scars that most of the surviving uninfected people chose to move away. Natalie and Emily grieved over the loss of their parents—Natalie feared this last shock would be too much for Emily to handle but it was as if so much had happened that they were both a little numb—and knew they would be among those who left. Will needed to pack up his laboratory and move on as well.

Will checked the Demon Trap and the warped visage of Rudy frozen inside as soon as he was back in the remains of his lab. Rudy had fallen to the Dark Lord but he was, after all, just a lonely little misguided kid who'd had a moment of weakness. After learning about Edward and about April's mistake—and after nearly giving in himself—Will intimately understood how easy it was to succumb. Someday Will would figure out the antidote his father had used and release him from the Demon Trap, patch him up enough so that he'd be able to live some semblance of a normal life. Though he had a sneaky feeling that even if he "cured" Rudy, the little guy would always have a devilish streak in him. Besides, he couldn't waste Rudy, he just couldn't. The little guy was his friend. He actually had a friend now. A demon freak friend, but a friend.

And he had Natalie, and Emily—they seemed to come as a package deal. Will would have to protect them but he more than welcomed the challenge. Remembering Natalie with the tri-blade, he realized that with a little training—if Natalie wanted it—they might even be able to protect each other.

Will thought about Edward and wished he could have saved him. He would never forget Edward; Edward would always be his real father where it counted, deep inside his heart. And Will would make his killer—the beast that had violated April and sired Will—pay.

Will thought about his newly revealed "father" (how he detested using that word, how he hated even *thinking* he was the offspring of that creature). Teenagers were supposed to buck horns with their parents, but in Will's case it had been taken to the extreme and there was surely more to come—a whole lot more. He suspected that the blast inside the cathedral had not been fatal to the Dark Lord and that they would meet again on the moral and physical fields of battle. Will knew his fate was singular and extraordinary and he was doomed, some might say damned, to an existence of perpetual war.

But maybe he didn't have to feel sorry for himself. Maybe being the son of the Devil could have its advantages. Who was to say he couldn't use his demonic powers for good? No one could tell him what to do, he was free to follow his heart. And his heart told him that he had been given this gift for a purpose, and that purpose was to protect and defend those who were predominately good-hearted and pure. As for the others, those who would join forces with the Dark Lord to further their egotistic desires, well, they would have someone to answer to. And that someone was the New Kid.

Will packed up his crates for shipment, loaded Natalie and Emily into a car along with Rudy in the Demon Trap, and drove off in search of a new beginning.

ABOUT THE AUTHOR

 Screenwriter/filmmaker Temple Mathews, a graduate of the University of Washington and a producer at the American Film Institute, has written dozens of half-hour animation TV episodes and several animated and live action features and direct-to-DVD and video films. Mr. Mathews has sold scripts and/or worked for hire at every major studio in Hollywood. His credits include the Walt Disney animated feature films *Return to Neverland* and *The Little Mermaid II*, and the MGM feature film *Picture This!* Mr. Mathews lives in Santa Monica with his daughter, Manon.